Blood Communion

BLOOD COMMUNION

A Tale of Prince Lestat

The Vampire Chronicles

ANNE RICE

ILLUSTRATIONS BY MARK EDWARD GEYER

Alfred A. Knopf

New York

2018

THIS IS A BORZOI BOOK
PUBLISHED BY ALFRED A. KNOPF

Published in the United States by Alfred A. Knopf,
a division of Penguin Random House LLC, New York,
and distributed in Canada by Random House of Canada,
a division of Penguin Random House Canada Limited, Toronto.

www.aaknopf.com

Knopf, Borzoi Books, and the colophon are registered
trademarks of Penguin Random House LLC.

Grateful acknowledgment is made to United Agents LLP on behalf of
Caitriona Yeats for permission to reprint an excerpt of
"The Circus Animals' Desertion" by W. B. Yeats.

Library of Congress Cataloging-in-Publication Data
Names: Rice, Anne, [date] author.
Title: Blood communion : a tale of Prince Lestat / by Anne Rice.
Description: First edition. | New York : Alfred A. Knopf, 2018. |
Series: Vampire chronicles
Identifiers: LCCN 2017058218 | ISBN 9781524732646 (hardcover) |
ISBN 9781524732653 (ebook)
Subjects: LCSH: Lestat (Vampire), 1760– —Fiction. | Atlantis (Legendary place)—Fiction.
| Spirit possession—Fiction. | Vampires—Fiction. | Paranormal fiction. | GSAFD: Fantasy
fiction. | Horror fiction. | Occult fiction.
Classification: LCC PS3568.I265 B64 2018 | DDC 813/.54—dc23
LC record available at https://lccn.loc.gov/2017058218

Front-of-jacket photograph by FlamingPumpkin / E+ / Getty Images
Back-of-jacket illustration by Mark Edward Geyer
Jacket design by Abby Weintraub
Illustrations by Mark Edward Geyer

Manufactured in the United States of America
First Edition

Dedicated
to
my mother
Katherine Allen O'Brien
And
to the memory of
my friend,
Carole Malkin.

"I love; therefore I am."

Blood Communion

Chapter 1

I'm the vampire Lestat. I'm six feet tall, have blue-gray eyes that sometimes appear violet, and a lean athletic build. My hair is blond and thick and hangs to my shoulders, and over the years it has become lighter so that at times it seems pure white. I've been alive on this earth for more than two hundred fifty years and I am truly immortal, having survived any number of assaults on my person, and my own suicidal recklessness, only becoming stronger as the result.

My face is square, my mouth full and sensual, my nose insignificant, and I am perhaps one of the most conventional looking of the Undead you'll ever see. Almost all vampires are beautiful. They are picked for their beauty. But I have the boring appeal of a matinee idol rescued by a fierce and engaging expression, and I speak a brand of easy rapid English that's contemporary—after two centuries of accepting English as the universal language of the Undead.

Why am I telling you all this, you might ask—you, the members of the Blood Communion, who know me now as the Prince. Am I not the Lestat so vividly described in Louis's florid memoir? Am I not the same Lestat who became a super rock star for a brief time in the 1980s, publicizing the secrets of our tribe in film and song?

Yes, I am that person, most certainly, perhaps the only vampire known to just about every blood drinker on the planet by name and by sight. Yes, I made those rock videos that revealed our ancient parents, Akasha and Enkil, and how we might all perish if one or both of them were destroyed. Yes, I wrote other books after my autobiography; and yes, I am indeed the Prince now ruling from my Château in the remote mountains of France.

But it's been many a year since I addressed you directly, and some of you weren't born when I penned my autobiography. Some of you weren't Born to Darkness until very recently, and some of you might not believe in the story of the Vampire Lestat as it's been related to you—or the history of how Lestat became the host to the Sacred Core of all the tribe, and then finally, released from that burden, survived as the ruler upon whom order and survival now depend.

Make no mistake, the books *Prince Lestat* and *Prince Lestat and the Realms of Atlantis* were penned by me, and all that they related has indeed happened, and those many blood drinkers described in the two books are accurately portrayed.

But the time has come for me once again to address you intimately and to shape this narrative in my own inimitable and informal fashion as I seek to relate to you all that I think you should know.

And the first thing which I must tell you is that I write now for *you*—for my fellow blood drinkers, the members of the Blood Communion—and no one else.

Of course this book will fall into mortal hands. But it will be perceived as fiction, no matter how obvious it may be that it is not. All the books of the Vampire Chronicles have been received as fiction the world over, and always have been. The few mortals who interact with me in the vicinity of my ancestral home believe me to be an eccentric human who enjoys impersonating a vampire, the leader of a strange cult of like-minded vampire impersonators who gather under my roof to engage in romantic retreats from the busy modern world. This remains our greatest protection, this cynical dismissal of us as real, true monsters, in an era that just might be more dangerous to us than any other through which we've lived.

But I will not dwell on the matter in this narrative. The story I'm going to tell has little or nothing to do with the modern world. It's a tale as old as tale telling itself, about the struggle of individuals to find and defend their place in a timeless universe, alongside all the other children of the earth and the sun and the moon and the stars.

But it is important for me to say—as this story begins—that I was as resentful and confused by my human nature as I'd ever been.

If you do go back to my autobiography, you'll likely see how much I wanted humans to believe in us, how boldly I shaped my narrative as a challenge: Come, fight us, wipe us out! There ran in my Frenchman's blood only one acceptable version of glory: making history among mortal women and men. And as I prepared for my one and only rock concert in San Francisco in the year 1984, I did dream of an immense battle, an apocalyptic confrontation to which elder blood drinkers would be awakened and drawn irresistibly, and young ones incited with fury, and the mortal world committed to stamping out our evil once and for all.

Well, nothing came of that ambition. Nothing at all. The few brave scientists who insisted they had seen living proof of our existence met with personal ruin, with only a precious few being invited to join our ranks, at which point they passed into the same invisibility which protects us all.

Over the years, being the rebel and the brat that I am, I created another great sensation, described in my memoir, *Memnoch the Devil*, and that too did invite mortal scrutiny, a scrutiny which might have seduced yet more hapless individuals to destroy their lives arguing that we were real. But that brief damage to the fabric of the reasonable world was corrected immediately by clever blood drinkers who removed all forensic evidence of us from laboratories in New York City, and within a month all the excitement stirred up by me and my Blessed Veil of Saint Veronica was over, with the relic itself gone to the crypts of the Vatican in Rome. The Talamasca, an ancient Order of Scholars, managed to obtain it after that, and subsequent to their acquiring it, the veil was destroyed. There's a story to all that, a small one anyway, but you won't find it here.

The point is—for all the fuss and bother—we remained as safe in the shadows as we'd ever been.

This story—to be precise—is about how we vampires of the world came together to form what I now call the Blood Communion, and how I came not only to be Prince, but to be the true ruler of the tribe.

One can assume a title without really accepting it. One can be anointed a prince without reaching for the scepter. One can agree to lead without really believing in the power of oneself to do it. We all know these things to be true.

And so it was with me. I became Prince because the elders of our tribe wanted me to do it. I possessed something of a charismatic ease with the idea, which others did not share. But I did not really examine what I was doing when I accepted the title, or commit to it. Instead, I clung to a selfish passivity in the matter, assuming that at any moment I might tire of the entire enterprise and walk away. After all, I was still invisible and insignificant, an outcast, a monster, a predatory demon, Cain the slayer of his brothers and sisters, a phantom pilgrim on a spiritual journey so narrowly defined by my vampire existence that whatever I discovered would never be of relevance to anybody, except as poetry, as metaphor, as fiction, and I should take comfort in that fact.

Oh, I enjoy being the Prince, don't get me wrong. I loved the rapid and totally egregious restoration of my ancestral Château and the little village which lay below it on the narrow mountain road that led to nowhere—and it was an undoubted pleasure to see the great hall filled each evening with preternatural musicians and dancers, flashing exquisite white skin, shimmering hair, costumes of extraordinary richness, and countless jewels. One and all of the Undead were and are now most welcome under my roof. The house has innumerable salons through which you can wander, rooms in which you might settle to watch films on giant flat screens, and libraries in which you might meditate in silence or read. Beneath it are crypts that have been expanded to hold perhaps the entire tribe in darkness and safety, even were the Château itself attacked in the daylight hours and burnt over our heads.

I like all this. I like welcoming everyone. I like taking the young fledglings in hand and welcoming them to our closets from which they can take any clothing they need or desire. I like watching them shed their rags and burn them in one of the many fireplaces. I like hearing everywhere around me the soft uneven rumble of preternatural voices in conversation, even argument, and also the low, vibrant rhythm of preternatural thoughts.

But who am I to rule others? I was anointed the Brat Prince by Marius before I ever set foot on that rock music stage decades ago, and a brat I most surely was. Marius had come up with that little label for me when he realized I was revealing to the Vampire World all the secrets he'd bound me under penalty of destruction to keep. And a legion of others have picked up the title, and they use it as easily now as the simple appellation Prince.

It's no secret to the elders far and wide that I've never bent the knee to any authority ever, that I smashed up the coven of the Children of Satan when I was taken prisoner by it in the 1700s, and that I broke even the most informal rules with my rock music adventure, and deserved a good deal of the condemnation for recklessness that I received.

I didn't bow to Memnoch either.

And I didn't bow to God Incarnate, who appeared to me in the airy spiritual realm into which Memnoch dragged me, all the way back to the narrow dusty road to Calvary in the city of ancient Jerusalem. And having given short shrift to every being who had ever tried to control me, I seemed a most unlikely person to undertake the monarchy of the Undead.

But as this story begins, I had accepted it. I had accepted it truly and completely and for one simple reason. I wanted us—we, the vampires of this world—to survive. And I didn't want us clinging to the margins of life, a miserable remnant of bloodsucking vagabonds, battling each other in the wee hours of the night for crowded urban territories, burning out the shelters and refuges of this or that enemy, seeking to destroy one another for the most petty of human or vampiric concerns.

And that is what we had become before I accepted the throne. That is exactly what we were—a parentless tribe, as Benji Mahmoud put it, the little vampire genius who called to the elders of all ages to come forth and take care of their descendants, to bring to us order, and law, and principles for the good of all.

The good of all.

It is extremely difficult to do what is good for all when you believe that "all" are evil, loathsome by their very nature, with no right to breathe the same air as human beings. It is almost impossible to conceive of the welfare of "all" if one is so consumed with guilt and confusion that life seems little more than an agony except for those overwhelmingly ecstatic moments when one is drinking blood. And that is what most vampires believe.

Of course I'd never bought into the idea that we were evil or loathsome. I'd never accepted that we were bad. Yes, I drank blood and I took life, and I caused suffering. But I wrestled continuously with the obvious conditions of my existence, and the bloodlust of my nature, and my great will to survive. I knew full well the evil inherent in humans and I had a simple explanation for it. Evil comes quite simply from what we must do to survive. The entire history of evil in this world is related to what human beings do to one another in order to survive.

But believing that doesn't mean living it every minute. Conscience is an unreliable entity, at times a stranger to us, then ruling the present moment in torment and pain.

And wrestling with uneasy conscience, I wrestled as well with my passion for life, my lust for pleasure, for music, and beauty, and comfort and sensuality, and the inexplicable joys of art—and the baffling majesty of loving another so much that all the world, it seemed, depended on that love.

No, I didn't believe we were evil.

But I'd taken on the argot of self-loathing. I'd joked about traveling the Devil's Road, and striking like the hand of God. I'd used our contempt for ourselves to ease my conscience when I destroyed other blood drinkers; I'd used it when I chose cruelty for convenience when other paths had been open to me. I'd demeaned and insulted those who didn't know how to be happy. Yes, I was determined to be happy. And I fought furiously for ways to be happy.

And I had settled—without admitting it—for the old sacrosanct idea that we were inherently evil and had no place in the world, no right to exist.

After all, it was Marius himself, the ancient Roman, who had told me we were evil, and that the rational world had no place for evil, that evil could never be effectively integrated into a world which had come to believe in the true value of being good. And who was I to question the great Marius, or realize how lonely his existence was, and how dependent he was on keeping charge of the Core of vampiric life for those whom he so easily branded as evil?

Whatever my confusion on it, I played no role in a social revolution for blood drinkers. No. It was someone else who questioned the old assumptions about us with a childlike simplicity that changed our world.

Benji Mahmoud, Born to Darkness at the age of twelve, a Bedouin by birth, was the blood drinker who transformed us all.

Made by the powerful two-thousand-year-old Marius, Benji had no use for ideas of inherent guilt, mandatory self-hatred, and inevitable mental torment. Philosophy meant nothing to him. Survival was all. And he had another vision—that the blood drinkers of the world could be a strong and enduring tribe of immortals, hunters of the night who respected one another and demanded respect in return. And from that simple conviction in Benji's audacious appeal, my monarchy was eventually born.

And it is only in an informal and carefree style that I can tell you how I eventually came to terms with being the monarch.

You will find the tale filled with digressions, and there may be times when you suspect the digressions are the story. And you may be right. But whatever the case, it's the tale I have to tell about how I came to accept what others had offered to me, and how I came to know just who we creatures of the night really are.

Oh, don't worry. It's not all interior reflection, and inner change, so to speak. There is action. There is intrigue. There is danger. And there were certainly surprises for me.

But let's get into it, shall we?

As the tale begins, I am still struggling very much to meet the demands of Court life, to find some balance between the expectations of the Council of Elders—and my own wild desires to enhance and enrich the Court, which was attracting blood drinkers from all over the world. I haven't come close to believing in the Court in a profound way, merely riding the passion of the belief of others, and I think I know what it means to be Prince, but I don't.

Did I expect the Court to last? No, I really didn't. I didn't because every effort I'd ever witnessed to forge an enduring refuge for the Undead had eventually failed. And a lot of those coming to Court felt the same way. "This too shall pass," they did not hesitate to say, even as they wished us the best.

But I wanted the Court to last, I really did.

So let me begin the narrative on a night when Marius, the ancient Roman Child of the Millennia, in a fit of pique became impatient with what he referred to as my "nauseating buoyancy and optimism" about the world in general.

There was a ball that night in the great hall of the Château, as there almost always is on a Friday night, and it was snowing (it is snowing all through this novel), and things had been relatively simple and busy at Court for the last two to three months, and I was in a very happy disposition, believing that all was going extra specially well. Yes, it would all come crashing down eventually, but for now it was going well.

Marius, watching the dancers under the soft golden radiance of the chandeliers, said to me in a hard cold voice,

"Ultimately they will all disappoint you."

"What the Hell are you talking about?" I asked. His words had struck me with great force and I wanted to get back to listening to the music, and watching the dancers move to the music, and watching the snow fall beyond the open doors to the terrace. Now why did Marius, sitting on the bench beside me, have to say something so ominous?

"Because, Lestat," he said, "you have forgotten something absolutely essential about our nature. And sooner or later they will remind you of it."

"Which is what?" I demanded. I've never been a courteous pupil. "Why at a time such as this must you invent difficulties?"

He shrugged. He folded his arms and he leaned against the plastered wall behind us, gazing off into the ballroom. His long white-blond hair was swept back from his face and fastened with a gold clip at the nape of his neck, and he had a contented, relaxed look about him in his loose red velvet robes that was entirely at odds with the way he was ruining the moment for me.

"You've forgotten," he said, "that we are by nature killers. No, listen to me. Just listen." He placed his hand on mine but kept his eyes on the dancers. "You've forgotten that what makes us distinct from human beings and always will is that we hunt human beings and we love killing them. You're trying to make us into darkling angels."

"Not so. I never forget what we are."

"Be quiet," he said. He went on talking, eyes moving over the room slowly. "Soon you're going to have to accommodate what we are," he said. "And the fact that we are simpler creatures than human beings, allowed only one supreme creative and erotic act, and that is the act of killing."

I was resentful. "I haven't forgotten this for one solitary moment," I said, glaring at him. "I never forget it. How can I forget it? What I wouldn't give just now for one ripe sweet innocent victim, one tender—." I broke off. I was maddened that he was smiling.

It was only a small smile.

"Whyever do you bring this up now?" I asked.

"Don't you know?" he replied. He looked at me. "Can't you feel it?" His eyes fixed on me and he seemed effortlessly sincere and almost kind. "They're all waiting for something."

"Well, what else under Heaven can I give them!" I declared.

Something interrupted us that night.

Something came between us.

I no longer precisely remember what it was. We were interrupted. But I didn't forget that little exchange on the shadowy margins of the ballroom as we watched the others dance.

But several nights after, right at sunset, I awoke to the disturbing news that a gang of ugly blood drinker mavericks had terrorized an old immortal in the wilds of Louisiana who was appealing to me for help, and also that our beloved friends, the immortal Children of Atlantis, a tribe of strange beings with whom we shared the shadows, had deserted their new compound in rural England for the shelter of Gregory Collingsworth's great pharmaceutical towers outside of Paris.

Matters for the Prince, and the Prince went to it. And this is the story of all that followed.

Chapter 2

The slaughter of the band of rebel mavericks in Louisiana was inevitable. They'd been warned to stay away from New Orleans, where they'd been known to bully other blood drinkers and wreak enough havoc to make the local news. And this time, not only had they fractured the peace to attack the estate of an older immortal appealing for help, but they'd broken into my townhouse in the Rue Royale, stolen clothes from my closets and chests there, and stupidly slashed to pieces a minor but beautiful Impressionist painting which was dear to Louis.

Now, you probably know full well who Louis is and what he means to me. But for the newer fledglings, I'll say a few words here on that subject.

Louis de Pointe du Lac was a landowner in French colonial Louisiana when I gave him the Dark Blood sometime before the close of the eighteenth century. A little while after that, largely to bind him to me, as I loved him very much, I brought a child vampire into our family, and the three of us lived together in relative peace for sixty years in the old French part of New Orleans.

All of this was described in full by Louis in the very first of the Vampire Chronicles, published over forty years ago. Louis told the story of his life in that book, and also the story of his quest to find something that would give his painful existence as a vampire some meaning. It was a tragic story with a tragic ending. And it was Louis's outrageous lies about me, intentional and unintentional (some people should not be granted a poetic license), that prompted me to write my own autobiography and tell the secrets of Marius to the whole world.

Well, Louis and I have been reunited a number of times, and this time around, at the Court in France, our reunion is enduring. He left that Impressionist painting behind at my request in our old flat in the Rue Royale, and now these miserable miscreants had senselessly destroyed it.

But it was the appeal of the older vampire which compelled me to make the trip across the Atlantic to settle the score. An immortal totally unknown to me, by the name of Dmitri Fontayne, had written to me on parchment with India ink in a gorgeous old hand to recount how this band of rebels had tried to burn down his house in the bayou country, stolen his horses, and ruthlessly murdered his two mortal servants.

This could not go unpunished.

So off to Louisiana I went, along with my two bodyguards, Thorne and Cyril, of whom I have become increasingly fond, and it's a good thing, because they go with me everywhere.

Now, there used to be a vital reason for this, as there was a time when I carried the Sacred Core within me, the intelligence named Amel, to whom every vampire on the planet was connected. Had I been destroyed during the time, all the blood drinkers of the world would have perished with me.

But I no longer carry within me the Sacred Core. Indeed, no one does. Amel has been liberated, and his intellect now resides in a new flesh-and-blood body, provided for him by our fellow immortals, the Children of Atlantis.

Once this was accomplished, I had expected to lose Thorne and Cyril. I fully expected them to announce that there was no reason anymore for them to protect me. But quite to my surprise they both demanded to remain with me. And the Council of Elders formally asked them to remain, explaining that I was still the Prince, and the continuing vitality of the Court depended on me.

This was a little bit of a shock, and not an unpleasant one. It marked a deepening of my awareness of how very much my presence was required at the Château, and I couldn't bring myself to complain about being needed, respected, and wanted.

So off we went, the three of us, to find the miscreants on the prowl in New Orleans.

I will not recount how we annihilated them. I took no pleasure in it. I ascertained in each case that the rebel had indeed been warned, was determined to make mischief, believed we old ones to be bragging about powers we didn't possess, and then I destroyed them. I used the Fire Gift—or the telepathic ability to set them ablaze—and coupled with it a strong telekinetic blast that smashed their heads to pieces before they went up in smoke. I did not want to make them suffer. I wanted them gone. They'd had their chance to travel the Devil's Road and they'd gratuitously hurt another blood drinker for no good reason and murdered humans dear to him.

But it bothered me, all this. The leader of the pack, the last to die, had asked me by what authority I was to take his life, and I didn't really have a good answer for him. After all, I'd been the Brat Prince for decades, had I not? The question burned. Of course I could have rattled off a litany of reasons, but I didn't.

And when it was done, and nothing remained of these unwise fledglings except pools of dark grease on the rooftops on which they'd fallen, I felt faintly disgusted, and desperately thirsty.

Thorne, Cyril, and I spent an hour hunting. My craving for innocent blood was as usual damn near unbearable, so I settled for the infernal torment of the Little Drink from any number of tender, fetching young victims in a darkened nightclub, packed before the stage on which a folk singer sang tender laments with a southern drawl that made her sound faintly British.

After that I walked. Just walked. Walked on New Orleans pavements which are like no other pavements in the world, some of flagstone, some of herringbone brick, some of fractured and fragmented cement, many dangerously ruptured by the roots of trees, and some overgrown with tall grass, and others slimy with velvet-green moss, and some even set with old street names in blue letters.

New Orleans, my New Orleans.

I finally went back to my flat, and inspected the ruined painting. I left a note for my local attorney to have it restored, commended him on doing what he could to clean up the flat, and then sat in my favorite gilded armchair in the front parlor, in the dark, watching the headlamps on Royale float across the wallpapered ceiling. I love the sounds of the French Quarter on mild nights . . . laughter, chatter, gaiety, Dixieland jazz drifting out of open doors, rock music pounding somewhere—an eternal carouse.

The following night, we went into the bayou country to find the residence of Dmitri Fontayne, the blood drinker with the elegant handwriting.

Chapter 3

I was in love with the being the moment I glimpsed the house and the great black iron picket fence surrounding it. Such high fences these days are often made of aluminum, and they just don't look the same as iron. But this fence was indeed crafted from true iron and very high, with gilded pickets like the great fences and gates of Paris, and I loved that mark of care, including the heaviness of the arched gate as I opened it.

Down a relatively short drive lined with majestic oaks stood the house itself, with high front steps of marble and galleries upstairs and down running across its broad façade. Graceful two-story Corinthian columns punctuated these galleries, giving the place a Graeco-Roman grandeur that suggested a temple.

I figured the place had been built in the flush years right before the Civil War when rich Americans threw up such immense houses in desperate competition with one another, using the native cypress wood and stucco to produce an edifice that appeared to be all of marble when it was not.

I caught the scent of the oil lamps before I marked their soft mellow light behind the heavily figured lace curtains, and I stood for a moment on the bottom step looking up at the fanlight above the broad front door. All the scents of Louisiana, so familiar, so enticing, descended on me: the raw fragrance of the magnolias blooming in abundance on the nearby trees, and the deep perfume of the roses in the garden patches along the galleries, and jasmine, night jasmine of such a sweetness that one could drift off into endless dreaming just breathing it in, and remembering long-ago nights, and life moving confidently at a slower pace.

Steps in the hall beyond, and then a figure in the doorway, imperially slim, as the poet says, and with hair like my own, long, so blond it was almost white, gathered back in the fashion Marius and I had popularized at Court. And a hand raised with the flash of a ruby ring beckoning for me to enter.

I hurried to accept the welcome while Thorne and Cyril drifted off to make an inspection of the property, as they so often did.

As soon as I clasped his hand, I liked this blood drinker. His eyes were not large, but they were radiantly blue and his smile animated his entire face.

"Come in, Prince, do come in," he said in very precise English, sharpened by an accent I couldn't place.

He was my height and indeed quite thin, wearing a narrow-waisted modern coat and an old-fashioned lace-trimmed shirt over flannel trousers, and wingtipped shoes polished to a mirror luster, with string ties.

He drew me into a broad central hallway, paved in black-and-white marble, and then into a great spacious double parlor, so common in old plantation houses, which had become a library lined with books of all ages. A center table stood in the second parlor, and there we sat down to talk.

By then I'd glimpsed a dining room across the hallway, with a long oval table and English Chippendale chairs. That room too was lined with bookshelves.

Quaint glass oil lamps scattered here and there on the periphery of these rooms provided warm light. The highly polished heart-pine floors were lustrous. Those old floors had never meant to be bare, but rather an under flooring for carpets or parquet. But the poly-mer lacquer had rendered them hard and beautiful and they gave an amber glow to the room.

"Please call me Mitka," he said, "and your bodyguards are most welcome to come in. My name is Dmitri Fontayne. I'm part Russian, part French. I was made a blood drinker in the time of Great Cath-erine in Russia."

This delighted me. Vampires in the main don't volunteer their age or their history this readily, and he seemed entirely trusting when he came so easily to the point.

His mind was entirely in accord with his words, and these words particularly fascinated me. I don't think I'd ever encountered a blood drinker with quite this background. And there was a great deal I wanted to tell him about Louis suddenly, Louis who was immersed in the novels of Tolstoy, and had myriad questions about them which no one cared to answer, and how much Louis would love him right off.

But I came back to the moment.

"Mitka, my pleasure," I said. "And you know who I am. Lestat will do, though it seems the world likes to address me as 'the Prince.' Don't worry about Thorne or Cyril. They know I want to talk to you alone."

"As you wish," he said. "But they mustn't go far. You have enemies."

"If you're speaking of Rhoshamandes, I know all about him and his latest activities. . . ."

"Ah, but there are others, Prince," he said. "Please tell them to remain near at hand."

I did as he wished, sending a silent message to the others, who were prowling around the stables now, having a good time with the horses, which were apparently splendid, and which they wanted to ride.

"Which enemy is this? You do know the band of mavericks in New Orleans has been annihilated?"

"Yes, I do," he said. A shadow passed over his face, and he looked down for a moment as if he were murmuring a prayer for the dead, but I caught nothing, and then he surprised me by quickly making the Russian Sign of the Cross. Like the Greeks, the Russians touch the right shoulder before the left.

As he looked up, his face brightened beautifully and I felt a kind of elation that was all too common of late, simply being here with him in this ornate parlor surrounded by hundreds of enticing volumes, and feeling the night air through the long open windows to the south. Roses again, the scent of roses in Louisiana is perhaps stronger than anywhere else, and then there came on the breeze a great drift of green fragrances from the nearby swamp, all so redolent of life.

I had to get myself in hand. Fits of laughter, I'd always struggled with at odd moments, and fits of rage occasionally, but now it was spells of elation, as if the common comforts of the world were miracles.

A passage came to me suddenly from Tolstoy, something that Louis had read to me, something that Prince Andrei Bolkonsky was thinking as he lay close to death. Something about love, love making everything possible, and then Louis's strange comment that Tolstoy's first two great novels were studies of happiness.

"Ah yes," said the blood drinker opposite me with irresistible enthusiasm. "'Happy families are all alike,'" he said quoting the famous first line from *Anna Karenina*. Then he caught himself. "Forgive me. I make it a matter of courtesy not to ransack the minds of those I've only just met. But I couldn't help it."

"No need to be concerned at all," I said. I looked about the room. Too many topics of conversation pressed in on me and I tried to find some order. What had we been talking about? Enemies. I didn't want to talk about enemies. I started to talk about all that I saw before me, the inevitable Philadelphia wing chairs flanking the marble fireplace, and a tall secretaire punctuating the bookshelves, a lovely piece with inlaid designs and mirrored doors above the flap of the desk.

He was at once brightly happy over this. And something mad occurred to me, that every single time I ever encountered another blood drinker in friendship, it was as if I were meeting and entering an entire world. Seems I'd read somewhere, or heard it in a film, that the Jews believe each life is a universe, and if you take a life, well, then you are destroying a universe. And I thought, Yes, this is true of us, this is why we must love one another, because we are each an entire world. And with blood drinkers there were centuries of stories to tell, millennia of experiences to be related and understood.

Yes, I know what you're thinking as you read this. All this is obvious. When people suddenly understand love they can sound like perfect idiots, true.

"This enemy is a creature named Baudwin." Mitka's voice startled me. "An unsavory creature but a powerful creature, ancient, as ancient perhaps as Marius or Pandora, though I couldn't myself tell. He was on the prowl in New York at the time that you came there, and made an enemy of Rhoshamandes, and were proclaimed the Prince. I haven't seen him, however, in over a year."

"It's a pleasure to meet you," I said. "I'll meet this Baudwin when the time comes. Let's not waste these moments on him, though I appreciate the warning."

There was no need for us to discuss the obvious, that if this Baudwin was of the same age as Marius or Pandora, he would destroy me in a moment with the Fire Gift just as I'd destroyed the mavericks in New Orleans. It was sobering to realize that there might be any number of such creatures whom I hadn't come to know yet, who knew of me. I liked to believe that I met all of the Children of the

Millennia and had a fair idea of who hated me and who did not. But I'd never heard of Baudwin.

"I love your house and all you've achieved here," I said, pushing the darker thoughts from my mind. It was enough to know that Cyril and Thorne were paying heed to every word we said.

"I'm so happy you approve," he responded. "I wouldn't call it a restoration, since I have used some modern materials and made some distinctly modern choices, but I've done my best to use only superior materials throughout." He too seemed to forget the darker thoughts and his face was fired with enthusiasm now, and as so often happens, the human warmth and the human lines came back to it, and I could see what sort of man he might have been. Likely thirty years of age, no more than that, and I noted how very delicate were his hands with which he gestured easily, and all of the rings he wore—even his ruby ring—were made with pearls.

"It's taken me years to acquire the furnishings," he said. "I remember in the beginning when I first came here in the 1930s, it seemed easier to find the very high-quality survivals from the eighteenth century—paintings, chairs, that sort of thing."

He talked on easily of the bones of the house being excellent, and the old plaster falling away to leave bare-brick chain walls. Chain walls are walls that went all the way down to the ground rather than a foundation, and I had not heard that term in many years.

"The house was a total ruin when I first happened upon it. You understand I had no idea you were in New Orleans in those times. I knew there were blood drinkers about, but I knew nothing of them until many decades later when I read all of your stories, and I was riding on the old road to Napoleonville when I saw the house on the night of a bright moon, and I swore it spoke to me. It beckoned me to brave the wreckage and come inside, and once I did I knew I must bring it all back to its former glory, so that some night when I finally left it, it would be infinitely better than I'd found it, and I'd left my stamp upon it with pride."

I smiled, loving the way his voice flowed with such easy sincerity and excitement.

"Ah, you know these old heart-pine floors were never meant to be bare, but we finish them with polymer now and they are hard and have an amber sheen."

"Well, now there are no vandals to torment you," I said. "And I'll see to it that none dare in future. I think what happened last night in New Orleans will be known far and wide. I didn't leave anyone alive to tell the tale, but such happenings are always known."

"Yes, they are," he said. "I knew when they died." And that shadow came across his face. "I mean no harm to other blood drinkers. If I'd known when I came to Louisiana that you were here and you needed help, I would have come to you. I had been in Lima, Peru, for many years, well, almost since I'd made the crossing centuries ago, and America was so new to me, so startlingly new."

"I can well understand that you'd never want to leave this house," I said. "But why don't you come to Court? I wish that you'd come."

"Ah, but you see, I have an enemy there, quite an implacable enemy, and I'd be arranging my own demise if I came."

He said this last with seriousness but not with fear.

"In fact, I must confess I welcome the opportunity to put the matter before you so that perhaps you can prevail upon this enemy to allow me to come to Court and leave me alone."

"I'll do more than that," I said. "I'll settle the matter. Tell me who this is."

I liked him. I liked him very much. I liked his lean face and his well-shaped animated lips and his soft blue eyes. His hair, though blond, had a pearl-white look to it; and his eyes had a pearly look as well. His jacket was light blue, and he had chosen pearl buttons for it, and of course there were those rings on his right hand. Why, I wondered, only on the right hand? If a man wears three rings on his right hand, then usually he wears two or three on his left.

I couldn't read his mind as he looked at me, but I knew he was pondering this enemy, and I admired the way that he could keep his thoughts veiled. His expression was attentive, and pleasant. Finally he spoke.

"Arjun," he said in a soft voice.

"Well, of course, I know him."

"Yes . . . I've read . . . in the two books. And he is there at Court, isn't he? He's with the Countess De Malvrier."

Countess De Malvrier was an old name for Pandora, a name that belonged to an earlier existence and a name she never used now. And yes, Arjun was at Court with her and, to the best of my estimation, making her life rather miserable.

Arjun had been roused from the earth by "the Voice," who happened to be the spirit, Amel, inside of us, coming to consciousness and desperate to destroy some of those vampires connected to him. But all this was history now. And Arjun, unprepared for and uninterested in the modern age, lodged at Court rather like a patient in a madhouse, gazing about him with menacing eyes and clinging always to Pandora.

There had been times when he seemed restored, pleasant, ready to begin to embrace a new existence, but these periods had become infrequent, and Arjun frightened many of the other vampires who lacked his age and power.

"I've read the latest books over twice," Fontayne said. "And I have the hope that Arjun has softened towards me, but I wouldn't want to put this unexpectedly to a test."

"Why is Arjun a threat to you?" I asked. "Explain the whole thing. Give me as much as you can so that I can talk to him and really obtain a resolution."

A sudden memory surprised me—of that maverick in New Orleans demanding of me in a rage, "By what authority do you do this to me?"

I felt a shiver and tried to shake it off. "I want to be of help," I said.

"You have the authority of the Council of Elders behind you," he said now with great sympathy. He reached out for my hand. "That is the source of your authority and also the needs of the entire Court."

I liked him so much. I saw no reason to conceal it. His generous expression, his easy speech, all this was pleasant, as was his house with its books gleaming on the shelves in the gentle light.

"I have my doubts," I said. "But I behave as if I had none, and I'll behave that way with Arjun, if you'll put the case before me."

"Of course. I assure you I'm innocent of any wrongdoing," he said. "I have never done anything intentional to displease Arjun."

"So let me know what happened."

"I was in Saint Petersburg in the 1700s," he said. "Great Catherine was enchanted with European society then, and my father had been a Parisian, and my mother a Russian countess. Both were dead, however, when I sought a position serving Catherine's court. I spoke Russian and French naturally, and also English as well as I speak it now. I gained a position almost immediately as a translator and later working as a French tutor to a noble household, and from there I answered the advertisement of the Countess Malvrier. Hers was one of the most lovely houses in Petersburg then, on the English Embankment, entirely new and lavishly furnished, but she was reclusive and seldom appeared in society and never invited anyone into her home.

"My first meeting with her was shocking. She had me come up to her bedchamber. She was wearing a simple nightgown of white gauze and in her bare feet, standing by the fireplace, and she asked me to brush her hair.

"I was stunned. There were female servants all over the house, and plenty of male servants too. But I hadn't the slightest intention of refusing her. I took the hairbrush and I brushed her hair."

I saw it as he spoke. I saw Pandora etched by the light of the fire. I saw that she was trembling, and her face was drawn and her eyes were large with hunger and pain.

"She wanted me to be her librarian, she said, and to go through boxes and boxes of books. Seems she'd collected these books over many years and from all over the world. Now I know of course that she'd been collecting them for centuries. She asked me to put these books in order, to fill the shelves of her drawing rooms with them." He stopped and gestured to his own library. "This is so small by comparison, but then those Russian houses were so very grand. There was unimaginable wealth in Russia then, and such a great appetite for European art."

"I can imagine it," I said. And again I saw Pandora looking straight at me as through his gaze. I saw Mitka standing behind her with the brush in his hand. Her hair was long, brown, rippling with waves, falling over her shoulders as if she were an illustration in a Pre-Raphaelite painting. I could smell a heady incense in the room, something Eastern and exotic and intoxicating. The only illumination came from the flames of the fire.

"Yes," he went on, "and finally she said that even more important was that I read to her in French, that I read the works of Diderot and Rousseau. She wanted me to read scientific works to her in English—and to know about all things European but most especially the Enlightenment, le Siècle des Lumières. She abruptly stopped talking of this and asked me to explain John Locke to her, and what was the appeal of David Hume? She wanted to know all about Voltaire.

"Of course none of this in itself was out of the ordinary really in that the Empress Catherine was in love with all of these very same European writers and thinkers, and all the Court was cultivating an interest to follow the Empress, whether they cared about such things or not.

"Seemed for months on end I read to her, aloud, nightly, sometimes from sunset to the early hours of the morning. Of course I never saw her in the day and I wasn't surprised. I usually worked on ordering the library until noon. Then I'd sleep, and sometimes especially in winter she woke me well before I was supposed to be called.

"I didn't care. I adored her. I fell in love with her. She told me that she did not want for this to happen, and that her lover was demanding and cruel, and might appear at any time. I won't dwell on this, but I did have fantasies of killing him. But I assure you, I never sought really to harm him. All this was, well, poetic."

I laughed. "I understand," I said. He smiled gratefully and continued:

"When he finally did appear, I hated him immediately. He was Arjun; he dressed then entirely as a Russian, and the first time I saw him he was piled in furs and wearing leather gloves and had just come in from a storm. It was close to midnight and I was talking softly to the Countess about a possible trip to Paris, assuring her that she would love such a thing, and she kept saying what she always said to any of my suggestions, that it was absolutely impossible, and that I must make Paris real to her, and I was doing my best to describe it when in came Arjun.

"He told me to get out of his sight immediately, and thereafter for the next year, I saw the Countess only in the library and when she was appropriately dressed, and then only for about three hours of an evening before she and Arjun went out.

"I was fiercely jealous but kept it to myself. After all, I had no title, didn't come from a great family, and had only a small income that was less than half of what I was being paid for my work.

"I did everything I could to stay out of the way of the master when he was home, to appear busy regardless of the hour, and to keep to my room whenever I could. But this wasn't enough. Often when the master appeared I was told to go out.

"Alas, we still encountered one another, once at the ballet, another time at the opera, and then again at a ball. Then it became all too clear that I was going to run into Arjun wherever I happened to go in Petersburg, and finally one night when I came home unexpectedly and caught the master and the mistress in the middle of a huge argument, Arjun turned to me, and in a fit of snarling rage, drew his saber and ran me through with it. I couldn't move or speak. The blood was pouring out of me. He was laughing. He had the servants lock me in my room.

"I was dying, there was little doubt of that, and I was in a rage that no physician had been sent for, but within a few minutes I was too weak even to get off the bed. I thought this was the end, and as I was thirty-four years of age, I was bitter and disconsolate and in a lot of pain.

"Suddenly I heard loud voices on the floor below and then the sound of the great front door of the house being slammed, and I knew that the murderer had gone out. Perhaps now, I thought, someone will help me.

"Within seconds, the door of my room opened and the Countess was there. She examined my wound and then she very simply told me to trust her in what she did next and I would have the power to live until the end of time.

"I almost laughed. I remember I said, 'Countess, I will settle right now for living through this night.'

"I couldn't even form a sensible question to all this, when she lifted me in her arms and began to draw the blood out of my wound and into her own mouth. I fainted or went into a swoon.

"I don't recall seeing anything, or knowing anything, or having any veil lifted on the mysteries of life, only a kind of warm ecstasy and then a drowsiness in which my death seemed inevitable and a fairly simple step. I tried to make some sense of what she had done to me, and I decided she was trying to make it easy for me to die, and she certainly had. I no longer cared. Then she lifted me up again and this time she tore open her left wrist with her teeth and forced my mouth against the gash.

"You know what this was like, the taste of her blood. And the sudden ravenous thirst triggered in me by this. I drank the blood; I drank it as if it were wine going down my throat; and I heard her voice speaking to me, low and steady, without stop. She told a simple story of her life. I don't recall expression in her voice, or even a cadence. It was like a golden ribbon unfurling, to listen to her, and feel this blood coursing into me, as she went on about the great blood drinker who had made her, Marius, and how deeply she loved him and how they'd been lost to one another, and how she had traveled the world. She spoke of powerful blood drinkers like herself. And some of those names I've found since in your books. Sevraine was the name that I most distinctly remember. She spoke of seeking refuge in the halls of the Great Sevraine. At some point, she spoke of India, of temples and jungles in India and of encountering the Prince Arjun and of bringing him over, and of how he had become the cruelest of lovers, giving her the worst torment she'd ever known.

"There came a moment when I was no longer drinking blood. I was seated on the side of the bed looking at her as she hastily put me in a long fur-lined coat to hide my bloodstained garments and then we went out into the night.

"The predicable things happened. I took my first victim. A poor beggar all but dead from the cold. I died the death, as she put it, the vile fluids streaming out of me, and then it was home again in haste to my rooms, where I bathed and dressed in fresh garments, and then she took me into the closed-off east wing of the house, and found a hiding place for me and told me not to stir from that spot until it was safe. She had explained to me about the paralysis that would come over me when the first light shone in the sky. And I slept that strange unearthly sleep we know in which I dreamed of her, and of embracing her, and of a passion that had no real meaning for her, wanting her desperately and vowing to take her away from Arjun.

"Arjun went into a rage when he learned what she had done. I could hear him easily when I finally opened my eyes. It seemed he was destroying the entire house.

"I couldn't listen to this and do nothing, though she'd told me of his immense strength and the powers he had to destroy with his mind, though she'd warned me that he and she both possessed the power to burn objects and persons at will.

"I came out of my hiding place and rushed towards the central portion of the house, determined to fight him to the death.

"But he was gone. She met me, and led me back into her bedroom. There was no time, she said, to provide for me as she had wanted to do. But I must listen to what she said. She undid the strings from one of her pillowcases and into this she poured all the jewels that were on her dressing table, emeralds and pearls and rubies and bracelets of gold. And to this she added all the coin she had in her rooms. And then she gave me the name of the bank through which she would provide an income for me, and told me what code words I was to use to claim it.

"She was just finishing these instructions, and I had the pillowcase sack in my hands, when in came Arjun, quiet and as huge as a tiger, I would imagine, but then I've never been surprised by an actual tiger, and there he was, flashing with menace. He terrified me."

I saw Arjun as Fontayne had seen him.

Arjun was a big man, dark of skin, with remarkable black eyes that made me think of opals. He had ink-black hair that was mostly a knotted and tangled mass these days and he roamed about the Château in a long ornamented gown called a kurta with silken pajamas under it, his feet bare.

In Fontayne's story, Arjun was splendidly dressed as an eighteenth-century gentleman in shimmering gold brocade and lace with breeches and white stockings and shoes with bejeweled buckles, his hair hidden by a crimson turban. His face was hideous, deformed by rage and hatred.

" 'I'll let you live,' Arjun said, 'for one good reason, that she will make my existence Hell if I do to you what I want. But if I ever lay eyes on you again, Mitka, I will burn you alive.'

"And having said this in his soft dark voice, he turned this power of his, this evil power to immolate living creatures with his mind, he turned this power on a great painting on the wall and I saw it turn black and wither, and then burst into tiny flames as it fell in smoking fragments to the floor. 'You will die like that,' he said to me, 'and slowly, and you will be crying for me to end it before I do. Now go, get out of here.'

"The Countess nodded to me, and told me firmly not even to look at her, but to do what Arjun told me.

"And this is why I cannot come to Court, Lestat, because if he is there, he will do what he promised to do on that night."

I reflected on this for a long moment. I was about to respond when he spoke again.

"I swear to you," he said. "I have never done anything to offend him. Yes, I did love her, and I did covet her, but I swear to you that I did nothing to invite his enmity. He was offended at my very existence and simply maddened to learn that she had given me the Blood."

"I understand," I said. Again I reflected, and then after a long time I said this:

"He is at Court and he is difficult and cantankerous. He is a thorn in the side of Marius. I will go to the council and tell them this story and then I will ask for him to come in and tell us if he has any objections to your coming to Court. I will let him make the choice, either to accept your coming, or to insist that you don't. And if he does insist that you cannot come, that he will destroy you if he sees you, well, I will demand to know why. If you've told me the truth, he will have no good reason. And it was for disputes like this that my authority, whatever its source, was made. I'll do my best for you. I will insist that he agree to forgive whatever injured him in the past."

I could see that he was anxious and filled with misgiving. In a low voice he began to say that perhaps this was too much to ask of me.

"No," I said. "This is why I am the Prince, so that all disputes of this kind can be settled, and so that all can come to Court and in peace. You let me do what I must do. And I am confident that I'll be sending for you very soon."

He shuddered all over as if he were about to cry and then he rose to his feet, came towards me, and lifted my right hand and kissed it.

I stood and we walked out of the parlor together. I suppose I had some vague idea of going back to New Orleans now, but really I didn't want to leave Fontayne.

It was far too late of course to return tonight to France.

"But you trust in me," I told him.

"There is one thing more," he said in a whisper.

"What is it?"

"I've never . . . I don't know how . . . I cannot make the crossing of the sea as you do."

"Oh, yes, you can," I said. "Don't worry about this. I'll come back for you and I'll show you how to do it. You're older than I am. You'll learn quite fast."

I did not want to go. He sensed it.

An absurd thought came to me, that being here with him, being in his house, simply sitting at a table in his parlor and talking to him, it had all felt natural and good, as if in spite of the topic of our conversation we were simply human beings and all the dark world didn't exist. I was ashamed of this. Why did we have to be "like human beings"? I demanded of myself. Why could we not simply be blood drinkers together? And there came over me again the realization of how new it was to me to love others of the tribe and accept them as beings that had a right to be alive as I was alive.

I looked at him, at his shining eyes, and his congenial smile, and he took my hand and said he wanted to show the house to me.

We remained together for several hours after that, during which we walked through many rooms and I admired not only the endless book collection that flowed from room to room, but many of his paintings, including a few Russian painters of the nineteenth century I'd never heard of before. Fontayne told me that his most valuable paintings were not here in this house, that after the attack of the mavericks, he'd put them in a vault in a New Orleans bank, but that he might bring them to Court if I would accept them. I was delighted.

For me, this was a lovely time. I was overflowing with affection for him, called him Mitka easily, and finally did ask the inevitable simpleton questions, "Did you really know Catherine the Great herself?" and "Did you in fact speak to her?"

"Yes" was the answer to both, and the questions sparked a long reverie about what it had been like in Saint Petersburg in those times, and how much he'd enjoyed the balls at Court, and the passion of the Russians for all things French. Of course the Revolution in France had had a mighty impact, yet life in Russia had remained stable and it had been unthinkable that revolution would occur there.

We might have continued that conversation for a year.

We walked about outside the house, through the gardens which were crowded with flowers and vines that blossom at night, and I saw Fontayne's stables, including the wreckage of the one which had been burned, and only towards the end of the night did he confide to me that the mavericks had destroyed a young woman whom he wanted to bring into the Blood.

I felt this like a sword to my heart. I was furious.

"And why they did this I have no idea," he said. "Why come after me? Why trouble me? I never hunt in New Orleans. Why destroy those mortals who were attached to my house?"

I wished the little beasts could have been brought back to life so that I might kill them all over again. I told him so.

"And I was only waiting for your approval to bring her into the Blood," he added. "You know, I wanted to meet you, to get your permission."

This silenced me, but it was not the first time a blood drinker had volunteered this complete acceptance of the Court and my position as the sovereign.

"Surely you will be making rules as to who might be brought into the Blood," he said as we kept walking. "Surely you will set some standards."

I didn't answer. I knew that the council was considering this very thing. Yet all of us agreed that the right to make another blood drinker, to transform another human with our own blood, was such an intensely personal and intimate and emotional act that we did not know how to go about imposing a law on it. I tried to say something to that effect.

"It's rather like telling humans that they cannot have children."

I could see that he was now in such deep pain he couldn't talk. We continued down a long garden path and made a round of a large pond filled with monstrous goldfish, flashing under the light of many Japanese lanterns along the shore. Finally he said, "Well, what's the use of speaking of it now? They destroyed her. There was nothing left of her when they had done their work. I cannot, I will not, dwell on it, wondering what were her last moments."

I wanted to ask if the girl had known what he had planned, but why cause him more misery? I thought of my own architect back in the village on the mountain below the Château, and my own plan to bring him over, and I thought I should act on that immediately.

Since time immemorial, immortals had tormented other immortals by destroying human beings under their protection.

Finally, I asked him about this Baudwin, whom he'd characterized as my enemy. I asked if Baudwin had had any connection to the mavericks whom I'd just wiped out.

"No," he said. "Baudwin is ancient, and I don't know him. He came to me with one purpose. He had heard about the books you've written and the Court and wanted to know what I thought of all this. When I didn't respond to his outrage at the idea of a monarchy or a Court, he appeared to lose interest in me. I didn't have an easy moment in his presence. He was too old, too powerful." He paused, looking at me, and then he said, "It's hard for me to believe that young and old can congregate at the Court."

"Well, they do," I said. "The lion and the lamb lie down together there." I shrugged. "This is the spirit of the Court. The old rule of hospitality prevails: all blood drinkers are welcome. All immortals are welcome."

He nodded.

"Someone has to break that peace to be cast out," I said. "And if Arjun cannot accept your coming, then he will have to leave."

"I've encountered so few blood drinkers over the years," said Fontayne, "and always with discomfort and suspicion. My existence has been lonely almost beyond endurance. But this Baudwin troubled me. There was something childish and foolish about him. He claimed descent from a legend. Perhaps he left because I didn't find him all that interesting myself and he sensed it."

Descent from a legend?

But it was time, finally, to return to New Orleans. Cyril and Thorne suddenly appeared at a polite remove, and I knew of course by the lightening sky and the song of the morning birds.

I kissed Fontayne on both sides of his face, and promised him I'd resolve the issue with Arjun as soon as I could.

It wasn't until I was alone with Cyril that he confided to me in a whisper that Arjun was no more and that was all he knew about it.

When we reached the flat in New Orleans, there was a voice message for me on my landline phone. It was from Eleni in New York.

"Lestat, you're needed now at Court. Armand has already gone ahead. Seems Arjun has been destroyed by Marius."

Chapter 4

The following evening, I crossed the Atlantic in record time, entering the Château by means of the old tower—the only one of the four towers that had been still standing from my time before the restoration of the entire castle.

The house was eerily quiet—the orchestra was not gathered, the ballroom empty—and I was told immediately by Louis that Marius had not spoken a word since the "catastrophe" happened, and that he and all the council were waiting for me.

But before I continue with the story of Arjun's death, or any story for that matter, I want to bring you up to date on the state of the Court and the village and what had been happening there.

As many of you know, I began years ago to restore the Château in which I had been born, and the deserted village that lay on the mountainside just below it. These ruins were in a very remote part of the mountains of France, and I had paid immense sums to the architects and workmen whom I lured to this neglected spot and challenged them to re-create the Château not as it had been in my childhood, with one of its four towers left standing and only a few habitable rooms in its central portion, but to rebuild the Château as it had originally been after the Crusades, when my ancestors were at the peak of their wealth and power. And on top of this I wanted modernization with electricity throughout, and the entire structure plastered inside by master craftsmen, and floored with the finest hardwood parquet, creating what might have been an eighteenth-century gentleman's restoration of the place.

For years I did not visit myself, but made decisions from heaps of photographs sent to me wherever I was in the world, and I opened the coffers for the complete furnishing of the place in the most expensive and beautiful reproductions of eighteenth-century chairs, tables, beds, et cetera. To all this I added an immense collection of Persian and Aubusson rugs and tapestries. Windows were fitted with double sashes and heavy glass to insulate them against the cold, and even the old crypts beneath the place were refurbished and divided into proper rooms paneled in marble.

When I first set eyes upon the place after so many years, it was as if I were dreaming. All four towers had been fully rebuilt, and the village itself, little more than a steep winding high street, was walled in eighteenth-century-style shops and townhouses, and even a few manor houses had been redone in the countryside.

Surely I'd given permission for all of this, but I had paid little attention to the master plan or the requests over the years. And I fell in love with what I saw before me.

A small population of craftsmen and artists lodged in the village, and regarded my coming as an event, and I struggled not to disappoint them, clothed as I was in a long fur-lined cloak, with pale lavender glasses over my eyes, and my hands sheathed in gloves.

Complaining of the bright light everywhere we went, I soon seduced them with the notion that the village would best be understood and appreciated by candlelight, and they must forgive me for wanting to see it that way.

Through some fifteen little structures we went—by candle-light—as I admired the meticulous re-creations of the tailor's shop, the butcher, the baker, the cheese maker, the drapers, and all the other buildings which had once made up the small community, but the great prizes were really the inn, of which I had the most painful and joyful memories, and the church, which was so magnificently restored that a Mass might have been said at the altar, without anyone realizing that the place was not consecrated.

The craftsmen lived comfortably in the flats above all these various museumlike shops, and worked together in large studios in the manor house just beyond the boundaries of the village—and a great map was shown to me of all the land I owned and how much work there was to do to create the old fairground where the yearly markets had been held, and perhaps erect another inn, a much-larger inn for the inevitable public who would flock to this spot to view the entire re-creation.

Of course, I had to disappoint them. I had to tell them that the Château would be inhabited by a secret order of men and women who met to discuss philosophy and music and escape the modern world, and that there never would be a time when the public would be invited here. I could feel their disappointment when I explained all this. Indeed it was almost anguish. Some of these people had devoted their entire careers to this one project, and there was nothing now to be done but to give them more work to do, to let the village develop to serve their community as well as ours, and to pay them handsomely for it so that they would go on working in obscurity in this strange realm beyond time and the modern world.

Gold was the secret. Salaries became bribes. A physician was sent for and maintained to serve the local needs. Food and drink were supplied at no cost; and the inn at night was a place where all could eat and drink without very often receiving an actual guest, but of course some guests, some very unusual guests, the Children of Atlantis, did come later.

There was a great deal more work to be done—stables to be

built, horses to be bought, an immense network of greenhouses to be erected for the growth of flowers for the Château and fruit and vegetables for the village.

And there were egregious lies to be told, but without any sort of boast—that is, told grudgingly—that we as a secret order imported all our own food, and those visiting the Château would bring their special dietary needs with them.

To my surprise, the head architect of the group, Alain Abelard, with whom I soon fell in love, and with whom I am still in love, was familiar with my books, and had a collection of my old rock videos, and completely respected my persona as a vampire, and thought the whole thing charming, marveling at the wealth American and British rock stars make that could support such a magnificent enterprise.

In his quiet and generous soul, I could see that he was convinced I'd someday open all this to the public. My hope was that I could bring him over into the Blood. But not right away. There was still too much work to be done.

When I first walked through the restored Château, I experienced emotions I couldn't contain. I dismissed the mortal guides and went from room to room on my own, remembering far too much of what all this had been like in the time of my mortal life.

Gorgeous salons with silken-paneled walls and plaster curlicues and Savonnerie carpets on the floor now replaced the miserable bed-chambers we'd occupied in those days.

A lovely banquet room lent itself to being the Council Chamber of the Court, and the architects were still working upon the many apartments throughout the structure, and their modern marble bathrooms, replete with sunken tubs and spacious showers.

Vampires adore modern baths; they love standing in a flood of heated water, thoroughly cleansing the dust from themselves, and then shaking the water out of their hair, and drying their preter-natural skin with luxuriant towels before warm little fires. Well, the

Château had such a bath for every apartment or suite or bedchamber. We give off no scent, absorb no precious oils, and often take up the clothes of our victims precisely because they do carry a human scent and this disguises us as we drift through the crowded taverns, bars, and dancing clubs, but there is no one on the alert for us anyway.

The great hall where my family and I had once dined, quarreled, listened to the demands of the villagers and the farmers, and hovered around the single fire we could afford was now a great palatial ballroom with ample space for an orchestra of vampires, which soon came to be, and some five thousand or more dancers.

At later times when the entire household assembled in this room, there might be two thousand present in the ballroom. No one ever counted, except our resident doctor, Fareed, who is, to this very moment, still trying in vain to calculate the actual size of the blood drinker tribe. His most recent guess is four thousand.

But then three thousand have at times come together at the Château. The fact is no one knows what blood drinkers sleep in the earth or lurk on the periphery, as this one described to me most recently by Fontayne— this "enemy" named Baudwin.

Now let me explain how the Court itself became established and organized. I've described some of this in the other two recent books published since I became Prince, but I want you all to be acquainted with how things worked.

And how things worked evolved quickly once I had thrown open the Château to all, and the word went out from one telepathic mind to another, and to all a guarantee of safety was given, so long as they would come with goodwill and respect for us.

My fellow hosts in this were the elders I'd only recently come to know and love—Gregory Duff Collingsworth with his family of Chrysanthe, Zenobia, and Avicus; Dr. Fareed and his maker, Seth, the son of Akasha; the ravishing beauty known as the Great Sevraine, who had for some time been a friend of my beloved mother, Gabrielle; and the Children of the Millennia cherished by me for so long, Pandora and Marius. Jesse Reeves and my beloved David Talbot also came to reside at the Château, and eventually so did the young fledglings of Marius, the pianist Sybelle and the creator of the vampire broadcast that did more than anything to awaken us and unite us as a tribe, Benji Mahmoud.

Antoine, my old fledgling from New Orleans, had been reunited with us and became the conductor of our orchestra; and from an alpine refuge that had been a closely guarded secret for over a thousand years came many more musicians brought into the Blood by Notker the Wise, for music was of such importance to him that it had become his way of moving through eternity.

There were many others, Bianca, a long-lost love of Marius; Davis, of the old Fang Gang; Everard de Landen of Italy; Eleni, who had long ago been my friend at the Théâtre des Vampires; and Allesandra, a powerful immortal who survived the fires that had ended so many of the old Children of Satan who had dwelt beneath the great cemetery, Les Innocents.

There were chambers aplenty for all of these, and they came and went as they chose, and over time began to remain for longer and longer periods.

But through the doors every night for a very long time there drifted new blood drinkers, many penniless and living from victim to victim, and a great many too young to live in the remote mountains where the Château was located.

I would not permit ever any blood drinker to prey upon the mortals of the surrounding villages or towns, and so that meant that many of the young who were unable to take to the air and travel with confidence just under the clouds could not stay with us unless protected by an older vampire who could shepherd them regularly to the thick hunting grounds of Marseille or London or Paris.

But such a Court needs structure eventually, maintenance, and even enforcers who can rid the Court quickly of those who come with no respect whatsoever for what we were seeking to achieve.

And a staff evolved, without my much tending it, due to a young fledgling from America named Barbara.

Barbara like every blood drinker who crossed the threshold had a story to tell that would fill two volumes, but it is enough to say she had one hundred and thirty years in the Blood, and had lost by violence the two elder vampires who had made her, forming with her a household that had endured into this century. It was not the Burnings as we call them which had destroyed her beloved elders, but a random violent raid by one of those marauding blood drinkers who slaughter others for territory.

Barbara and her makers had lived in a venerable old wooden Victorian home in a small university town in the Midwest near enough to several cities for easy hunting. Theirs had been a quiet life enduring for decades under the same roof, with Barbara or one of the others undertaking to teach at the university from time to time, and now and then traveling. In this little group, our books, the Vampire Chronicles, had been studied over the years with skepticism but respect, and it was to me that Barbara came when a maverick burnt down the old home of her makers, destroying them with it.

Barbara had been in the city of Saint Louis at the time, to attend a symphony, and came home before dawn to witness the conflagration.

She remained near the ruins only long enough to ascertain without doubt that her makers were truly dead and gone, reduced to ashes amid the rubble, leaving behind only their unmistakable clothing.

And then Barbara accepted the invitation to all, broadcast night after night by Benji Mahmoud to come to the Court in France as a guest, or to ask for justice.

It had taken Barbara great difficulty to cross the sea. She'd traveled as far north as she could on the American continent and then taken a plane to London, and from there another to Paris, from which she'd driven into the mountains searching for several nights before she came upon the restored Château filled with lights above a perfect village slumbering as if it were under an enchantment.

It was curfew of course that was responsible for what Barbara saw as she drove up the high street. No one among the mortal colony was then allowed out after a certain hour, except to go and come from the tavern in the inn, which Barbara passed making straight for the broad bridge over the moat that surrounded the castle.

I'd not been there when she first came, and did not meet her until a week later. I was immediately drawn to her. She had been in her fifties when the Blood restored her to a more youthful appearance, turning most of her gray hair black again, and banishing forever a crippling disease in the joints that had been making the slightest movements ever more painful for her. She dressed in simple, heavy tweed jackets and long skirts with brown boots to the hem, and pinned her hair back with a diamond barrette, her only adornment. She had a long narrow face that was almost gaunt, with eyes that were immense, and thick black eyebrows drawn quite straight above her eyes and a full ruddy mouth. Her skin was very dark for a blood drinker, and she told of a Greek and Italian heritage and an infusion of African blood through one of her grandmothers.

I liked her at once. But more than that, I was impressed by her. She found the Court astonishing and she had gone to work doing all manner of things that needed to be done, from polishing mirrors, to beating rugs, to unpacking crates of new bronze statuettes (I was always ordering such things) and antique Chinese vases, to fixing taps that were broken, and righting paintings that hung crooked, and cleaning out chimneys that smoked, and picking up garments scattered about and trying to find the apartments of their owners.

And though the cleaning of the Château at that time was the duty of several mortals who resided in the village, Barbara assured me that there was no need for such exposure.

"I am in love with this Court," she said, "and I can provide what's needed for all of you if you will allow me to do it." She'd seen what was obvious, that certain vampires who had wandered in, and clung uncertainly to the shadows, would do anything to become a vital part of the household. Many had skills from their long-ago mortal lives that could be revived now to good use. Only a word from me and their loyalty and submission would be unstinting.

Within a matter of months, Barbara began organizing a staff of quick, eager blood drinkers who attended to every conceivable need while being the eyes and the ears of the council everywhere. Barbara established a log of which apartments belonged to whom, and which were empty, and how many solitary rooms there were, and saw to the endless supply of beeswax candles and fresh flowers and wood for the fireplaces.

She kept my wardrobe, though I never dreamed of asking her to do such a thing, sewed buttons on my coats, and even mended a great velvet cloak that I refused to give up, though it had become too fragile for wearing.

Fareed was particularly delighted with Barbara's innovations, as he wanted to know the history of each blood drinker who came to Court, insisted on taking a sample of the creature's blood and studying it for what distinguishing characteristics he could find in it.

Barbara brought the guests to Fareed; she explained to them what was expected. She spoke in a soft, deep compelling voice to all with uniform politeness. And her fluency in French and German was very helpful.

Fareed had made many vampire family trees on his computers, and other complex charts, creating as best he could a picture of the common parents shared throughout history and throughout the world by the blood drinkers. His dream was to eventually trace the ancestors of every fledgling all the way back to the primal fount, but his lists and graphs were filled with strange names and blanks, and only occasionally some name common to more than two unrelated wanderers.

We all agreed this was valuable information. Volumes were compiled for every single name ever mentioned, with a brief history of that blood drinker even if he was no more than a character in the wild stories of a ragged vagabond.

Fareed wanted to take Barbara away to his offices in Paris, but I wouldn't have it. But Barbara found the perfect blood drinker assistants for Fareed and his staff of doctor blood drinkers.

At Court, she continued to create new and refined positions of service, lists of duties, and saw to the matter of incomes for all of these many workers, and that the young ones were under the guardianship of elder vampires who could take them to Paris and Marseille to hunt. She trained ladies' maids and gentlemen's valets and had a collection of drivers to take members of the Court over the miles to concerts or operas or films in the nearby cities.

Indeed, Barbara created such a network of supporting staff that I began to wonder how we had lived without them.

And the Château was soon spotlessly clean from its highest and smallest tower rooms, to the spacious open crypts of its cellars.

It was Barbara who found dungeons I hadn't known existed, under the foundations of the southwest tower.

Excitedly, she took me down the coiling stone stairs to this strange stratum beneath the earth, where the walls oozed damp, and actual prison cells remained with rusted bars and heaps of debris that for all I knew might once have been human remains.

Long narrow air shafts brought the faint light of the moon to some of these places.

"All this should be cleaned and restored, Prince," she said. "You never know when you will need this."

"A dungeon, Barbara?" I asked.

And there was Marius at my shoulder telling me firmly that Barbara had a point. He gave the order for it to be done. New bars, new locks.

"You see a different future than I see," I said to Marius.

"The problem is that you don't see the future at all," said Marius. And he made remarks very like those he'd made to me most recently about "our nature," and what I was denying about it.

"If you ever think I'll keep a pack of hapless mortal victims down here, you've really misjudged me," I said.

The strangest expression came over his face. Then he turned to Barbara. "Come with me, darling," he said. "I'll give you the specifications for what we need here."

Very soon we became accustomed to blood drinkers who voluntarily assumed the position of servants, showing profound respect for all of us as surely as my father's old servants had back in the eighteenth century, and for much the same reason.

We had been beggars in those days, one of the poorest families of the peerage, but those old servants whose ancestors had served us for generations had counted themselves blessed to live under the roof of a marquis and have a bowl of porridge to eat every day, a place at a kitchen fire, and meat on holidays. I cannot recall a single one of them, young or old, ever setting out to make his or her fortune in the cities of France where men and women and children starved to death during the harsh winters.

"Just let us stay here. We will do anything." Barbara recounted that plea over and over. She organized the tasks, the chain of command, banished curious mortals altogether from the Château, and saw to it all knew the rules of the house, and committed themselves to "service."

Barbara's last innovation had been livery. I had fully expected the elders and more modern members of the tribe to be outraged at the idea, but they weren't. And we soon found ourselves accustomed to a staff dressed in spotless black velvet suits and gowns, and addressing the rest of us as "sir" or "madam," "monsieur" or "madame."

Of course I was always "the Prince." And now and then I heard someone referring to me simply as "the sovereign."

The sovereign.

A small group of clerks was developed by Barbara. They kept the records, paid the taxes, opened such mail as came, and answered the only landline phones in the Château, which were on their desks in their cellar office.

And Barbara, presiding over all, wore a rich and lovely black gown with a string of natural pearls at her throat, and that diamond barrette holding back her hair, ever stepping out of the shadows when I needed her.

So this is the Court to which I returned, in which some six hundred blood drinkers were lodging, and a place in which I felt at home as I'd never felt anywhere in my entire existence except perhaps, perhaps, in my old flat in the Rue Royale in the nineteenth century, when Louis sat in an armchair by the fire reading the French newspapers and Claudia, in her puff-sleeved dress of white gauze, played the sprightly joyful music of Mozart on the pianoforte.

"Out, out, brief candle." Such comforting remembrance can turn in an instant to agony.

Chapter 5

So Arjun is dead?" I said as I came down the stairs from the tower. "Where's Barbara?"

But it was Louis who met me. Louis was his usual rumpled self, his silk tie askew, a layer of palpable dust on his shoulders and on his once-shining shoes, and he began explaining matters in a whisper as if that had the slightest meaning in a building filled with creatures with telepathic powers. Not even Barbara could get him to attend to his appearance.

I put my arm around him and we moved through the various deserted salons making our way to the Council Chamber.

"What happened was not Marius's fault," Louis said. There was a pained expression on his usually serene face and a slight tremor to his lip. "Arjun attacked Marius," he said. His voice was a near whisper again, but I realized that it was what Louis did, lower his voice the more emotional he became. "It had to do with Pandora," he went on. "Arjun wanted to take Pandora away and Pandora did not wish to go, and Marius warned him to leave her alone or 'face the consequences.' They went out there somewhere near the woods to have it out. But everybody could hear Arjun thundering at Marius, excoriating him for his interference, and his wild protestations of his love for Pandora."

I could easily hear this, though in fact I'd never heard Arjun raise his voice except in the story told to me by Fontayne.

"And Pandora, what was she doing?" I asked.

"Weeping. Weeping in the arms of Bianca." He sighed. "Somehow or other she had become the very personification of the conflicted, passive, suffering woman, utterly incapable of defending herself. They've become like two wives to Marius, Bianca and Pandora—and Arjun was restless and wanted to leave. He claimed to have been reborn, ready to confront this new world, and he ordered Pandora to ready herself to go back to India with him."

"She didn't want to go with Arjun."

"No, obviously not. But she seemed unable to say so."

"Did you see what finally happened?" I asked. We were drawing closer to the Council Chamber, and I'd spied a very few vampires about, mostly sitting together in small groups in the shadows, as if someone had forbidden them to move or speak or dance or sing or read or do anything. Barbara stood outside the room with her black leather-bound notebook in her arms waiting for me.

"No," said Louis. "I didn't, but others did. I had my hands over my ears. I was trying to read. But all are in agreement Arjun shoved Marius, dealt him a vile blow to the face, and sent the fire at him. Marius sent the fire right back and utterly obliterated Arjun."

Countless thoughts crowded into my head. What was really going on here? Why was the house so ridiculously quiet, and what was on the minds of all the vampires who now sat silent in shadowy corners? What was on the mind of the council?

I thought again of Fontayne, actually waiting for some sort of permission from this Court before bringing a young mortal woman into the Blood, and that maverick hissing at me, "By what authority do you do this to me?" and I figured there was nothing to be done but for me to enter the Council Chamber.

I went in, and took my usual place at the head of the table nearest the door. Barbara took a seat to my right, away from the table and against the wall, and opened her notebook and prepared her old-fashioned fountain pen for writing. Louis took his usual place at my right hand at the table.

Marius was in the chair to my left, but he had moved it away from the table and he sat facing the assembly, but not looking at it, with his arms folded. He was wearing his usual long red velvet tunic. And he hadn't bothered to cut his hair, which he often did on rising, and it hung in a great mass around his face and to his shoulders. He was frowning.

He did not acknowledge my presence.

The crystal chandelier above was on its highest power, flooding the room with merciless light, and sconces along the walls were also lighted with their tiny candle-flame electric bulbs glowing. And no one in this illumination looked even remotely human. It was an assembly of immortals, some of whom might easily have provoked the label of monster. But they all looked perfectly fine and beautiful to me because their preternatural skin and glittering eyes were completely familiar.

And there were two creatures here who were not blood drinkers. Not at all.

Now for those of you new to this narrative, I'll tell you who was assembled in the room in some detail.

At the far end of the table sat Gregory Duff Collingsworth, the eldest vampire among us now, who looked as he usually did, very like a Swiss or German businessman. He wore a simple gray suit and a red tie, and his arms were folded across his chest; he nodded to me with a quick and agreeable smile. His hair was always clipped short, and for all I knew then, it could never be anything else, as our hair never grows once we're made and, if cut, grows back overnight. He appeared cheerful and happy to see me.

On his right was Seth, who very likely was the next in age, having been made a vampire by Queen Akasha some thirty years or so after Gregory. And he wore a simple black cassock like a Catholic priest, his black hair trimmed very short, and his black eyes fixed on me as if he were not really seeing me. Beside him sat Dr. Fareed, our beloved scientist and physician, an Anglo-Indian with beautiful green eyes, in his usual white doctor's coat. He was scribbling on a legal pad of yellow paper with his black fountain pen. The scratching of his pen was the only sound in the room. Beside him was Sevraine, born a thousand years after the Blood had come to Akasha, making Akasha the first vampire. And Sevraine, known by everyone as the Great Sevraine, looked the part with her glorious hair coiffed with pearls and diamonds. Her jeweled tunic of dark green silk looked very much like the kurta or sherwani worn by Indian males. And there were enough genuine diamonds and rubies on it to constitute a great fortune.

"Good evening, Prince," she said as soon as I was seated. "We're glad to see you've returned."

"Thank you, *chèrie*," I said at the risk of being condemned for patronizing women with easy endearments. But I hadn't had time to restrain myself.

On the other side of the table, right after Louis, came David Talbot, my fledgling, in his Anglo-Indian body, dressed as usual in a modern suit of brown wool with a caramel-colored shirt and golden tie, his wavy black hair short and combed. He too appeared to be making notes of some sort on paper, but his pen made no sound.

To his right was Jesse Reeves, made by the great Maharet, a painfully thin birdlike woman who in life had been pale and freckled and was now as white as alabaster, her rippling copper hair streaked with white, a woman who looks more ghostly than human due to her natural pallor infused with the powerful blood of the twins, Maharet and Mekare, who had been as old as Gregory. Then came Teskhamen, the Child of the Millennia who had made Marius two thousand years ago in a Druid forest. He wore the same type of bejeweled tunic as Sevraine, only his was of black velvet and studded all over with beads of black jet, rather than jewels, which gave it a wild glitter.

And next to him sat two immortal creatures also made of flesh and blood who weren't human, the first being Amel—Amel the spirit that had thousands of years ago fused with Akasha to produce the first vampire, and who had connected all the vampires of the tribe to that host body—Amel, now in the slender well-proportioned flesh-and-blood body of a young male, with thick curly red hair and green eyes that were fixed attentively on me, his beautiful face breaking into a generous smile as I looked at him.

And to his right the female Replimoid, the Child of Atlantis, the stunning dark-skinned Kapetria, who had constructed Amel's body for him, a being made on another world and sent to our Earth aeons ago, equipped with great genius and cleverness and conscience, who had awakened in the twentieth century from a tomb of ice to go in search of her ancient brethren. Kapetria's quick dark eyes were fixed on me, and she too smiled. Her thick wavy black hair was long and free to frame her face, and she wore, as she often did, a doctor's white stiff, starched coat, like that worn by Fareed, and her arm was around the figure beside her.

This was Pandora—Pandora who centuries ago had made the unfortunate Arjun and become his slave rather than his mentor; Pandora who often radiated a sadness so dark and bittersweet that it invited tears in others. She wore a black robe and a black veil, and her eyes were closed as if she were dreaming. Her head was bowed and her two hands were clasped on the shining mahogany of the table. I could see very little of her curly brown hair. And not a sound emanated from her. Bianca, at her side, was also silent, with downcast eyes.

And there was Armand with his arms folded, studying Marius, his auburn hair carelessly veiling his face, his brown eyes narrow and focused.

Minds locked.

"All right," I said. "It's obvious that you've all been waiting for me." I wanted to ask all sorts of questions and, first and foremost, why Amel and Kapetria were here, but as I was glad to see them and Marius began to speak at once, I listened to him.

"Well, of course," said Marius in an abrupt and hostile voice. He turned to me and brought his chair up to the table. "I've broken our laws," he said. "I've struck down another blood drinker and burned him until there was nothing left of him."

Silence. No one else spoke up.

"So of course," Marius went on. "I'm waiting for your judgment, and the judgment of all assembled here. I accept that Kapetria is one of us now, and is here due to this matter, and as for Amel, well, yes, Amel, our beloved Amel—." He stopped. His eyes misted and he swallowed as if his voice had dried up in him, and then fighting his emotion, he said, "Our beloved Amel has a right to be here too now."

"Stuff and nonsense," said Gregory. "There is no need for this meeting or any judgment." He sounded completely human. If one were to go by centuries in the Blood, Gregory ought to appear the most unearthly of all of us. But the very opposite was true. Because of his centuries of maneuvering in the mortal world, building a vast pharmaceutical empire, he had taken on a human varnish that was as thick and concealing as any emollient any of us used to pass for human, and his demeanor and his voice were completely human. His skin was tanned by his carefully planned exposure to the sun while he slept through the paralysis of the daytime, and he had the polish of a great executive used to giving orders to others and gracious to all. He went on talking,

"Everyone here understands exactly what happened," Gregory said. "No one here has questioned what Marius did. Marius is the one questioning Marius."

"That's ridiculous!" said Marius. "I murdered another blood drinker. I broke the very rules that I've written as binding for all of us." He looked from me to Gregory. "Yea gods," he said angrily, "are we to make rules for young blood drinkers throughout the world and break those laws ourselves in moments of passion?"

"Any of us would have done the same in the same circumstances," said Seth in a low voice. He looked at me and continued in a calm and even voice. "Prince, there were witnesses, though all of them were young. But they agreed on what they saw. Arjun attacked Marius, taunted him and insulted him, and threatened his life. Arjun sent the fire at Marius with a stream of curses, and Marius retaliated. Just as I would have retaliated."

Another silence fell. Behind me, the doors opened and I saw Cyril and Thorne come into the room and take seats along the wall. This was never a good sign, but I wanted to remain attentive to the council.

Sevraine spoke up.

"Arjun was terrorizing Pandora," she said. "For this blood drinker, Arjun, women are not persons. Arjun asked for what happened to him."

"Pandora, do you have anything to say?" asked Jesse. She looked to the others. And then to me. "Should we not hear from Pandora?"

Pandora didn't stir. She didn't open her eyes. She might have been a statue.

Bianca, beside her, quite close to her, attuned it seemed to the mixture of grief and confusion that must have been making this miserable for Pandora, did not move either.

Armand remained silent but I could see now he was angry.

"Marius," I said. "What would you have us do?"

"Something should be done," Marius said. He bowed his head. "Something should be said. Something should attach to my breaking rules to which I mean to hold others with mortal consequences. I broke the law."

"Ah, the Roman, always the old Roman," said Pandora in a soft voice. "Always the man of reason." She opened her eyes and looked straight forward. "Arjun tormented me for centuries. And you have rid me of him and I am thankful. I didn't want for him to die, no, I didn't want anything for him that was bad, but I longed with all my soul to be free of him."

"But you couldn't do anything about it yourself, could you?" Marius blazed. I had never seen him so angry. He was glaring at her across the table. "You couldn't stand up to him yourself. No, and so I had to do it, I had to stand against him and his brutal assumptions and cover my hands in blood when the survival of our tribe is now the only thing under Heaven I care about!"

He brought his right fist down on the table. I feared the wood would splinter, but it didn't. He clenched this fist and I caught the scent of the blood coming from his palm.

"Listen to me," said Seth. "Surely no law we make will ever deprive a blood drinker of the right to defend himself against one who attacks him with the fire."

"I could easily have restrained him," said Marius. He was quivering with rage. His head was bowed and he rubbed his hands together now as if he couldn't control the gesture. "I could have restrained him and—."

"And what? We would have another Rhoshamandes on our hands?" asked Gregory. "He might have come back at any time and sought revenge on Pandora or on you or on all of us! He broke the peace, Marius. You have rid us of one not made for these times, and not made for the enterprise here that is dear to us."

"I agree," I said without thinking. Then I realized they were all looking at me. "I agree, and this our enterprise, as you put it, Gregory, is everything. We want this Court to endure. We want the tribe to endure, and Arjun was not a being who cared about this, not if he sought to take Pandora from here by force."

"And that he did," said Pandora. Again her voice was soft, as though she were engaging in another conversation. "And I am grateful to be free. And Marius, I beg your forgiveness that I couldn't free myself of Arjun. I beg your forgiveness that I lacked the strength, but I was his maker and his mother as well as his lover, and simply could not do it."

I knew this to be true. I had not paid a great deal of attention to Pandora or Arjun in the last year or more, but I had seen and heard enough to know that Arjun made Pandora miserable, and that her misery was increasing, and that she clung to the Court in the last few months, choosing not anymore to travel with Arjun, even as far as Paris.

"I should have had your strength," Pandora continued, looking at Marius. "But I don't have it. And so you did this thing for me, more out of disgust—."

"Oh, don't deceive yourself!" he fired back at her.

She paused and then went on, "Perhaps more out of disgust for my weakness than any—."

Marius made a sharp derisive sound and looked away from her.

"For whatever reason," I said, "it's done. And I rule based on all you've told me that it was done with good reason and in self-defense, and that this be the end of it."

"I heartily agree," said Gregory. There were murmurs of assent all around, even from Amel.

"Is there anyone who objects to this?" I asked.

Marius rose to his feet.

He looked at me and then at the others.

"I am sorry for what I did," he said. "I am sorry for my impatience, my rage, and my weakness. I'm sorry that I struck down Arjun. And I want you to know, I want all to know, that I believe we must abide by the laws we make for one another. We the council, we the elders, enjoy no exception to these laws, no special prerogative to break them. I am sorry and I give you my word that I will never again in wanton rage take the life of another blood drinker."

Again there were murmurs of assent from everyone.

Amel seemed deeply moved by all this, and seemed on the edge of tears for a moment, but then this was very much his way, to have the easily kindled emotions of a young man, though he was far older than any of us. He looked up at Marius plaintively as if he wished with all his strange unnatural heart that he could do something to stop the torment Marius couldn't conceal.

"Then it's done," said Pandora.

She too was looking pleadingly at Marius, but he would not look at her.

"And now," she said, "you can despise me for this as well as for so many other things."

"That is too trivial and foolish and self-indulgent to deserve a response," he said. "I thank you all for your forgiveness."

"Then we can get to the more pressing matter," said Gregory.

"And what is that?" I asked. I wanted now more than anything in the world to tell them about Fontayne, to tell Pandora about him, and have her assurance that I might bring him to Court, but I could see all eyes on me now, even the eyes of Pandora.

"Rhoshamandes," said Gregory, looking directly at me. "Lestat, you must give the order to put an end to Rhoshamandes."

Chapter 6

Iwas quietly infuriated. Rhoshamandes. Five thousand years in the Blood. Living on his own private island of Saint Rayne. Visited from time to time by his fledglings, Eleni, Allesandra, and cohabiting with his lover, Benedict. A blood drinker who clearly despised me for what I had done to him in the past, after his murder of the great Maharet, and while he was holding my son, Viktor, captive. A blood drinker who had agreed to leave us in peace if we left him in peace.

"Why in the world are we talking of this again?" I demanded. "What's happened?"

For a moment, nothing was said, and it was easy for me to understand why. We had argued this out over and over again. They, one and all, were for the destruction of Rhoshamandes, and I alone had held out against it, insisting over and over again that Rhoshamandes had been formally forgiven for what he had done to Maharet and that he had done nothing to break the peace, committed no act of aggression against us.

It maddened me that I could not get any of them to understand what it meant to me to pass judgment on a blood drinker who had walked the earth for thousands of years, who had seen empires rise and fall, and worlds I could only imagine—to strike down such a being for an error he had made due to the enticements of a spirit voice that had lied to him and manipulated him and goaded him to attack Maharet and destroy her.

But never was there the slightest bit of understanding. Most of the council was positively adamant that Rhoshamandes should be destroyed, and those who seemed to care very little weren't in disagreement.

"Amel," I said. "This is the first time, to my knowledge, that you've been at this table. Can't you speak up for Rhoshamandes?"

"Lestat, why would I do that?" he asked in his boyish voice, his face suddenly flushed as he looked at me. We had seen each other many times in the last year, and I had grown used to him in this new immortal body, and at times it was as if the spirit, Amel, that bizarre and terrifying being, had never existed.

"Because it was you, you coming to consciousness, Amel, who goaded him into killing Maharet. Have you forgotten that?"

This was a painful moment for the others, and I could see it. They were gazing at Amel uneasily, as if they had not forgotten, not for a moment, the ancient spirit that he had been, and were unable to trust the youthful red-haired Amel who sat before them. They seemed not reassured by his obvious emotions but suspicious of them. But Amel had always from the very first moment he uttered a coherent word in spirit form been a victim of his emotions. And he was now.

I found myself deep in my thoughts, remembering that it had not been two years ago that, at a table like this one at Trinity Gate in New York, these very immortals had spoken of imprisoning the spirit Amel in some chamber of fluid in which, blind and deaf, and unable to speak, he might have lapsed back into a mindless existence of torment. I tried to drive this from my mind because this was not a time to speak of this, but the Replimoids, whatever their immense powers, could not read our minds, and Amel, who had once been our central mind, so to speak, who could move from mind to mind among us, was now for all practical purposes a Replimoid.

What was that like, I wondered, for this strange incarnate spirit who had been in a physical body now for months—walking, talking, reading, perhaps making love, living as an enfleshed immortal again—to be sitting amongst us now, the blood drinkers of the tribe he had created and inhabited and sustained for centuries? Thoughts like this do not lead to easy or simple conclusions. They persist in me because I am driven to go to the root of things. And I wanted to understand everything that was happening now, and the emotions I could feel all about me were sadly as real as words or actions.

No. I wasn't going to linger on this, the baffling relationship between this person whom I loved devoutly and the blood drinkers who didn't share that love or even understand him.

If Amel remembered that council of cold immortals dispassionately discussing his fate—when none of us knew precisely what he was, or whence he'd come, or why or how he'd fused with a human being to make the first vampire—he didn't let on.

He'd been there, that spirit, inside of us, binding us to one another, binding us to a host, speaking in our minds when he chose, wheedling, and deceiving, and setting blood drinker against blood drinker. And he had sought to charm Rhoshamandes, to set him against Maharet, and he had succeeded. And into her lair, Rhoshamandes and his lover Benedict had gone to strike her down with such a brutal blow that I could scarcely bear to think of it.

I let my eyes fix on Jesse Reeves, Maharet's beloved niece and fledgling, and slowly her eyes turned to me, and I caught the message:

Rhoshamandes must be put to death. There is no alternative. It is you, Lestat, who do not understand.

"Destroy him," said Amel, suddenly, impulsively, his face flushing red. "Destroy him before he destroys you or before he destroys *us*."

"That's why we're here, Lestat," said Kapetria. This was the first time she'd spoken at this meeting. "We're here because Rhoshamandes has begun to cast a shadow over our lives, and we cannot breathe easy in that shadow. Rhoshamandes does not mean to let us alone."

"Let's explain what happened," said Amel. He turned and looked at her and took her right hand and kissed it. He looked back to me as he spoke. "We've withdrawn from our colony in England. We've retreated into Gregory's laboratories in Paris. We are living in hiding now with Gregory's protection, because at every turn, for the last week, Rhoshamandes stalked us, watched us, found some reason to talk to us, entered our private rooms, seemingly appearing out of nowhere as ancient ones can do, and never left us a moment's peace."

I was crestfallen. I had assured everyone that this would never happen. Rhoshamandes had assured me that he would leave the colony of the Children of Atlantis alone.

I had spoken to him directly about this, and he had given me his word. He had said, "I have no interest in these creatures. I acknowledge that you wish to protect them. I am not a menace to them. I have nothing against them. As long as they leave me alone, I will leave them alone."

Now this.

Kapetria appeared more troubled than I had ever seen her. I have always thought her powerfully beautiful, with her flawless bronze skin, her exquisitely sculpted features, and her thick wavy raven hair. Her eyes had an immediate warmth that I found reassuring and always had. And she had proved her loyalty to us. She had proved it more than once, but most spectacularly when she removed the spirit of Amel from my physical body, leaving my mind and body intact.

She could easily have destroyed me in the process. But she had postponed this act until she knew well that she could achieve it while sparing my life.

"You know how very much we love our colony," said Kapetria

directly to me. "You know how we sought to learn from you and from Gremt in founding it."

Of course I knew. And I loved what the colony had become.

Kapetria with the assistance of Gregory and Gremt had bought an abandoned asylum in rural England, along with a stately manor house quite close to it, and a large stake in a nearby village much larger and more vital than my small re-created village here in France.

The Replimoids had established a "health spa" as a cover for their activities, completely renovating the asylum and developing their laboratories there. They refurbished property in the village, invited new business interests, and renovated the ruined church and established a bequest to fund a vicar in residence.

This was the sure way, Gremt had told them, of thriving among mortals, to show great generosity to the locals of the neighborhood, to become a force for good amongst them so that they could easily forgive anything they saw that might incite suspicion that an alien species was in their very midst.

This was simple for the Children of Atlantis who had only good feelings for human beings, and were in fact People of the Purpose, in their mind—the purpose being to do what was good for human beings.

I'd visited the British community several times in the last few months, astonished by the progress made by the colony which now numbered sixty-four Replimoids, including thirty clones of Kapetria and thirty clones of her three brothers, Garekyn, Welf, and Derek.

Now, if you've read the most recent stories in the Vampire Chronicles, then you know how these creatures multiply, and how it was discovered by accident when Rhoshamandes held one of them prisoner—it was Derek—and severed Derek's arm. They multiply through the process in the plant kingdom that is called branching, in that once a limb is severed, it develops into an individual who is a clone of the parent body from which the limb was taken, while the parent body regenerates a replacement limb. This gives them, of course, a remarkable reproductive advantage in this world, and for that reason some of our tribe thought that for the good of the world the Replimoids should be destroyed.

Armand had been the one to most forcefully put forward this idea, right in the presence of the Replimoids, and continuously when they were not present. As he watched the colony grow to sixty-four in number, he voiced his warning again and again.

"Destroy them now or you will regret it later," he had said. "We were humans before we were blood drinkers. How can we let this species menace the human race?"

Armand had said nothing all this while. But I could see his cold, merciless eyes fixed with their characteristic apparent innocence on Kapetria, and I imagined a stream of malevolence flowing from him, but he was letting nothing of his mind or heart be known.

Rhoshamandes had never expressed this view to me—an inherent horror of the Replimoids—but as Rhoshamandes had five thousand years in the Blood, undoubtedly he knew of Armand's feelings on the matter. Rhoshamandes could spy on us telepathically over great distance, and surely he knew that we were discussing putting an end to him right now.

Of course, he might not be listening to our conversations. He might be piloting one of his boats in the northern seas, or sitting in an opera house somewhere in Europe enveloped in the music. Or perhaps he was simply indifferent to us now and did not care what we said.

I had, after all, assured him that we would never move to destroy him if he left us all alone, and "all" included the Children of Atlantis.

I was deep in my thoughts on this, as I'm relating them to you, when Kapetria spoke up, and because I was not looking at her, but had been looking at Armand, I heard her voice quavering for the first time. I heard a weakness in it, a fragility I had never heard in her before.

"Five nights ago," she said, "as if he knew you would be crossing the Atlantic to your old home in New Orleans, Rhoshamandes appeared for hours walking in the village, or sitting in the church, or even strolling on our own grounds."

"Every night," Amel interjected, "we have a service for Vespers in the chapel, and more and more of the villagers are attending it, and I love to attend it, and there he was suddenly, this tall, heavily wrapped figure in a hooded cape, in the back pew for the entire service, and then walking slowly up the village high street and off into the woods."

"It was unnerving, this sudden attention," said Kapetria putting

her hand on Amel's arm perhaps to silence him or calm him. "But I spoke to him politely, I made a point of it, and he was artificial when he spoke with me, smiling artificially and saying how very nice it was . . . nice to see us so very close to his home. Of course I told him that I didn't see the southern part of England as so very close to Saint Rayne, but he said that for a creature such as himself, it was a matter of seconds to cross the distance. And then in a rather solemn way he wished me well."

"He spoke to others," said Amel. "He even went out of his way to stop Derek in the village—and you know Derek is terrified of him!"

"Yes," said Kapetria. "Derek is convinced Rhoshamandes was stalking him, and one of the times when he stopped to speak to Derek he asked about Derek's regenerated arm. He said something ironic about their sharing this form of suffering, that you had 'hacked off' his arm as he had 'severed' Derek's arm. But of course it was such a 'fortuitous' event, was it not, for how long mightn't it have been before we ever discovered that we could multiply in this simple way? He made some cold observation that you had been the author of the discovery, as you were the one who had 'hacked off' his arm in the presence of immortals he had known thousands of years ago when the world we share now could not be imagined. And he went on to say that this was too often the case with your blunders . . . what was it? . . ."

". . . That somehow," Amel said, "Lestat manages to profit by his blunders as no other creature he's ever known, and not only had you profited but the Children of Atlantis had profited as well. He asked if you still carried the ax inside your jacket."

"Derek couldn't answer his question about the ax," said Kapetria. "He laughed and laughed under his breath. Derek was utterly undone by all this. But it was two nights ago that he frightened me and I am not a being who is easily frightened. I dare say I lack an intelligent understanding of fear." She hesitated.

"What did he do?" asked Armand suddenly.

Kapetria looked directly at Armand for the first time.

"I was in my study," she said. "I'd been working all evening in the laboratory, and at last I had some time to rest, and was tired, and I came in and flopped down in a chair by the hearth. I was cold, shivering, and rubbing my arms and about to give up when suddenly the oak logs in the fireplace burst into flame. There was a roaring sound as it happened, a crackling and roaring, and then I saw *him* sitting in the chair opposite me, just as if he'd been there all the time. It was as if he possessed magical powers, and I was defenseless against them. Magic by which he could invade our most private rooms."

"It was not magic," said Gregory. "It was simple speed you cannot imagine, and of course surprise."

"Well, whatever it was, I was frightened," said Kapetria. "I gained an insight into what people mean when they speak of being frightened. You could even say that it was a good thing, because I learned from it what it means to be frightened. . . ."

"Well, that's exactly what he wanted you to be," said Marius, "frightened, and that's why he came unbidden into your study and ignited the fire."

"What did he say?" asked Gregory.

"Well, at first nothing. And I said nothing. I looked at the door to the hallway and saw it was open, and imagined that he had moved through that doorway silently and speedily so that I hadn't seen. . . ."

"That's what he did," said Gregory. "That is all he did, Kapetria, and we all have that power, and that skill."

"So he left without saying anything?" Marius pressed.

"No," she said. "He finally broke the silence. He asked if I was not going to welcome him to my parlor, as he called it, and I said without thinking that it was not necessary apparently as he had come into my private study of his own accord. Then for the first time, the first time since his strange visits had started, he said something positively menacing. He told me in a low voice, a cold and hostile voice, that he found us all irritating and did not want us in England.

"I asked him if he was telling me that we should go, and to that he replied that he would leave that to my judgment. 'You are very enticing to blood drinkers,' he said, 'with your ever-regenerating blood, and it is really quite amazing that Lestat has received you and your cohorts as equals and put you under a protection which he can't guarantee.'"

"That's exactly what he said?" I asked.

"Yes," she replied. "And we immediately left for France, all of us, that night by plane, landing in Paris well before morning. And we were all safely relocated to our old lodgings in Collingsworth Pharmaceuticals before the sun set."

"Yes," said Amel with a deep sigh, "behind walls of steel in the very interior of a tower in which we have no windows, but are apparently quite safe."

Amel looked at Gregory. "And Gregory has accepted us again with his usual generosity, even agreeing to wait for the whole story until you returned."

I sat back in my chair. I couldn't conceal a disgusted look.

Everyone was silent for a moment and then David Talbot and Gregory began to speak at once. Gregory gave way to David.

"Listen, my beloved friend," David said to me, leaning forward over the table as he looked at me, "you must put an end to this being! Now wait, before you answer. I was a mortal man not fifty years ago, Lestat, a human being that recently, and a human being who had lived for seventy-four years before he lost his original body, assumed another, and saw that body transformed by the Dark Blood. I well remember all the moral lessons of being human, and I'm telling you—you must give the order immediately for the destruction of this creature. You're gambling with your life and the lives of the Replimoids and you are gambling with the lives of all those here."

"And he is somewhere listening to every word," I said.

"All the more reason," David said.

"Give the order," said Gregory.

"Give the order," said Sevraine.

"Give the order," said Seth.

Jesse merely raised her right hand without a sound and nodded her head.

All of them gave their assent by gesture or a few words, except for Armand. His eyes were fixed on me.

"Why in Hell do you hesitate?" Armand said. "Where is the despicable villain who destroyed the coven of the Children of Satan in a single night?"

"Oh, for the love of God, I did no such thing," I said. "It was your taking me prisoner that brought me into your coven, and I struck down no one. Don't bring up old grudges. That doesn't help."

From the far side of the room, I heard Cyril's voice. "Get rid of him, boss," he said. "Get rid of him. He is too dangerous and too foolish and too without a soul."

No one on the council made any objection to my big disheveled leather-clad bodyguard speaking up. In fact, Marius expressed his agreement with the assessment at once.

"That's it precisely," said Marius addressing me. "He has no soul in him to control a body that has grown in unspeakable power for thousands of years. Nothing tempers his shallow brittle view of the world."

"All right." I put up my two hands. "Let me understand this, Marius. You, you who are demanding a public censure of some sort for your destroying Arjun, you are saying that I must reverse my decision now on Rhoshamandes because he has harried the Replimoids and violated the sanctity of Kapetria's private study to discomfort her with a string of badly chosen words?"

"You know all the old arguments," said Marius.

"And you've heard my response to them," I replied. "What has changed is not sufficient to warrant the reversal of a prince's pardon, not as far as I can see."

"He means to destroy us," said Kapetria. "He plays with us like a restless cat."

I shook my head, and tried to withdraw within my own soul for a moment of pure thought on this matter, but found myself looking into Amel's eyes.

I'd never seen such a look of distress coupled with malice as I saw on his face now.

His lower lip was trembling in a boyish way, and then he spoke. "Do you know what it means to rise from a long wretched slumber from which you've tried to wake again and again, and then to roam in darkness, searching for light at one remote station after another along the great roadways of an invincible country without a name?" He was trembling all over. And his voice trembled.

"Imagine it," Amel said. "Imagine a mind gradually awakening to its own contours as a mind, a mind struggling to grasp that it was once a person, a creature, a being . . . and struggling to make sense of what it could hear but not see, and then see but not see completely . . . amid a cacophony of voices that never ceased speaking." He broke off. He put his hand to his forehead and looked down for a moment as if struggling violently with himself.

"Amel, I'm listening to you," I said. "I understand."

"What he wants to tell you," said Kapetria, "was that on those endless journeys up and down the threads of the web the vampiric blood had created, he knew what seemed to him innumerable minds, and amongst those minds, he knew the mind of Rhoshamandes, and knew it to be selfish, small, brittle, and easily seduced."

I nodded.

Amel had recovered himself. He looked at me again. "I know him," he said, his voice raw. "He's a monster. Kill him before he kills you. If you die, Lestat, if you perish, if you let that unspeakable—."

Kapetria put her arms around him, around this body that she

had created for him, and kissed him, her hand stroking his hair. "He understands," she said. And again. "He understands."

There was a pause. I felt the same reluctance I'd always felt to condemn Rhoshamandes. But I struggled to find a more persuasive way to express my deep feeling—that though his behavior had been aggressive and obnoxious in the extreme, he had done nothing to merit the penalty of death.

It was Sevraine who broke the silence. Sevraine was a dazzling blood drinker; her face had the perfection of a statue, and her hair, like Pandora's hair, often resembled a veil. As she spoke now, she stared before her, her voice low and steady.

"I know Rhoshamandes," she said. "I've always known him. I knew him when he was a mortal man. I know him now. If he were a younger blood drinker, say, with only five hundred years in the Blood or even a millennium, this would be a different matter. He abhors conflict, and is, in a very real sense, a coward.

"But you've provoked him, Prince, and what maddens him even more is that Benedict, his lover, is drawn to you." She looked at me. "Benedict is in the ballroom now waiting for the music to begin. Benedict was here last night also. And as Rhoshamandes loses his hold on Benedict, he grows ever more irritated and restless and angry. And his powers are too great for his mind, especially now that he has tested them and knows just what destructive forces he can command."

I nodded.

"He is a thoughtless, shallow being," Sevraine added. "Were he to retreat, to seek some part of the world where he might live in peace and never hear of you or the Court, it would be different. But he hovers, clawing at his own wounds."

"All right," I said. "I understand what you're saying, all of you. But I can't simply reverse my decision. I am going to go to Louisiana now, to bring to Court an old fledgling of Pandora's, and when I return, I will make the decision, I promise you."

I stopped. I was painfully aware that Benedict could no doubt hear every word uttered in this room, that Rhoshamandes could hear if he had a mind to want to hear.

"For now," I said, as if addressing Rhoshamandes himself, "the being is safe. He has not broken the peace. And he still enjoys our protection."

I rose to my feet and gestured for Thorne and Cyril to follow me.

As I reached for the handle of the door, I reflected on how very simple it would be for them to do what they wanted without my assent, and why they insisted that I give the order. But that is how it was and they weren't going to take the burden of this decision from me.

On my way to the north tower, I passed through the ballroom. I saw Benedict and I embraced him. He was shaken, miserable, obviously, but he embraced me in return.

"How goes it with Rhoshamandes?" I asked.

"He's getting used to things, Lestat. Truly he is," Benedict said in a pleading voice. "I've urged him to come to Court, to see all of this for himself. He will in time, I know he will." He kissed me. It was sudden, a full kiss on the lips. I saw fear in his eyes. I saw pain. His face was boyish, as was Amel's, and he had the same tousled hair, only of a different color, and a voice that was youthful.

"I want for all of us to prosper," I said.

I had reached the battlements before I thought of Pandora. I had not even asked her whether she wanted Fontayne to come to Court. But I had seen her face in my last minutes at the council table, and it seemed to me there was an agreeable smile on her lips. Surely she knew where I'd been and where I was going now.

Suddenly as I stepped out into the cold wind, I heard her right behind me.

"Yes, bring him to me, Lestat," she said. The wind was filled with the green scent of the forest. Snow was coming, and I welcomed the beauty of it. Her garments were whipped and pulled by the wind.

"I took an immediate liking to him, Pandora," I said.

"That's your gift," she said. "You love everyone."

"Love," the overused word; "love," the most popular word of the twenty-first century.

I wanted to talk further, to tell her of all my recent reflections, that we had to love one another, respect one another, stop using our own loathsome nature as blood drinkers to justify the cruel treatment of one another, that I was in love with the world just now, and, yes, as Marius had told me, not allowing for our true nature perhaps, having to ignore it. And I wondered what Cyril and Thorne thought of all this, traveling with me every night, being at my side, rarely speaking except in the most practical way.

But I merely kissed her, and was thankful with all my soul that she wasn't suffering over the loss of Arjun.

Off we went, Thorne, Cyril, and I—traveling west into the night as the sun set over the distant coast of North America.

Chapter 7

It was early evening as we approached Fontayne's magnificent house in the bayou country. I wanted to enter the estate in the proper way and paused outside the gates to ring the bell, which I heard echoing within the house. Once again, I admired the high iron fencing. And the entire look of the great Greek Revival house with its high columns and flowering vines enchanted me. At the same time, I sensed something. I heard something.

"Someone with him," whispered Thorne. "Let us go ahead of you."

"No, we're not leaving him," said Cyril.

I felt his powerful arm slip around my back and his right hand come down on my shoulder. No one knew how old Cyril was, not even Cyril, and to the simplest questions on the matter he gave absurd or foolish answers. Illiterate, and cynical by nature, he kept no history of himself in his heart and had none to share with anyone else. But I had no doubt of his power.

I sent out the message to Fontayne that we had come and were approaching the door. But nothing came back to me.

Nevertheless I moved down the wide path between the rows of oaks, climbed the marble steps, crossed the porch, and lifted the brass knocker. Three times I knocked and Fontayne opened the door.

He stepped back for me to enter, but his face was cold and hard, and with his eyes, he sought to give me a signal. He flashed his gaze to the right, once and then again. Someone was here. Someone was behind him.

As I walked into the room, I saw no one.

"So glad you've come as you promised," said Fontayne, and those eyes of his gave me the signal again, though his mind was obviously desperately locked. "I've had a visitor," he said.

"Rhoshamandes?" I asked.

A violent roar filled the air, like the roar of a beast, and Fontayne was thrown suddenly right up against me. I felt an appalling heat press me against the closed door, and smelled the flames before they engulfed me. I was blinded by the fire, then felt myself rising in the air.

"Go, go for the sake of your life," Fontayne cried. The fire was everywhere. The walls were opening as if torn by a hurricane.

Thorne had both of us in his arms as we broke through the ceiling above and then the outside wall, splintering and crashing through burning wood, and suddenly we were high above the burning house, and then the house was gone, and the clouds were swallowing us as we sped east at a velocity I had never dared to travel.

I clung to Fontayne, and Thorne carried me. I pushed Fontayne's face against my chest, and covered his right hand with mine, and the wind was so fierce it seemed to be ripping my hair from me.

It was now impossible to think or speak or send even the sharpest telepathic message. But I knew we were headed back across the Atlantic, and I prayed that Cyril was safe right beside us.

I lost consciousness before we reached the Château. It was the speed, the cold, the violence of it, and the exhaustion from having just made the journey in the other direction.

And I woke, numb and disoriented, in a large room at the top of the northeast tower.

It was one of those rooms seldom sought or used by anyone. I found myself sitting on the floor, on a thick Oriental rug, and I saw the fire lighted and the candles of the sconces lighted as if by sorcery and the windows shut up against the night.

Fontayne lay on his back, apparently lifeless. His clothes were burnt black and I could see a dreadful burn on the side of his face.

As for me, I too had been burnt, and the heavy fragments of my damaged coat fell off me onto the carpet. I ran my fingers through my hair. I felt no burns on my skin.

Thorne was towering over me.

"Where is Cyril?" I said.

"Never mind," said Thorne. "Cyril can take care of himself and he'll get that bastard. Shall I give this one blood?"

I nodded. He sat down, and cradled Fontayne in his arms, making a bizarre Pietà as he bit into his wrist and pressed the wound to Fontayne's lips. Fontayne looked so fragile.

Pandora was in the room, and Marius with her, and Bianca, and Gregory.

Gregory helped me to my feet. My assistant Barbara was there, and she had a fresh coat for me and helped me into it.

Pandora fell to her knees and gestured for Thorne to give Fontayne over to her. She rose to her feet holding him in her arms. She opened a wound in her neck and put his mouth against it.

She turned away from us and walked off into the shadows carrying her man-child with her, and retired into a darkened corner.

Barbara was brushing my hair, and Gregory was looking me over for burns.

"Who was it?" Gregory demanded.

"It was not Rhoshamandes," said Thorne. "It was another, another named Baudwin."

"Baudwin!" repeated Gregory in a shocked whisper. He was in his usual business attire, and gave off the scent of an expensive man's cologne, his face immediately troubled at this news. "I thought Baudwin was long gone," he said.

"So did I," said Thorne. "But not so, and Fontayne warned us of him when we first came to him."

I was pretty much restored to myself, and I sat down now beside the hearth in a modern armchair, which was thankfully soft and made of yielding leather. Still half frozen from the journey, I extended my hands to the fire.

"Baudwin," I said, "and he sought to destroy both of us, me and Fontayne."

"Cyril sent the fire right back at him," said Thorne.

Seth came into the room.

"It's all over now," I said, looking up. "No need for alarm, but we lost a magnificent house to this utterly ridiculous assault." It struck me as ironic that none of us possessed the telepathic power to stop a blaze that we or others had started. And we had no telepathic gift to heal our own wounds, did we?

Pandora brought Fontayne to the fire, and seated him opposite me. His hair was loose and disheveled, and in his thin white shirt and dungarees he was shivering. Pandora knelt beside him and removed his black boots and tossed them to the side. She rubbed his sock feet with both her hands soothingly.

I was for letting him alone, for letting him warm up, for letting Pandora do her work, but the questions began immediately. Gregory with his arm on the back of the chair wanted to know what had happened.

Seth wanted Thorne to take him back to the place where the assault had occurred.

"Give Cyril time," said Thorne. "Cyril can handle that fiend. Cyril will be here soon."

Everyone was then talking at once, including Fontayne, and then all fell silent to listen to Fontayne and he told the story.

"He arrived last night. He told me that he would destroy me

if I did not cooperate with him. My powers were no match for his. There was nothing I could do to drive him out of my house. I was powerless under my own roof. The next night he knew you were coming."

"What does this fiend look like?" asked Gregory. "How old is he?"

"He came out of the British Isles," said Thorne, "made before me, and he always claimed descent from a legendary blood drinker, and no one believed him." His red hair and red beard were covered in ice still, but he seemed impervious to the cold, merely standing there in his heavy black leather jacket.

"And who was that legend?" I asked.

"Gundesanth," said Fontayne. "His maker was Gundesanth."

Gregory and Seth laughed out loud. I heard the laughter of Sevraine. She stepped into the light of the fire and kneeling beside Fontayne's chair she began to massage his hands as Pandora continued with Fontayne's feet. Both Pandora and Sevraine were in long dark shimmering gowns and flat slippers and had a rather angelic look to them. Only such beautiful blood drinkers revealed their bare shoulders, arms, and bosoms as these two did now in these low-cut and clinging garments, and I found it distracting.

Two hundred and fifty years in the Blood and I still respond electrically to the erotic charms of vampire men and women.

Barbara stood behind the chair brushing out Fontayne's hair, and I could see that all of this tender care was positively astonishing to him. He looked helplessly from one to the other of these seemingly gentle creatures. Barbara had a meekness about her and a plainness to her in her high-necked sweater and long wool skirt, but seemed quite indifferent to anything except restoring Fontayne.

"All right, who is Gundesanth?" I said looking up at Seth. "Are you great ones going to explain or go on chuckling and laughing with one another?"

"He was a monster by all reports," said Seth. "I never laid eyes on him. But I knew even in the early years after I was made that every maverick who had fled the blood priesthood of my mother claimed to be made by Gundesanth."

"I knew him well," said Gregory. "I knew him before he defected from the Queens Blood—before you were made," he said to Seth. "But I've never heard tell of him in the last two thousand years in this world, never even a mention of him."

I wasn't sure what I wanted to learn first—more about Baudwin, or more about Gundesanth.

"Well, it was his claim, this Baudwin," said Fontayne. He seemed much restored. His cheeks were ruddy and he had stopped trembling. "He hinted to me that his master himself would soon rise from his slumber to destroy the Court. He claimed this was inevitable."

"And if that was the case," Thorne said in a low, harsh voice, "why the Hell didn't this Baudwin wait for his master?"

Laughter all around. Except for Fontayne.

His hair was now groomed and he sat back in the chair and looked at me directly. "This Baudwin is a big creature, rawboned, and with pale eyes. No facial hair, and the yellow hair of his head clipped short when he came to me. I could see on the second night that he was cutting it off when he waked and with little concern for how it appeared. He was almost in rags, what people today call rags, soiled clothes all mismatched, a shabby torn dress coat, and a workingman's blue denim shirt and a muffler of knitted wool. He looked completely out of place in a furnished room. He paced back and forth demanding of me again and again how 'this fledgling Lestat' had the audacity to establish a monarchy among the Undead and why he hadn't been destroyed for the effrontery. He said there was very little in the realm of the Undead that could rouse his beloved maker, Gundesanth, but this Court would undoubtedly do it. He demanded allegiance of me, but I wouldn't give it. I expected to perish by his hands, but I couldn't give it. I didn't want to die, you understand, but I hadn't the power to deceive him on the matter. I was trying to marshal my powers, follow the descriptions in your books, attempting to tap into gifts of which I'd never known before I read your books, and then he announced you were coming.

"'You must meet Lestat and talk to him,' I said. 'You'll be charmed by him. He means no insult to anyone.' He laughed at me. Then I heard your approach."

I nodded and murmured my thanks.

"So nothing, absolutely nothing, was said of Rhoshamandes?" asked Gregory. "You're quite sure of this?"

"Yes, I am," said Fontayne. "Nothing, absolutely nothing. But then this being guarded his thoughts from me, though I couldn't keep mine from him. I rather hated him. And I hate him now for trying to destroy you." He looked at me.

I nodded, and gestured for him to remain calm.

"It was all my worst fear," said Fontayne, "why I've lived a life away from other blood drinkers, looking to mortals for affection, which I must say can destroy one's soul over time."

He looked up at Pandora, who was now standing beside him. He gazed at her as if she were a goddess, and so she seemed.

"And Arjun, madam?" he asked her in a soft polite voice. "Has he accepted my coming here?"

"Arjun is gone," said Pandora. "You must never worry about him again, Mitka. I'll take care of you now." She looked at me with soft brown eyes, and a trace of a smile on her pink lips. "I'll see to everything."

"If only Cyril were back here!" I said. I saw troubled expressions on the faces of the others. And only then did I notice Louis, and my mother, in the far doorway.

How long they'd been there, I had no idea. My mother looked at me, and her simple expression said what it so often said. *So you're alive, unhurt.* And then she disappeared. I gestured for Louis to come in, to meet Fontayne.

Thorne was saying that I needn't worry about Cyril.

I had enough strength in me to introduce my two friends, Louis and Mitka, and then I had to be alone. I had to sleep. The journey back and forth had been too vigorous and too draining.

I excused myself, and said I was going to my own private apartment. And so I did. I fell down on the bed, for all the world like an exhausted mortal man, and slept, waking more than once with the sudden apprehension that I was on fire, consumed with fatal heat, only to realize I wasn't and slip into sleep again.

Outside a light snow had begun to fall, and I dreamed of the warm nights of Louisiana and the tall knifelike banana trees swaying in the wind in the courtyard of my old house, and I dreamed of the oaks that led up the pathway to Fontayne's house and I saw the house a hideous ruin in my dreams and I hated this Baudwin, whoever he was, and wanted to destroy him. He had done in one instant what Rhoshamandes had never done to any of us.

Through my sleep, I heard Barbara come into the room. I saw her bend to put a waxen taper to the logs in the fireplace. I heard her fasten the steel shutters over the blowing snow. I wanted to rouse myself, say, No, please let the soft snow drift into the room with its tiny flakes, its white flakes that melted as soon as they touched the carpet or the damask of the chair, or the velvet of the coverlet beneath me. If Cyril perished at the hands of this monster, Baudwin . . . I found myself dreaming, dreaming of Louis and Fontayne talking together, and then in my dream I knew that they were, that they were in the library adjacent to this very room, and that they were already loving one another, that Mitka spoke a language that Louis understood, and then I drifted off, deeper and deeper. *I am in my home. I am in my father's house which has risen from the ruins. And the snow is falling, and my kith and kin are around me, and we will endure, all of us, we will not let anyone destroy us.*

From far away came a Strauss waltz, and the low hum of vampiric voices, and Antoine's violin. And a memory slowly drew me in—of my old friend, the friend of my mortal years, Nicolas, play-ing his violin in Renaud's little theater, and the audience, that small packed audience, clapping thunderously for him. I saw his brown eyes, eyes somewhat like Pandora's eyes, and I saw his sly smile at me as he turned again to the stage. I smelled the oil of the foot lamps, and the dust and the scent of humans, and out of the smoky darkness came the deadly word, *Wolfkiller.*

And where is that blood drinker now, who sealed my fate then before going into the fire himself? He is a ghost and he lodges with the Children of Atlantis, and maybe they are making for him a new body. Or maybe he is in this room, or in this dream, invisible, and filled with anguish. . . . Sleep, sleep so deep that the dreams can't find you, the dreams that will not let you rest. Sleep.

Chapter 8

They woke me two hours before sunup to tell me Cyril had returned with Baudwin, and I should come quickly.

The prisoner had been taken to the newly discovered dungeon below the restored southeast tower.

I found all the usual members of the household in the large room directly above the barred cells. The significant elders, Seth, Gregory, and Marius, were there, along with Dr. Fareed, Sevraine, and Armand.

Cyril was unharmed, though his black leather coat had been singed, I could see. But he had a mischievous expression on his face, and his hair, tousled by the wind, was hanging in his dark bright eyes.

"There you are, boss," he said, "the fiend who tried to burn you. He's all yours."

In their midst on the stone floor lay one of the grimmest sights I'd ever beheld—a being almost entirely wrapped in what seemed to be strips of black metal.

This creature was lying on his side. Only his legs below the knees were free, sheathed in filthy brown boots, and they moved restlessly, while all the rest of him was bound in these black coils all the way to the crown of his head.

"Ah, yea gods," I said. "The pickets of the iron fence!" Cyril had removed those and used them to tightly wrap the head and shoulders, and arms of this being against his back, and his legs together to the knees. He'd made a mummy of the creature in iron coils, between which there was not the slightest opening.

Cyril stood over the being and gave a triumphant laugh. "Baudwin, at your mercy, my lord," he said. "He gave me a devil of a time, but I got him. And wrapped up like this, he can't send the fire against anybody unless he wants to roast his own head."

"But how is that possible?" said Seth. "I've never heard of such a thing."

"Neither have I," said Marius.

"There's a lot you don't know," said Cyril. "But in olden times we knew it. Bind up a blood drinker in iron and he can't make fire or send force against you. He can't even call to others."

No one looked more amazed than Dr. Fareed.

Sevraine was also laughing along with Cyril. "How very clever, of course. It locks the energy in."

"That's it," said Cyril.

"Good Lord," said Fareed. "I'm devoted utterly to studying our anatomy, our psychology, and all our gifts—entirely from a scientific standpoint. And I never dreamt—."

"And let me tell you something else," said Cyril, "and remember it. If he can't see you, he can't send any force against you either. But I didn't take out his eyes. I was tempted to, but this was simpler. And the iron fence was there. I was in a hurry to bring him back here to find out what he knows."

"But surely he can still send out the word, and the word might reach his maker, if his maker exists," said Gregory. "I must confess I did hear tell of this in the later times after the Mother and Father had gone silent. Seems I remember prisoners whose heads were bound in iron. Like the medieval armor that came later. But I thought it was a form of torture. I never thought that it could contain his powers."

"Do you hear any thoughts coming from him?" asked Cyril. "I don't."

Fareed took out his iPhone and began to tap in some message to himself or another. "Iron masks," he said, "from the armorer in Paris. Iron masks."

I almost laughed. Here we stood on the first floor of a great refurbished dungeon, and Fareed was texting the armorer in Paris who had made the ax which I still carried under my left arm inside my coat. The armorer had in the last two years meticulously and wondrously restored all of the old armor I'd gathered from the ruins of my father's house.

Now all through the Château suits of armor guarded doorways or graced shadowy corners, with their eyeless helmets and hands sheathed in mail. How many times in my childhood had I heard tell of this or that ancestor who had worn such armor in the battles for the Holy Land in which my family had made its name?

And now this craftsman of ancient armor would make us iron masks.

Quite suddenly, the whole little informal assembly fell quiet.

A muffled voice was struggling within the iron wrappings to be heard.

"You will pay for this, all of you," said the voice, through clenched teeth. "My maker will burn you to cinders and I shall watch."

"It's almost morning," said Cyril. "And I'm tired. Which cell do you want for this one?"

"*Mon Dieu,*" I whispered. "So now I preside over a dungeon into which blood drinkers are thrown to languish without a trial?"

"Boss," Cyril said, pushing his way towards me until he was right in front of me and glowering down at me, which naturally enough I hated. "The monster tried to burn you alive, you and your fancy

little friend Fontayne. He burnt up that fancy house you loved. People came from the nearby town to put out the flames, but they didn't have a chance of saving it. Isn't that enough for you? What makes you so—damn, if I only knew the words! What makes you so crazy? I love you—only you, nobody else ever—only you, and I'll always do all in my power to protect you but you are . . . you are . . ."

"Past all patience," said Marius in a low sardonic voice.

"Yes, that's good enough," said Cyril. "Past all patience, whatever the Hell that means. Sounds fine."

"How old are you really, Cyril?" asked Gregory.

Cyril waved away the question. That's what he always did when asked about his past.

I well understood why Gregory wanted to know. How could one calculate the strength required to turn iron bars into coils, coils of uniform shape, it seemed, with not a slice of light dividing them, encasing a being entirely in iron? Each one of us was a mystery when it came to power, and for some reason many blood drinkers would never confide their true age.

Cyril was one such, and would never speak of memories. When Fareed sought to enter Cyril's personal story into his records, Cyril would give no cooperation. Yes, he'd made Eudoxia, the female vampire destroyed centuries ago as described by Marius, he would admit to that, because it was in the books. And I had picked up little things from him here and there, but he was a mystery overall.

He was glaring at me now, his muscular arms folded, his dark eyebrows knit in a scowl. "Prince, this is all good what you've done here," he said. "All this is good. I do not want to go back to living in caves, and sleeping in dirt, and staying clear of other blood drinkers as if I were a tiger on the prowl. No. But you must realize that those who try to harm you have to be destroyed."

"I know, Cyril," I said. "I understand."

I went down on one knee beside the prisoner. I studied the iron coils which bound him. "Here," I said. "Strip away this one, so that I can get to his throat."

From behind the iron came a muffled voice. "I loathe you and despise you. You will pay for what you have done to me."

Cyril bent down, picked up the prisoner in his left arm as if the prisoner weighed nothing, and then unwound the coil of iron that was closely binding his chin and his neck. You would have thought it was licorice candy, it was so simple for him, until it clattered on the stone floor.

I stared at the quivering flesh and the Adam's apple pulsing.

"Why did you try to destroy me?" I asked.

"You have no authority," he said in a muffled murmur, "to rule the blood drinkers of this world, beings who've thrived for centuries before you were even born. Your Court will be destroyed."

"And why is that?" I asked. "Why should it be destroyed?"

"This is excruciating," said the bound one. "At least remove the bonds from around my legs. Let me move my legs."

Cyril shook his head. "Keep him as he is. He's very strong. Give him no room to flex and break the bonds. He can turn his head now and that's a bad thing. I'll put the iron back when you've finished."

"Did you drink his blood?" I asked Cyril.

He shrugged. "I saw in it what he wanted me to see, great splashy pictures of the wonderful Gundesanth. He's a liar. Gundesanth never made him."

"You're the liar," said the prisoner. "My name is Baudwin, Lord of the Secret Lake. And Gundesanth made me before you ever opened your eyes on this world."

Gregory drew closer to the prisoner.

"Baudwin, did Rhoshamandes put you up to this?"

"I do not know Rhoshamandes," said the prisoner. "Oh, I've heard tell of him. Seen him. I stay clear of him. He stays clear of me."

"Well, then who did put you up to what you did?" asked Marius. He had been watching everything in silence. He came forward now as he spoke.

"No one put me up to it," said the prisoner. "You offend me, all of you, and there came a chance to destroy you and I took it. I will have the chance again."

"And why should we give you that chance?" I asked. "We have done nothing to you."

"You made this Court and you make rules here. You are as offensive to me as the old Children of Satan, and worse. Whereas they were penitential and stupid, you are clever and rich. You're too visible to the world, and blind to your own folly. You and everyone with similar designs beg to be destroyed. Those allies of yours, those dark creatures from the early world, those creatures should be destroyed as well."

"Why not end this now?" asked Cyril.

"But we've done nothing to you," said Marius, ignoring Cyril. "We do not force our rules on those who don't want to join us. We settle disputes only when we're asked. And we do try to do what's just."

"My maker will come for me," the prisoner said. "My maker will hear my cries."

"No, he won't," said Cyril, "and if he were living and like to come, he would have come."

"And who is your maker?" Gregory asked.

"You know who he is. Gundesanth. You knew him, Nebamun, and he knew you. He was the third blood drinker made by the Mother, of the primal blood. He was made before you were made. He rode the Devil's Road from one end of the world to the other, burning out the mavericks."

"And by what authority," I asked, "did he do that?"

"The Queen's authority, as they were renegades from her priesthood," said the prisoner.

"Ah, but you're lying," said Seth. His voice was soft but hard and hostile. "Do you know me, Baudwin? I'm Seth, the son of the Mother. And you know as well as I that Gundesanth became a renegade and he hunted down and burned mavericks for his own pleasure."

"What I'm saying is Gundesanth made me, and when he finds out you're holding me prisoner, he'll come for me. Don't you think he can read your thoughts even now? You've wrapped me in iron so I can't summon him. You're very clever, all of you are clever, but you can't keep the Court and the news of the Court from anyone, especially not Gundesanth."

"Where is he?" asked Marius. "I should like very much to meet him. We all would."

"We didn't part enemies," said Gregory. "Santh was my friend until he left the Mother. I knew he was leaving. I didn't betray him. Santh never raised his hand or his weapons against me."

"He hates you, Nebamun. He's told me so."

Gregory looked at me. He shook his head. "None of this makes sense. It's a fact, I can't really probe his mind when he's wrapped in iron, but he's lying. I know he is. I can tell by his voice."

"Let me go," said the prisoner.

"Why on earth do you think we would let you go?" I asked. "So you can try to kill me again?"

"I will do that, you can be sure."

I sat back and drew his helpless body up close to me. He groaned and kicked, slamming his boot heels against the stone floor.

I touched his neck, which filled me with revulsion, and then I bent and sank my fangs into him, resisting a wave of nausea, and the blood flowed quickly into my mouth.

It was hot and thick, much like the blood of Marius, but not the nectar of Seth's blood, and immediately I heard his curses, his invectives, his evil predictions rushing at me, but what I saw was a great blond-haired blood drinker with green eyes, mounted on a magnificent warhorse caparisoned in gold. His hair was thick and long and blowing in the wind, and a look of jubilant malice illuminated his face as he gazed at me through the blood. I saw and heard fire all around him. The sky was lurid with fire. A terror seized me. I felt myself running on foot. I saw a mace coming at me, an iron ball on a chain, the very weapon I'd used over two hundred years ago to slay the wolves that had surrounded me on my father's mountain, and I ducked and fell facedown on the earth. Horses were all around me. I felt someone lift me and with both my fists I pounded upon the handsome, malicious face and yanked at the hair. A low rolling laughter deafened me. I was sick, sick unto death, and fell back and, turning my head, vomited the blood on the floor.

I shoved him away from me onto the stones. I tried to stand, but the nausea rose in me again and I went over to the corner, put my hand on the wall, and more of the blood came out of my mouth. Someone held on to me, steadying me, and I realized it was Cyril. But Marius was beside me, and Sevraine's long graceful hands were flashing in front of my face. She put a white handkerchief to my lips. The sickness wouldn't pass.

Had this ever happened to me before, the blood of a blood drinker sickening me as if it were poisoned? I couldn't remember.

"Gundesanth will destroy you," said Baudwin.

"Be quiet, you bloody demon," said Cyril, and kicked the iron-bound body hard, rolling it over on its front.

"Put him in the cells," said Marius.

"Why not simply put an end to it here and now?" asked Seth. His voice was soft as before, but he appeared as full of revulsion as I felt.

"No. I have an idea on that," said Marius. "No point in wasting his death."

"Wasting his death?" I said. I leaned back against the wall. "What do you mean?"

"Just what I said. The sun's rising. Let's put him in the dungeon for now."

Cyril gathered up the iron coil, put it back around the prisoner's neck, and tightened it till the prisoner started choking and then carried him through the door that opened to the winding stone stairway that led to the barred cells below.

I was staring at Marius, trying to regain my equilibrium, trying to make the sickness go away. I heard the loud clank of a door or gate opened and slammed shut, and the grind of the key in the lock.

Cyril brought the old key ring to me. I stared at it for a moment in revulsion, and then I took it.

"I'll be the keeper of these keys," said Gregory, "unless you prefer."

"No, you take them," I said.

"Are you satisfied, Lestat, that we've given him a trial?" Gregory asked.

"Yes," I said. "Besides, he never asked for a trial, did he?" This sickness wasn't letting up. I reached out for Cyril. "Something's wrong with me. . . ." There was more I wanted to say on this question of a trial. The rebel didn't recognize our authority to put him on trial. But I couldn't think for the sickness. What had Marius meant by those strange words, "no point in wasting his death"?

"Ah, it's just he put a curse on you when you drank from him," said Cyril. "Come, let's go."

And we all left the dungeon. I was growing cold. The sickness was leaving me for the numbness of the dawn. Cyril all but carried me into my private cell and set me down on the marble shelf where I often slept beside the coffin.

I lay down because I couldn't prevent myself from doing it, and Cyril put my feet together upon the marble bed.

"You sleep, boss," he said. "Nobody's going to kill you. If Gundesanth were living, he would find you a companion for his soul."

"Why do you say that?" I asked.

He was silent. Then he said: "Gundesanth was an interesting talker."

Chapter 9

I opened my eyes. The day had died. The night had come, and I'd awakened from a dreamless sleep with the taste of nausea on my lips. I put my hand to my lips and felt the stickiness of blood there, and turning on my side, I vomited blood on the floor of my cell.

"When will this go away!" I said aloud.

I heard someone with me in my cell in the darkness. Someone I could not see. But a candle on the shelf burst into flame immediately, and as its feeble even light moved out like a vapor to extend itself to all corners, I saw the being, seated on the marble bench at my feet.

I swung my legs around and sat up, pushing back and away from the being instinctively and the better to see who he was.

I let out a gasp.

Seldom if ever in all my life had I seen a figure like this. It was a male being with dark rippling hair that came down to his shoulders and great glittering eyes. Above his rose-colored lips, beautifully formed lips, was a dark thick carefully trimmed mustache. And a rippling beard extended from beneath his moist lower lip. It had been trimmed to a thick rectangular shape.

He wore a robe of dark blue velvet trimmed in gold embroidery, made of actual gold thread, and studded with twinkling jewels.

"Beautiful," I whispered, and out of sheer delight at this great unique feast for my eyes, I laughed a soft reverent laugh. "Beautiful," I said again. "What are you? Who are you? How did you come to be here?"

I realized suddenly what sort of person he resembled, or just might be: a kingly being from an old Assyrian wall, a lord from the ancient lands of the two rivers, a lord who might have ruled in Nineveh or Babylon or some forgotten city long before, now erased by desert sands.

He smiled. And a familiar voice came out of him as he reached to embrace me.

"It's Gregory, beloved," he said. "It's Gregory as he looks when he rises before he shears off all the hair of his face, and clips the hair of his head. It's Gregory as I looked the night the Mother made me."

I was filled with delight. I couldn't quite explain it, that the explanation for this glittering splendor was so very simple. But it was most certainly Gregory and now I saw his good nature in his eyes, and as he smiled again, I saw his small pointed white fangs.

"Come here to me, Prince," he said. "Let me give you my blood. Let me give you the blood of the fourth blood drinker ever made."

I couldn't resist. It didn't even occur to me. I saw him rise before me and I lay back on the marble bed and he was stretched out on top of me, a warm gentle weight against me, and my fangs were pressed to his neck. I drank.

The cell vanished. I vanished.

There was only the night and the forest thick on either side of the ribbon of road that twisted and turned as it made its way amid these monstrous trees. How impossibly dark this forest that not a particle of moonlight could pierce its canopy, and it was in this darkness, just a few feet off the road and following it, that Gregory walked. He was the vampire Nebamun and he wore the leather armor of an Egyptian warrior, but his legs were wrapped and bound with linen to protect him from the northern cold, and a great fur cloak covered his shoulders, which he held close about him with his left hand. His hair was long and rich and thick to his shoulders, and his beard wild and unkempt.

Far off to his right, far away in the forest, he caught the flicker of light. It seemed no more than a spark in the distance, but he moved towards it, the brambles and tiny broken branches of the forest crushed beneath his leather boots.

Deeper and deeper into the woods he walked, pushing the shrubbery out of his path, deeper into the scents and sounds of the forest, when out of the perfect blackness there came a savage roar that shook me to the bone.

A monstrous pair of claws scratched at Nebamun, and a great gaping mouth filled with sharp white teeth closed over his head.

In a fury, he fought the beast, sending it hurtling away from him, rolling on its back, its fierce eyes red and gleaming, and its roar filled with fury, and Nebamun heard the clank of the chains that held the beast captive. He lifted his spear to kill it but waited, waited until he felt a hand close on his hand.

"Nebamun" came the whisper.

"Ah, I've found you!" Nebamun said. And the two blood drinkers embraced each other, their lips locked in a long kiss. For the longest time, in the darkness, they held to one another, Nebamun's lips moving over the face of the other, and again back to his lips.

"Santh, my Santh, my beloved Santh."

"Come with me," said the other. "I didn't expect you so soon." He led the way towards a pale uneven light, pushing the tall growth out of his path.

The beast roared and pulled on the chains that bound him. And every time, the roar sent a shiver through Nebamun. It was as bad as the roar of the lion in the African jungles.

"I knew that you left the stockade of the god at sundown," said Santh. "I didn't know you'd make such time."

"But how did you know?" asked Nebamun.

"I have my followers all through these woods," said the other.

They had come to the mouth of a low-roofed cave. It seemed impossible that any being would choose to live in such a place, but they'd gone only a few feet into it when the low ceiling opened up into a great cavern, and across that cavern they found another corridor through which they moved towards a distant light.

Finally, they came around a turn and found themselves before a roaring fire of forest wood and dead leaves. Above them the roof of the cave was covered with strange drawings—little men made of sticks just as children draw and great humped buffalo and the unmistakable image of a bear.

"What is the meaning of this?" Nebamun asked.

"No one knows," said Santh. "It's always been here. We hide in these places by day because the humans in these parts are terrified of them and won't come near."

Nebamun was glad of the warmth and drew as close to the fire as he could.

"Is all the world cold except for Egypt?" he asked. He looked at his friend, at his thick shaggy blond hair and beard.

"All the world where I was born," said the blond one. "Come sit down. Let me look at you. Ah, your wounds are healed already? We gods are amazing creatures!"

This sent them both into paroxysms of boyish laughter and they slapped their thighs as they laughed. "We gods!" scoffed Nebamun. They were doubled over with laughing.

They fell down on the soft earth, laughing, and they slapped their thighs as they laughed.

Nebamun's dark skin was like mahogany, but Santh's skin was a gleaming white. He wore only furs, a tunic of fur girded at the waist in leather, to which there was a sword attached in a bright golden scabbard, and a dagger in its sheath.

Again, they embraced each other, and moved along to a place where they could rest against the cave wall, yet have the fire very near to their feet.

"Well, if you knew I was coming," said Nebamun, "then you know why."

"Yes, but I don't know the why of the why" came the answers. "They want me to come back. They publish through the world that I am pardoned if only I return. They'll charge nothing against me if I come to temple in Saqqâra, but why do they want to pardon me? Why now?"

"The King and Queen no longer speak or move," said Nebamun. "They say it will eventually happen to all of us. We'll become as statues, we blood gods. But what do they know? They weren't there at the beginning. They don't know. So many things they don't know."

"Explain this to me," said Santh.

"They sit silent and have for years now," said Nebamun. "They don't take blood when it's offered. There is no reason anymore to keep them imprisoned in stone."

They both stared into the fire for a long moment.

"Then who is it that sends for me?" asked Santh.

"The Elder. The Elder would have you be the leader now if you wish it. And go throughout the world visiting the blood gods in their shrines, taking account of those that have gone mad, and doing away with them, and bringing new gods into the Blood to serve."

"Why haven't they offered this to you?"

"I refused it," said Nebamun. "I say the old religion is dead. I say it is meaningless. I say we are not gods, and never were, and we are not meant to pronounce judgment on humans. I say none of it matters now and I will not make new gods for old shrines."

"Then why did you come to bring me this message?" asked Santh.

"Because I wanted you to know there is no one now to hunt you. There are only foolish priests in the temple in Saqqâra, and even they don't believe it anymore. And I want you to know that if you want to come down to Egypt that you can. If you want to see Nineveh, you can."

"And you? What will you do?"

Nebamun didn't answer. He looked at his friend.

"I don't know, Santh," he said. "I don't know."

"You never found Sevraine, did you?" asked Santh.

"No." Nebamun shook his head. "I found Rhoshamandes once, but he knew nothing of her by the time I found him."

Again they stared into the flames.

"What do you want, Nebamun?" asked Santh.

"I don't know, Santh. I don't know." He picked up a loose stick for no good reason, and began to make scratch marks in the earth. He made a long line twisting and turning, which he thought of as a road. Not a particular road in a particular place. But the road of his life. "It's all finished, Santh," he said. "I'm tired. I don't know the people of Egypt now. I haven't known them for as far back as I can really remember, and the times before that, they're like a dream, a bad dream."

He could see by Santh's expression that he didn't understand. His green eyes were lively, and almost cheerful except for the sadness he felt for his friend.

"Stay with me, then," said Santh. "Don't go back this time. Stay here!"

A long silence fell between them. Nebamun realized he was weeping and he was ashamed. He felt Santh's arm over his shoulder, and he said in a soft voice to Santh, "This is your world, my friend, I have no world now."

A terrible sadness crumpled the face of Santh. He wasn't ashamed to cry. He hated the blood coming from his eyes and he wiped at it angrily with the fur of his sleeve, but he wasn't ashamed. "You cannot give in to this!" he said. "This is like a sickness, this feeling. You have to find a place somewhere. You have to find something. You and I were there at the beginning! Who's left who was there at the beginning? We must continue—."

Very softly through his tears, Nebamun asked, Why.

I woke.

I was sitting up on the bench. I could take no more blood, and as I stared at the candle I felt his blood and the power of his blood was beyond description. I could hear the wax slowly melting around the wick, and it seemed the breath I took into my lungs was like the moment before the death of the victim is about to come, and all my body is nothing but my mouth and the blood and the coming. I stared at the halo of light and color surrounding the tiny flame. I had never realized there were so many colors in that halo, that that halo was so large.

I turned and put my forehead down against Gregory's shoulder. I felt his hand come up to take mine, and I clasped his hand and then I reached past it and embraced him tightly.

"Is this sickness gone now?" he asked.

"Oh yes," I said. I closed my eyes.

"That was the last time I ever saw him," he said in a low confiding voice. "He begged me to stay, but I went home to Egypt. I made the long journey south again across northern Europe and down to the great sea, and around the sea until I reached Egypt, my Egypt, and I went down into the sands to sleep.

"Once, a long time after I'd risen and fallen in love with all the wonders of the Greek and Roman world, I met a blood drinker who told me that Santh was no more. Do I believe he made that scoundrel in the dungeon? I do not. I've heard so many claim to have been made by Santh or made by one who was made by him, but Santh was as miserly with his blood as I've been with mine. We don't make blood drinkers like us. We seek our partners and our mates among those already in the Blood, that is, sometimes. I have my Chrysanthe. And unlike Sevraine she has never left me. But Santh is gone, and it's been a thousand years since I've even heard somebody speak his name."

"Why did you come to me like this?" I asked. I was still holding him. His blood was quite truly a fire in my limbs. It was burning my heart. All the secrets of the world seemed inscribed in the pattern of the marble wall so close to my eyes.

"Because I knew you were weary and confused, and you hated for anyone to be condemned to the dungeon. And I know that Marius alarmed you when he said he had a design for what might be done with the condemned."

I couldn't deny it.

"And I want you to be strong," he said. "We need you to be strong. When you realize how much we need you, and how much you must be strong for us, then it will be easier for you."

"Maybe you're right. But as of now, I can't imagine it," I said. "I never dreamed of dungeons, or condemned prisoners, or passing sentence on an ancient like Rhoshamandes. . . . Oh, what's the use of saying any more?"

"You'll come to see it," he said. "You'll come to see that all we are doing will be defeated if we do not act in our own defense with resolve."

Words, I wanted to say, words and words. But I didn't want to offend Gregory, not for the world. For the first time I felt I knew him, knew him intimately, the way I'd once known Armand, over two centuries ago, when he had spellbound me and Gabrielle and showed us in that spell his memories of Marius who had made him, and how all that he loved had been lost.

"Come," he said. "Let's go. Benedict is here. He knows we're about to pass judgment. He knows. And he is not pleading for his master, and I don't know why."

Chapter 10

I had to have a thorough wash and a change of clothes before I confronted the throng in the ballroom. And so did Gregory, apparently, because he appeared at the same moment I did, his face clean shaven, his hair short, dressed in his usual costly business attire, winking secretively at me as we both approached a gift brought to me by Benedict.

A large rectangular dais had been brought into place before the right side of the orchestra for this gift—a dais that was not quite as high as that used by the conductor. And on this dais I saw a great medieval chair, made of oak, and ornamented all over with carving. The back and the seat were padded with red velvet.

It might have come from a cathedral. Indeed, I've seen popes photographed in such chairs. Winged lions crouched under the two padded arms, and above the cushion of the back was a pyramid of carved blossoms and leaves. The legs were beautifully turned. And over all the wood were the remnants of a thick gilding—with just enough gold polishing every feature of the wood to be elegant.

Benedict stood there watching me as I inspected the chair. He wore a monk's habit of dark brown wool, with a simple rope around the waist and great sleeves in which his folded hands were buried.

I reached out to him and he came forward and we embraced. He was warm from the kill, as we say, filled with blood, his boyish face so flushed it seemed almost human, and his hands were warm.

No such warmth emanated from me. Gregory's blood was as cold as it was powerful. Only human blood creates such heat.

"A monarch should have a throne," Benedict said. His voice was strained, faltering. He stepped back yet held my shoulders as if I were a schoolboy, and he kissed me on either cheek. "Prince," he said. His lip trembled.

"Thank you, my friend," I said. "Is Rhoshamandes with you?"

"No." He shook his head, and gave a short scoffing laugh. "I want to say my farewells in the Council Chamber."

"What farewells?" I asked. But he was already moving across the ballroom. The musicians were tuning their instruments. Nods and gestures of greeting distracted me. And I saw that some of the elders were following Benedict as I was.

When we reached the Council Chamber, I opened the door for Benedict and followed him in.

We were not a large group—only Gregory, Sevraine, Seth and Fareed, and Allesandra. But within a few moments, others joined us, David and Jesse, and then came Armand along with Marius and Pandora.

I sensed we were waiting for others to come. But only two more did, Bianca and Louis.

Louis continued to feel that he was out of place at these meetings, but I wouldn't hear of such an idea. He took the chair to my right as always. Benedict was to his right.

Marius sat at the far end of the table as he often did, and all the others were in random places.

"Thank you for coming," said Benedict. "I have reached the very end of my life, and I wish to say farewell before seeing to my death. I don't want to leave the world without a farewell to those here who have shown me friendship."

There was an immediate chorus of protests, the loudest from Allesandra and Sevraine, but Benedict immediately gestured for silence. His mouth became hard, which looked faintly absurd on such a youthful and sensitive face, and for a moment I thought he was going to give way to tears, but he merely remained quiet until all the others were quiet too.

"There are things I wish to say," he said. "Things I've learned. They will strike some of you as obvious, and perhaps ridiculous, but I want to say them, because they are things of which I'm sure, absolutely sure, and who knows when one of you or some of you may make use of my words?

"Well, the first thing I must say is that two are not enough. No. Two are not enough in this life. There must be others. We deceive ourselves when we think that two can be a secure partnership against the horrors of time. It's not true. And what you have created in this Court is a refuge and a shelter and a sacred place where any and all can find others with whom to form those ties that matter so much."

I could see Marius nodding to these words. Gregory looked suddenly sad, dreadfully sad. And for a moment in a flash, I saw him as he had come to me only an hour before as that great Sumerian king or angel; perhaps I would always see something of that shining hair and shining beard now when I looked at him.

"Don't ever think that two is enough," Benedict said. "Don't ever imagine it. And don't ever be crippled by believing that you cannot live without one other being, and only that being. You must have more than that to love, because loving, loving keeps us alive, loving is our best defense against time, and time is merciless. Time is a monster. Time devours everything." He shuddered. I was hoping against hope that he didn't begin to weep, because he didn't want to weep.

"I don't mean to keep you long," he said. He clasped his hands, running his fingers through one another, and pressed his hands anxiously together. His cheeks were suddenly red.

"And the other thing I must say, which is painful to say, is be careful when you strike a blow, be careful what type of blow you strike, be careful that you never, never, unless you must, strike a blow that another cannot forgive . . . such as the severing of a hand from an arm, or the severing of an arm from a shoulder—because that is a savage thing, that brings forth a hatred from the soul of the victim that is primitive and catastrophic."

"Oh, come now, Benedict," said Gregory. "Do you mean to say that the Prince should not have struck off Rhoshamandes's hand and arm when Rhoshamandes held Mekare herself captive, and had slain Maharet beneath her own roof? Surely . . ."

"I don't speak of justice now, Gregory," Benedict said.

Armand interjected before Benedict could go on.

"You murdered Maharet, you miserable coward!" he said. He was plainly seething with rage. "You battered her to death with an ax in the sanctity of her own house, and you come here expecting sympathy for your master. I don't care what the spirit moved either of you to believe. You're murderers of the eldest of our kind."

Benedict shut his eyes and put his hands over his face. He began to shake all over.

"Both you and your master should be destroyed!" Armand continued. His face flushed red.

Marius stood and came down the table to Armand and laid his hands on Armand's shoulders. But Armand rose to his feet and ignored Marius as if he weren't there.

I could feel the hostility blazing from Armand.

"I dreamed of some night going to her," said Armand. "I dreamed of hours, nights, weeks, months in her divine company," he said, his voice dropping low with its heat, his eyes fixed on Benedict. "I dreamed of asking her questions without end and roaming through her archives and her libraries. I dreamed of asking for her finest wisdom, and this you destroyed, you and your selfish fool of a master, you destroyed it, storming into her compound like barbarians with your weapons—."

Benedict was hunched over weeping, choking with sobs. But suddenly he rose to his feet, the blood streaming down his face.

"And you, you vile miscreant," he said back to Armand, "what did you do with your powers? Enslave the Children of Satan in rags and filth and rotten theologies under Les Innocents when you could have freed them to see the wonders Marius revealed to you, all the beauty of the world and its great art? Who are you to curse me? I'll tell you what else I've learned before I die."

"Oh, die and get on with it," said Armand. "Do you want my help?"

"Yes, I do," said Benedict. "But not in the way you think."

Allesandra had risen, and after a moment's hesitation she stood behind Benedict with her hands on his shoulders just as Marius stood behind Armand.

"I was the dupe of the Voice, and you know it," said Benedict, "and I was doing my master's bidding, I admit it. But she wanted to destroy us all, Maharet. She dreamed of it, of taking her sister with her into the volcano which would have destroyed us all."

"No, she didn't," said Armand caustically. "She had her moments of suicidal despair as we all do, that's all. She would have come round. Why didn't you and your master talk to her, seek to comfort her, seek to turn her from that darkness?"

"She would not have let us kill her if she had wanted to live."

Jesse Reeves's voice broke in suddenly. She turned in her chair to look up at Benedict.

"That is not true and you know it," she said. "Stop seeking to excuse what you did. You took my beloved Maharet by surprise. We are all vulnerable to surprise. Speed and surprise! And your blows fell on her body and on her soul."

"Very well, I admit it. Yes, it's true, all of it is true," cried Benedict. But he didn't look at Jesse. He was still looking at Armand.

And what a spectacle they made, the two of them, each Born to Darkness at such a young age, two "boys" facing each other with boyish cheeks and lips, and even boyish hair, two angels glaring at each other, and I realized as soon as the thought of it gripped me that Benedict was thinking this very thing.

"And now I'll tell you what more I've learned and want to share before I leave this world," he said. He looked at me and then back to Armand.

"Those of us made young," he said, "we never grow up. Five hundred years or a thousand. It makes no difference. Time gives us room to be forever stupid and blind with the confusion and passions of the young, vulnerable to the masters who made us and ensnared us."

"Oh, stuff and nonsense," said Armand. "I was never a child. I was a man before I was ever Born to Darkness, you imbecilic creature! Maybe you were a child, in your monkish robes, with your dark Christian longings, and maybe you still are. But I was never young. And I have learned through suffering and anguish and loneliness such as you, cowering in the shadow of your master, have never known."

Benedict was blinking as if Armand were a blinding light.

"I want to die now," said Benedict. "I want to die here among the young ones—." He pointed in the direction of the ballroom. "I've invited them to gather. I want to give them my blood. I want to take the sins of my master upon myself—."

"You are no Christ who can take upon himself the sins of others," said Armand. "You don't even know what you're doing with your staging of your own death. You bring a throne to the ballroom so the Prince will preside over your little spectacle, but you have no grasp of what you really mean to do."

"He's speaking the truth, Benedict," said Allesandra. "Please delay this dreadful step."

Allesandra had become more beautiful with every passing night, it seemed, since the Voice had called her forth from the catacombs of Paris, and she gathered Benedict to herself like a redemptive angel, her lovely hair falling all about her shoulders and his shoulders as she sought to embrace him. "Please listen to me, Benedict. Don't do this thing."

"There's no time anymore to waste," he said.

He reached inside his jacket and drew out a small silver box. He opened it and I could see the vampiric blood in it. The box was about half full of it, and it gave a gleam that mortal blood never gives. Closed up in a container as it was, vampiric blood stays liquid. He touched it now with the tip of his finger.

"Dr. Fareed, please come with me. I have something I must give you."

He put the box back into his inner pocket.

"And, Prince, please do preside if you will, and see my blood is not wasted. I beg you, don't let the flames take me. I'm in terror of the flames. Don't commit my remains to the fire until my blood is gone."

Without further ado he moved swiftly out of the Council Chamber, Fareed coming along behind him with Allesandra, and the rest of us following slowly as we approached the ballroom from which not a sound could be heard.

Chapter 11

Throughout the exchanges in the Council Chamber I'd heard activity in the ballroom, vampires gathering, cars entering the parking grounds, and feet ascending stairways, and others coming on the wind and entering through the terrace.

But even so, the size of the crowd astonished me. I think some thousand were assembled, and the orchestra sat waiting, and Antoine at his podium had his baton in his hand.

All eyes were fixed on us as we came in. I motioned for a path to be made, and in the center of this path Benedict stopped. He was facing Antoine. He was in the very middle of the room. And I saw now that lining both sides of this path were young ones—Sybelle and Benji, Rose, Viktor, and other fledglings who surely had been summoned by Benedict, and many I didn't know. Older fledglings were gathered here as well—vampires who had perhaps four or five hundred years in the Blood. And I suppose by that reckoning, I myself could be seen as a fledgling, and Armand too. But many of these had never had the blood of the ancients. Made by makers long gone from the earth, they stared at Benedict with rapt attention, and the spectacle suddenly chilled me to my soul.

I felt a wild impulse to call a halt. This was horrible, what was happening, what I saw in the faces on either side of us. But Marius took my hand now and led me towards the gilded chair.

"Don't stop it. Watch it and learn from it," he said.

"But this is wrong," I said to him in the softest whisper.

"No, not wrong, but what we are," he said.

He gestured for me to step up to the platform and be seated on the medieval throne.

I found myself obeying him and now he stood to my left with his right hand on my shoulder, my Prime Minister.

Benedict raised his voice to address the throng.

"In ancient times," he said, "when I was but a fledging in the Loire Valley of this country, in what we now call the Garden of France, I was welcomed into the sodality of the night by Rhoshamandes, and we lived in a great stone edifice which is long gone.

"When old ones in that time wanted to end their journey on the Devil's Road, they gave their blood to the rest of us, and so it is with me now and it's what I mean to do. I give my eyes first to Fareed that he may use them for some goodly purpose, but my body and my blood I give to you."

A great gasp went up from the spectators as he plucked out his left eye and then his right and put them into that silver casket before snapping it shut and handing it to Fareed.

The silence was like something that grew deeper and deeper by the moment.

Benedict continued, the blood trickling down his face, his eyelids fluttering hideously as he spoke.

"I beg you not to give my remains to the flames in those fireplaces until all blood is gone from me, and my head severed from my body and my heart silenced. And, Antoine, I ask you, give me music as it was in the old days. . . . Give me the *Dies irae, dies illa* . . . with the kettledrums, please, Antoine, and serenade me to my ruin."

Antoine's face was stricken with anguish. He looked at me, and I heard Marius tell him to do as Benedict asked.

And Antoine turned, lifted his baton, and at once I heard Notker's boy sopranos raise their voices in Gregorian chant to sing the song as I knew it, but with the savage beat of the drums.

The words came in Latin, but I knew the meaning.

That day of wrath, that dreadful day, shall heaven and earth in ashes lay, as David and the Sybil say.

Benedict stood with his head bowed. He slipped a knife from inside his long monkly robe.

"Come, Sybelle; come, Benji," he cried out. Then he tore open the robe and let it fall to the floor, revealing his entire naked body— a waxen image of a boy on the verge of manhood, the golden hair around his cock as bright and beautiful as the soft curling hair of his head.

"Come, Rose; come, Viktor," he cried out. "Come all of you young ones. Take the blood of a thousand years."

The hymn went on.

What horror must invade the mind, when the approaching Judge shall find and sift the deeds of all mankind.

With a movement so swift I didn't see it, Benedict slashed his left wrist, then his right, and then his throat. He plunged the knife into his heart, withdrew it, and it hit the floor clattering at his feet.

He vanished as the fledglings closed around him.

The mighty trumpet's wondrous tone shall rend each tomb's sepulchral stone and summon all before the Throne.

I sat there watching with the same sense of horror, of something unholy and hideous and yet beautiful, the music pumping through the heart of the kettledrums, as Allesandra and Eleni and Everard de Landen came up close to me, gathering to the left of the throne. They turned their backs on what was happening, Allesandra collapsing in Everard's arms.

"It's what he wants," Everard whispered. "That monster should be the one dying, not him."

The voices grew more urgent, the drums beating a faster cadence.

O King of dreadful majesty! grace and mercy You grant free; as Fount of Kindness, save me!

I heard the unmistakable sound of preternatural flesh tearing, of bones breaking. A ghastly roar rose from the crowd and I saw Benedict's head held aloft, like that of a prisoner executed by the guillotine, the empty eyelids still fluttering, and the music grew louder, the horns joining the voices of the singers, and finally the strings took up the grim song.

Out of the mass of blood drinkers, there wandered a fledgling I didn't know, a female in a velvet gown, with a severed hand to her lips, drinking the very last of the blood from its white flesh and then licking her lips. I saw her eyes open wide as the powerful blood flooded her senses, her blind gaze drifting over all in front of her until a great shudder passed through her, and she moved as if in a trance away to the far side of the room.

Others too were now moving away. But others hastened to pick up the fragments of the body which had been discarded. And I saw now as more and more abandoned the ritual that the limbs lay all scattered about.

"Come with me, Prince, please," sobbed Allesandra. "Help me gather them and put them on the fire."

I did as she asked. And Marius came with us.

It was finished.

We took up the broken pieces of what had once been Benedict and threw them into the flames. Marius held the head in both hands, then passed it to Allesandra, who held it to her breast, her fingers pressing into the golden hair.

"Come, it's over," whispered Marius to her.

I took the head from her, looked at the empty white face. Not a drop of blood remained to the hollow sockets. The head looked drawn and ancient.

I laid it as reverently as I could in the dancing flames.

There was nothing left now. Everard and Eleni had picked up the smallest remnants of flesh and brought them to us, and it was all done.

I stood there dazed. I couldn't grasp what had happened, even though I had seen it, that this Benedict, this beloved child of Rhoshamandes who had lived with him for over a thousand years, was gone—simply gone.

The music slowed. The hymn had finished.

I walked back to my new chair because I didn't know what else to do or where to go.

What would come now? The soft sad music of Albinoni in the Adagio in G Minor? That's what I wanted with all my soul.

But something different happened.

The orchestra broke into a riot of blazing sound. It was the pounding "O Fortuna" from *Carmina Burana*—with voices rising high above the roaring strings, and frantic drums.

From the shadows on all sides came blood drinkers to dance, skirts swirling, arms out, and the music moved away from its first theme into a dark and turgid waltz—a crashing and frenzied waltz fit for the denizens of Hell.

The room was quaking. Shrieks and ecstatic cries came from everywhere.

I put my hands over my ears and bowed my head. But I couldn't take my eyes off the great mass of dancers and their ecstatic movements, their voices rising to join the voices of the chorus.

I slumped back against the chair. I felt Marius's hand tighten on my right shoulder and his lips against the left side of my face.

"This is it. This is the dark part of us," he said, but not with spite, his voice soothing as though he meant only to comfort me. "We are killers and we thrive on death. It's the part of us you can't erase, not with all the love in broken Christendom."

I couldn't answer.

Allesandra dropped to the wooden platform at my feet and leaned back against my knees, crying. I looked down and saw she held Benedict's brown robe in her hands. She held it to her breast. I had forgotten about that robe. And something about the way she held it chilled me, brought back out of fractured and wounded memory a moment so painful I wanted to turn away from it; myself over a hundred years ago, holding Claudia's bloodstained dress, after her death in the cellar beneath the Théâtre des Vampires. I reached for Allesandra's hair. The music swallowed my thoughts, my memories, any meager attempt to reach beyond these moments.

Far down the hill, it must have roused the mortals from their beds, this dark savage dance. It must have been heard all through the snow-covered mountain valleys, this great dark surging waltz and all the searing preternatural voices mingling with it.

Through the fingers of my right hand I saw Louis among the dancers, his head back, his eyes closed, swaying with his feet in place, buffeted, it seemed, by the sounds around him, and Armand dancing with Sybelle in his arms, her silken skirts flying. And Rose and Viktor dancing as well, and others spinning like dervishes in their madness.

The Great Sevraine danced alone, a glittering figure in her shimmering white gown, lifting her arms with the grace of a ballerina, and beside her, in the very midst of it all, stood my mother, my Gabrielle, as if she were floating on the music. She wore her usual khaki coat and jeans, but her hair was loose, and she only smiled as hands reached for it, tore at it, picked it up, and let it fall in golden strands in the light of the chandeliers. Her eyes appeared glazed and distant as if the music was making her dream.

And where was Benedict? Where was his soul? Had his soul soared into the light, the eternal child, welcomed by some great forgiving power? Or had Memnoch, that evil and tenacious spirit, come to dazzle him with astral purgatorial nightmares?

A deafening crash shattered the dance.

The orchestra stopped. The voices stopped.

A great wind swirled through the ballroom, rocking the chandeliers on their chains, and snow descended in a soft silent avalanche of flakes.

I rose to my feet.

The crowd fell back away from the hearth on the far-left wall. Indeed the blood drinkers shrank into the corners.

I saw the Great Sevraine come towards me like a white comet. Gregory suddenly stood at my side, and so did Cyril, and Seth.

There—by the great fireplace on the left side of the ballroom—stood Rhoshamandes.

Chapter 12

Allesandra rose to her feet. It seemed no one else moved but Allesandra. She alone held out her hands with the blood-stained brown robe.

And the fire moved. The flames moved licking and devouring the white bones of the dead Benedict.

Rhoshamandes stood stock-still in his long velvet robe, only the tips of his black boots visible beneath the hem, his fair hair torn by the wind, and frost clinging to his arms and his shoulders. He appeared begrimed with frost.

He stared at the robe that Allesandra held in her hands.

Slowly she walked across the great empty dance floor, without making the softest sound, and held it out to him.

He stared at it as if he could not divine the meaning of it. And then his eyes moved to the fire, and he saw there the melting skull now cleansed by the flames of all flesh, the flames licking its empty eyeholes.

"Give the word," Gregory whispered in my ear.

"No," I murmured. "No. He must not be harmed. He's done nothing."

If Rhoshamandes could hear us, he gave no sign.

Allesandra wept in low hollow sobs. She moved to the other side of the great marble fireplace and looked down at the bones.

"He wanted it, my lord," she said. "He gave his blood to the young, as the old ones did in our first times together. It was his choice. No one harmed him."

Rhoshamandes looked up and away and then his eyes fixed on me.

His face for one moment was calm and still, washed clean of any visible emotion, and for all I knew he was staring at nothing, and certainly not at the blond Prince before the high-backed throne that Benedict had given him.

Then his face clabbered, clabbered like that of a child. His eyes quivered, and a soft shuddering moan escaped his lips. A roar broke from him that was louder than the music had ever been. A great openmouthed roar of pain such as no beast on Earth could ever make but only a feeling, suffering sentient being.

He clutched at himself with his own hands, hugging himself with his own arms, and the look of pain on his face was unbearable.

It was utterly unbearable.

If I were a painter I would never ever in all my life paint the image of that pain. I would never, never in all my life want to capture it. Let words try and fail and spare us all the expression of that agony.

"Now, give the word," whispered Marius.

"No, for the love of God, no. What has he done?" I whispered.

Rhoshamandes stared at me. There was no doubt now that he saw me. He didn't stare past me but at me. Sevraine stepped in front of me, and Gregory cleaved to my right side. I knew Seth was over my left shoulder.

Rhosh's lips twisted and struggled with the pain, and his eyes were pressed closed with blood tears and then they opened again. The emotion was drained from his face, and his eyes, which had never left me for an instant, were now filled with hatred.

Hatred I could feel across the width of the ballroom.

"You have done this to me," he whispered in a dry aching voice. "You have done this to me!" he shouted. And then he roared the words, "You with your Court and your cohorts, you have done this!"

Everywhere blood drinkers covered their ears.

Again, his face clabbered. He turned and reached into the fire, and grabbed up the skull and pressed it hard between his hands until it was nothing but powder. He rubbed the powder all over his face and his hair as he moaned, moaned over and over again.

I felt a great roaring blast of air come at me, a blast of searing icy wind, and I heard a sound as fierce as the blast, and saw a great swirl of color and movement. The far side of the room, the side wide open to the mountain and the windows, was suddenly broken out. The chandeliers fell with a crash to the ballroom floor, and screams rose all around me.

Rhosh was gone.

I sighed and put my hands to my eyes. I felt nothing but pity, nothing but sorrow for him.

Until five minutes later, when they told me that he had taken my mother with him.

Chapter 13

This is how it happened.

Gabrielle had been against the wall on the other side of me from the orchestra. She had drawn back there along with Louis and Bianca and Armand. Armand had been right beside her. And they had stood watching Rhoshamandes together. They knew I was safe, they said. That was their only thought, and Armand understood that I wanted no harm to come to Rhoshamandes.

Then they too had felt the wind, the noise of chandeliers smashed to the floor, and they had drawn together.

And only then did Armand, looking about himself to make sure of the safety of all he saw, realize that Gabrielle was nowhere in sight.

The word had gone out in a whisper. "Where is Gabrielle?"

And then Gabrielle's voice had come over the wind to Sevraine and Armand and Marius and a multitude of those who could, unlike me, hear her.

He has me. I can't get loose from him.

If she could hear any of us after that, she was unable to answer.

Speed and surprise. The words Jesse had used. *Speed and surprise.* Rhoshamandes had used both.

And with a sinking heart I sat on the ornate gilded throne realizing that my mother was likely already destroyed in payback for Benedict.

The Great Sevraine had gone after him, and Seth had gone with her—leaving Gregory to guard me along with Thorne and Cyril.

But Sevraine and Seth came back within the hour to report exactly what we all expected. They could find no sign of him anywhere. They left again, determined to search every room of his citadel on Saint Rayne. But I knew he would never be fool enough to go there and wait for the others to come after him.

I knew that, but it wasn't a thought. I was empty of thoughts. I was as empty of thoughts as I was of breath. I knew things, but I thought nothing.

I held the image of Rhosh's stricken face in my mind, and I heard his roar of pain, but I thought nothing.

Fortunately no one said anything inane, such as "Don't give up hope" or "Surely he won't hurt her."

Through all the whispering and rustling ballroom, as Barbara's people swept up the crystals of the chandeliers, and the broken links of silver and gold, as workers were already at work, plastering up the stones of the wall retrieved from the snow below, nobody said anything stupid.

And thankfully, no one asked, "Why on earth didn't you give the word to kill him? Why? Why? Why?"

Armand was crushed with grief that he had not prevented this. He sat on the dais weeping with Allesandra beside him.

And I sat on in the medieval throne, with my arms folded—with the life of my mother flashing before me, a silent torrent of images, words, and again I thought nothing, nothing, nothing. But I knew I could not bear the pain of this. I could not go on living if she were dead, she my first fledgling, first child of my blood and mother of my body. My life was finished.

Chapter 14

It had been three hours before dawn when Rhoshamandes took my mother.

Two hours later, Sevraine and Seth returned, saying that they had not found him in his castle on Saint Rayne, and his mortal servants, sweet guileless old mortals, had quite freely explained that their master had not been in residence for some time. It was their guess that he might be in France, but they truly did not know.

Sevraine had brought back the computers she found in the house, and papers purloined from his bedchambers. The beloved Children of Atlantis had been alerted right away to all that had taken place, and Fareed took the computers to them in their deep hideaway chambers at Collingsworth Pharmaceuticals, where Kapetria and Fareed vowed to search the hard drives for any clue to other places that Rhoshamandes might have established as residences.

I listened. I understood. I knew. I did not think.

Those who could reason and speak had concluded that Rhoshamandes would not stop his assault with my mother. And so Rose, Viktor, Louis, and Antoine, and Sybelle and Benji and Armand, had all gathered in the crypts close to mine for their rest, and would remain here after sunset as well, being guarded as I was. Marius had taken over the supervision of the Château, advising others under the roof to come to the crypts as well. There was ample space for them in the great warren we had dug out of the earth at the very beginning of our residence here. Those who didn't want to be confined were urged to leave the Château for their own safety. All agreed that no one was safe.

When I was finally led down the stairs, Louis came with me. In the darkened passage before my resting place, he embraced me and held tight to me, his lips pressed to my ear. I was aware of my hands moving over his hair, embracing his neck, drawing him ever closer, in a way I had never done in our long years in New Orleans. We joined in the posture of lovers, brothers, fathers with sons.

"I love you with my whole soul, and I will always love you," he confided to me. "You are my life. I have hated you for that and love you now so much that you've been my instructor in loving. And believe me when I say you will survive this, and that you must for all of us. You will survive because you always have and you always will."

I couldn't answer. I knew I loved him more than words could say, but I couldn't respond.

As I lay down, not in my coffin, but again on the marble shelf where I preferred to sleep of late, Cyril sat against the wall and fell asleep as if by will, and closing my eyes, I homed in on Paris where Kapetria, our lovely loyal Kapetria, was already hard at work, delving into the private fortune and wealth of Rhoshamandes.

Just before I lost consciousness, fighting it wildly and stupidly, I was aware of Gregory entering, dressed in a long robe once more with jewels embroidered around the neck and cuffs. I saw the jewels suddenly removed to a dark sky and twinkling like stars and I thought, She is dead, he has destroyed her, and how do I know? Because that's what I would have done. I would have destroyed her.

When I awoke, Gregory was sitting at the foot of my marble bed and all of his rippling hair had grown back, along with his thick mustache and beard. He was staring forward. Cyril was not with us. Cyril always woke before me, I had been aware of that for some time, and wasn't surprised that he had gone out. He detested being cooped up in crypts, he often said, and slept deep in caves rather than in the earth when he had a choice.

Again, I was numb with something so much worse than pain that I could hardly breathe. And I wasn't thinking. I was knowing.

I felt a raging thirst. No sooner had I recognized it than Gregory turned to me and welcomed me into his arms.

I wish I could put into words for you how very different vampiric blood is from human blood. Human blood is hot and salty and varies enormously in subtle flavor, often laced with spice and the aftertaste of food eaten, and it comes in spurts driven by the heart of the victim, unless one draws it out fast, which can rupture the being's heart.

Vampire blood is smooth, uniform in sweet delicious taste, finding the arteries and veins of the recipient as if it has a life of its own, which I suppose it does, and it varies only in thickness—from the luscious wine of a young vampire like Louis to the rich syrup of Gregory—or Akasha. I said once that it was like light, vampire blood, and it is.

It is as if I'm drinking light, to drink vampire blood, my senses being utterly confused, and in intermittent flashes, I see the great web of circuits of the body giving me the blood or my own body receiving it. Or perhaps both. Perhaps the circuits are congruent as I drink vampire blood. I don't know.

But as I drank from Gregory now, I saw no flaming images, no pictures, caught no story, only the outpouring of complete sympathy or what the modern world calls empathy. I felt so utterly loved and supported that it seemed my anguish was receiving its highest justice; he not only recognized the very depth of the torture I was experiencing but understood it and wished to take it to himself completely.

I drank until I couldn't take any more. But I wasn't conscious of pulling away. I merely awoke lying on my back in the little cell, with the door half open to the lighted corridor, and the blood heating me through and through so wondrously that I would have done anything to cling to that feeling forever.

Gregory sat on my coffin to my right. He had folded his arms and was looking about my cell with slowly moving eyes, as if he were an angel from an ancient Sumerian paradise deposited here to guard me and protect me.

He began talking. He told me that Kapetria and Derek and their helpful clones had broken into all of Rhoshamandes's complex financial networks, and not only discovered the sources of his immense wealth, but managed to freeze all access to it. They had hacked into all the computer systems of Rhosh's attorneys and destroyed the vital information needed not only to access and manage the wealth but also the data needed for personal communication with their powerful client. They had emptied half of Rhosh's bank accounts by late afternoon on this day, and would have all of his wealth transferred out of his hands by midnight.

They had also begun to shift into fictitious accounts the titles to all his properties, including the island of Saint Rayne with its great castle, a house in Budapest, which had formerly belonged to the blood drinker Roland, on which Rhosh had called a mortgage, and huge vineyards in France and in Italy, from which most of Rhosh's income had been derived, and new vineyards in California which had only lately been acquired, and small houses in random places, including Germany, Russia, and the southern Pacific islands.

I wanted to say, "But what if she is still alive?" But I said nothing. It was the first coherent and purposeful thought that had come to me since she'd been taken.

"Then he will come to sue for peace," said Gregory. He looked at me with his intense dark eyes, the flowing hair and beard giving him a spiritual authority that comforted me. "That is the idea," he continued. "There are as many ways to travel the Devil's Road as there are immortals traveling it," he said. "But for Rhoshamandes, the road is paved with gold and always has been. His bank cards are now of no use; his plane is grounded outside London, and everything of value on Saint Rayne has been taken."

He went on, explaining to me that just after Kapetria had come to us, which was now a year ago, the Children of Atlantis had been investigating Rhosh, in fear of the day when he might attempt to harm them. But they had found secrets today of which they hadn't known before.

"Wine," I whispered. "So it's from wine he takes his wealth." My voice was small and weak, a rather despicable voice.

"Yes, centuries ago he planted his vineyards in the Loire Valley," said Gregory. "The assault on his resources is total. But unless I've overestimated him, he has wealth stashed somewhere of which no one knows anything, no attorney, no lawyer, no land agent. If he doesn't, then he's a fool, and he always was a bit of a fool."

"Where do you think he is now?" I asked. My voice sounded strange to me, weak and spiritless. Not my voice.

"On the other side of the world, perhaps," said Gregory. "I've been searching for him since I opened my eyes. I've been sifting through the cities and the towns and the villages of the British Isles, the European continent, the land of Russia. And so has Seth and so has Sevraine. Sevraine is mad in her grief, mad. She paces like a panther, and pounds her right fist into her left palm, the safest place for the force of it. Avicus has come to join us. Avicus is ancient. And Flavius has arrived as well. These are mighty telepaths. They are mighty guards."

I didn't say anything more.

I heard footsteps in the passage and a soft knock at the door. The mingled sobs and curses of blood drinkers, angry whispers.

Gregory opened it and stood with his back to me so that I could see only the dim electric overhead lights in the passage.

Then Gregory closed the door and looked at me, the mighty Sumerian angel in his glittering garb.

"A small casket has arrived, by means of some mundane service in the mortal world. It contained a small vial of ashes. And a coat of khaki cloth, and wrapped in the cloth—was a long thick lock of hair tied with a boot lace."

I closed my eyes.

Images of my mother filled my mind. I saw her walking in her long winter garments of hundreds of years ago through the village street, and at Mass on her knees with the beads in her hands, asleep as she leaned against the stone column of the church.

I could not bear this. I couldn't breathe. I turned my face to the wall. *She never harmed you. You coward. You killed a being who did nothing to you at all.*

It felt just a little better to talk that way. I felt I was going to start weeping and I panicked.

Gregory's hands turned my face upwards, away from the wall.

His large black eyes were soft and wondering. I felt an immediate sense of dislocation. I was drifting. I was falling into sleep.

I felt his fingers close my eyes. "Sleep," he whispered, and I let the spell envelop me. "Yes," I whispered in French. I knew what he was doing and I drifted down and down into slumber, the sweetest slumber, snug in a bed of warm blankets just taken from the old hearth in my old room, and my mother was bringing the blankets up to my chin, and beaming down at me, her little boy, her useless, powerless little boy—and there came a blissful contentment muffling everything that was me in which nothing mattered, nothing was known, nothing was felt.

I dreamed I rose high into the Heavens. And it seemed that a great many marvelous things happened—that I met splendid beings and we conversed together and they explained to me the entire meaning of life. Out beyond the bounds of our solar system, they showed me all the universe. They explained how one travels from planet to planet, by the sheer power of thought. Why, that makes perfect sense, of course, I thought. A great feeling of understanding the most marvelous things enchanted me and sustained me. Of course, there would be no vast universe, I understood, unless we could travel it with such ease and, yes, every single thing now was clear.

Hours passed. Had to be. Because we are beings of time, and time never stops, and hours and hours passed as I roamed the stars.

A great rumbling noise awakened me. The very walls shook. I felt the stone roof was going to close in.

The door flew off its hinges and slammed against Gregory. He threw it aside, and was gone.

There was shouting, screaming. I felt the heat of an immense blast and saw flames in the darkness rolling upwards, a wall of orange flames, but they died down at once to cinders. Cyril lay on top of me, but I struggled against him as dust fell from the ceiling choking me and clouding my eyes.

I found myself standing in the stone passage yards away from my crypt, Armand's arm tight around me. Cyril had hold of us both.

Rose and Viktor stood there as well, along with the pale Sybelle and Benji Mahmoud, who for once was not wearing his fedora. I stared stupidly at them. I knew they were there, but I couldn't think. I knew they were still in their old finery from the last ball, and I knew they were terrified, though my son was doing his level best to conceal it. I wanted to show them a face of comfort and reassurance, but I couldn't move or speak.

The walls and ceilings were blackened with soot, and an acrid gas seemed to fill the air. Above there was more shouting and screaming and commotion. I closed my eyes and listened. Panic in the rooms above amongst those we knew and those we knew only little; and panic in the village.

The village. The village was on fire. I saw the flames in the minds of the blood drinkers rushing everywhere to save it. I saw the humans flooding into the high street as the townhouses burst into flame. I heard the engines of automobiles, and screams of terror.

And here it was almost dawn and I was helpless again, helpless in this miserable place in the earth, tormented by an enemy I couldn't hope to destroy yet every cell in my body burned with hate against him. I struggled to get loose. These were my people. I had to go to them. I had to get Alain Abelard, my architect, and the others to safety.

Cyril held me. So did Armand.

"Be still, boss," Cyril sobbed. "Be still."

Marius stood behind Cyril. Cyril was angry and flustered and covered in black soot. And the left side of his face had suffered deep scratches as if from the claw of a beast. His hair had been badly burnt, and his eyes were shot through with blood.

Marius turned his back to us, and stood watch on the passage and the stair.

"The village is on fire from end to end," Cyril said, but he didn't look at me. He didn't look at any of us. He was staring at the blackened floor, searching back and forth, back and forth as if for something lost in the soot. "Gregory is getting the humans out of it and sending them to Paris."

"But the sprinkling systems!" I said.

"Tanks burst, pipes melted," he said, eyes on the floor. "Don't worry about those mortals. No one is dead out there. They are on the way to Paris."

Then with his eyes still cast down, I saw his mouth twisted tight in a bitter smile and the blood tears rose in his eyes. He gave the hoarse awful sobs of a male who never weeps.

"What is it?" said Armand. He looked from right to left and behind us. "Marius, tell me!"

I looked at Armand. What was he talking about? What was it they were not telling both of us?

"Cyril?" I asked. I looked at Rose and Viktor. They were pale with fear, yet Viktor held Rose in his arms as if he could protect her from anything. Benji had his arm around Sybelle, and they too merely looked at Cyril.

"He took Louis, didn't he?" asked Armand.

Cyril covered his eyes with his huge hand.

"Boss, I tried to stop him. I couldn't even see him," he said. "Boss, I tried." And there came those deep, strangled sobs again.

I couldn't will myself to move, yet somehow I did, and I put my arms around Cyril, this great hulking figure who choked back his cries, both his hands on his bowed head.

"I know you did," I said. "I know."

"It was like he was made of the wind itself and the fire," said Cyril. "And the whole crypt was shaking. The earth was shaking, and all the doors were blown open and . . ."

"I know, I know," I said.

Marius turned around and looked at us. I could see he was struggling for calm. He had not changed his long velvet robe in two nights, and his face was tight and drawn, and devoid of expression.

He spoke but without emotion.

"He's going to pick us off one by one, no matter where we hide. We have to find him somehow. We have to find him now."

Armand went wild. He turned and began driving his fists into the marble with fury, cracking the marble tiles, the blood splattering everywhere, until Marius gripped him and drew him back away from the wall, and took both his hands and held them tightly in his own.

A long low moan came out of Armand.

Cyril had turned away from me as if in shame, and then taken up his station behind me.

Marius deftly turned Armand around and pressed Armand's head against his own shoulder.

He gave me a rather dry report that Kapetria had been unable to locate Rhoshamandes anywhere. There had been no attempted activity on his heavily used credit cards, no attempted withdrawals from his banks.

I knew that the monster had other resources. We all do, the clever ones, who don't wish to move through eternity like tramps. He had gold and jewels in hiding places. He had wealth undreamt of and unrecorded. And dwellings perhaps of which no one knew.

And now he had taken my Louis, my helpless Louis. Penetrated our most fortified refuge, and taken Louis away.

"Kapetria and Amel will not give up on this," Marius said. I don't think I had ever seen him look the way that he did now. He held Armand, who lay still against him, and he appeared dejected and in some dark place beyond anger. "They'll keep searching for clues to where he might be sleeping."

"Searching the whole world," Rose said. The sound of her uneven and fragile voice cut me, but I couldn't speak.

Viktor tried to comfort her. How completely human they both looked, immortals for such a short time, this splendid young male who had four inches of height over his father, and this delicate girl who had been saved from death so many times.

Her black hair was tangled and full of dust and specks of dirt and stone. And her dark blue ball gown was torn.

They were, all of them, dusty and windblown from the attack.

Benji stood there in his natty three-piece wool suit, looking around himself with feverish black eyes, his small face knotted with rage. His right hand appeared to move without his governance, pulling at his tie, dragging it from around his neck, and stuffing it into his coat pocket.

I knew they must have all been down here since sunset—and I'd been sleeping, charmed into deep sleep by Gregory, sleeping when they needed me and I had nothing, absolutely nothing, to give them.

My son was looking at me. But I couldn't meet his eyes because I couldn't tell him that I would protect him. I couldn't tell Rose that I'd protect her. What could I say to Sybelle or Benji?

Armand was like something broken as he lay against Marius.

Again, I was not thinking. I was merely knowing—and knowing

that Louis, Louis the most vulnerable of us all, was in the grip of that monster—or already dead.

I could feel the dawn creeping up on me, making me cold. Viktor took Rose with him into a large crypt that lay to the right off the passage. It was where they customarily slept when they were here, and not roaming all the great cities of the world, the cities they both wanted so very badly to see. Sybelle and Benji entered this crypt as well.

Gregory returned. Avicus was with him—tall brown-haired Avicus whose powers just might equal those of Rhoshamandes, and beside him Flavius, the ancient Athenian who was as old as Marius, short a few years.

And Barbara came last. I was ashamed. I had not even noticed that she'd been gone.

She told me that the house was all intact, and that anyone in residence was safe in the other dungeon. She had made sure of it herself.

"The other dungeon?" I was confused. "What other dungeon?" Again. I could not think.

I could see that Avicus and Flavius had only just arrived. Both were dressed in simple modern suits of dark leather, with high sweaters underneath and tall boots. They had been badly buffeted by the wind, their hair tangled, their faces exhausted, and the dawn was creeping into them as well. I knew all this. I didn't think about it or wonder why I noticed it. I just knew.

Thorne had just come down the steps, and he said that Baudwin in the old dungeon was unchanged, and maybe that is where we should hide, because that evil Rhoshamandes didn't know of that dungeon.

Marius said: "He knows. He is listening to everything. He knew of that dungeon when we discovered it. He knew when we put Baudwin in it. He knew."

Avicus told us that he would sleep with Thorne in the passageway. His was an agreeable voice, with a faint accent to the English, and there was no drama to his words. Flavius nodded in agreement, and Marius told them where they should take up their posts.

I heard myself ask, "Where is Fontayne?"

Seems Barbara explained to me that Fontayne was in the dungeon far down beneath Baudwin—two long coiling stairways down—along with Zenobia and Chrysanthe, and Bianca and Pandora. Notker was with them. Jesse and David Talbot were there as well. Spirits were with them, including Gremt, and Magnus my maker, and Hesketh. But the strongest guardian there was Teskhamen, who went back in aeons, as did Avicus and Cyril.

David. How in God's name had I forgotten David! David was my fledgling. He would go for David now!

"He's well guarded," said Marius. "This was all determined last night. You are not remembering. You are not thinking."

"That's true," I said.

He gestured for the rest of us to go into the large crypt also. And we obeyed without a word.

Marius came in with Armand, led Armand to one of the many large marble shelves along the walls, and Armand stretched out on it, on his back, and turned his face away.

Barbara found a place as well and appeared to lose consciousness almost at once.

There were candles scattered in high niches, giving the low-ceilinged room a kind of golden light. I stared at these candles. I stared at the flames, noting how some were small and some were large, and all were moving in the current of a draft.

I knew the cell was lined with granite and faced with marble because I had designed it and all the other crypts as I'd designed my own. Would granite keep back Rhoshamandes?

Viktor and Rose lay together on the floor beneath one of the shelves. Viktor had turned his back to the light and I could hear Rose's soft crying. Benji and Sybelle took their bed of marble together.

I considered many things, in this strange frame of mind in which no consideration had purpose, and realized that I was doing nothing at all.

I saw my mother, and I saw Louis, as if colored slides were being shuffled through my mind, and I banished these images, these salient moments as soon as they came.

"Cyril and Gregory will sleep with their backs to the door," said Marius. "I'll lie there. I bid you good night. I won't be sleeping for another hour, but I have nothing left to say to anyone."

Gregory was attempting to guide me to one of the resting places, but for some reason I wasn't able to move.

"Why didn't he take me?" I asked. It was that same small voice, that pathetic voice.

No one spoke. Marius closed the door on the passage and threw the giant iron bolts on it. What was the use of that?

"If he could come down here and take Louis, why didn't he take me?" I asked.

"I was with you," said Gregory. "I was guarding you. Louis was in the passage when Rhoshamandes took him."

"He was pacing back and forth and reading a book," said Marius. "At least, that was what he was doing when I last glanced at him."

Cyril had tumbled down to the floor and slumped against the door, his head in his hands.

"Speed and surprise," I said.

"Yes," said Gregory. He gathered me in his arms and we lay down together on a marble shelf, spoon fashion, my face turned to the wall. I was glad that he remained with me, though I knew he would soon take up his place by the door.

I listened to the candles. You can always hear candles if you listen carefully. And slowly the paralysis came, and the agony simply stopped.

Chapter 15

When the sun set, we talked amongst ourselves and agreed that Rose and Viktor had to remain below, but it was perhaps safe for Armand to go up and confer with Eleni and Allesandra and Everard, whom he had not spoken to now in two nights. They had repeatedly insisted that they were in no danger from Rhosh, and Armand thought they were wrong. They were in the far dungeon now.

"This being has gone mad," said Armand.

It was then that the next package arrived, a small gold casket this time, which contained a vial of ashes and Louis's favorite emerald ring.

A fledgling had brought it down to us, in the form of a simple parcel from the same courier service, in the hands of a wan fragile thing with flowing hair and a short flowered dress with puff sleeves. Her arms were white.

I'd turned my eyes away as Marius tore open the wrapping. But then I had looked back and seen the emerald ring.

It seemed altogether impossible that this pain would stop, and altogether impossible that it could go on.

"You never loved him," Armand said bitterly. I closed my eyes. "You were cruel to him. I protected him from you."

I heard Marius's soft murmur begging Armand not to say such things, and then Sybelle whispering to Armand that we all loved one another. That was the way now. And Rhoshamandes knew it, and could take any one of us and inflict unspeakable pain on the others.

"Cursed dybbuk!" Benji said. "Come on, now, Armand, don't torture him. Be wise. Be calm."

Talking. The fledgling's name was Marie, simply Marie, the oldest and most popular name in Christendom, and she had met the "man" and signed for the package as she had approached the Château. She'd never been here before. She'd only found us after a search. Marius told her she must stay now. She was immensely excited by all that was happening, but she had the good sense to be quiet.

I lay on the bench listening to the others.

Marius didn't want Armand to go to the other dungeon. Yes, said Marius, Eleni and Allesandra and Everard had told absolutely everything that they knew of their old master, Rhoshamandes, to Seth and Kapetria and her tribe. But Armand wanted to confer with them. Who knows? They might know something about Rhoshamandes, some little thing that others had forgotten.

The house was empty now, save for those in the far dungeon. And Marius said that Armand could not go to the dungeon alone.

Finally Marius raised his voice in exasperation, and told Armand to stay here, and the matter was settled, and if he dared to try to leave, he would deal him such a blow as he'd never felt.

Silence after that.

I wanted for all the world to sleep, but I would not ask Gregory for a charm now. I could not. I could not but lie on the shelf in the flickering candlelight and let the thoughts pass through my empty mind. My chest ached. My heart ached. My head ached.

Marius went out into the passage and stood guard with Avicus and Flavius—and one hour later, Rhoshamandes came for him.

Chapter 16

We heard the battle, but we could not see it for the smoke and flames, and the broken marble battering us from all sides. Marius's powerful voice rang out cursing Rhoshamandes. Doors were broken from their hinges once more, and the light bulbs exploded, and in the darkness we were thrown against the walls or the floors. I felt an intense heat pass over me, and I struggled to get to my feet as the broken and fragmented tiles swirled about the chamber.

Ghastly screams came from Sybelle and I managed to get to her and I fell upon her trying to put out the flames. Her hair and clothes were on fire, and the horrible roaring continued above, and I saw through Marius's eyes the ballroom above consumed with fire. Avicus and Flavius were in the midst of it. And once again, the stone wall was blown out, and the powerful sprinklers sent down a deluge.

I cradled Sybelle in my arms, not daring to touch her burned shoulders and arms. Her dress had fallen away. Benji came up behind her to shelter her.

Marius's strong telepathic voice came from far away.

Headed west . . . headed northwest at great speed.

And then there was silence.

What did it take to silence a being like Marius?

I heard in the dusty choking air the distant telepathic cries of those in the far dungeon. *Marius has been taken. Not Marius. Marius is gone.*

I looked about me in the fog of dust and swirling particles, and saw that no one else had been burned. But Armand had once again gone mad. He was beating at the walls again and howling. He was cursing me and calling me every name he knew in Russian or in French or in English and saying that I was to blame for all of it, always, that I had done nothing but destroy others all of my cursed existence, and now there were more deaths laid at my door, and I'd even brought Marius to ruin.

I stood staring at him, watching him pound on the walls, drive his fists into the exposed earth. I watched Gregory collect him and hold him tight and put his hand over Armand's mouth.

Cyril and Avicus were looking at each other, and Flavius started to go over and over it in a heated whisper, all that had happened, the glimpses, the fire, the blast that had knocked him on his back, Marius struggling with Rhoshamandes, then gone. He kept trying to grasp it, put it in order, the ballroom in flames, with the draperies ignited and the mirrors shattering, and the screams from the faraway dungeon that were outrage and grief.

Where was Barbara? Barbara came down the stairs declaring that the tanks and pipes of the sprinkler system had worked. The fire was out.

She looked positively normal with her hair still neatly held back by a silver barrette, and her long plain dark blue dress dusty but untorn.

She went into a closet that held all the many hand tools for those who worked in the Château.

And suddenly Cyril and Avicus were at work, along with Viktor, repairing hinges, hanging doors up again, and shoveling out of the way all the broken stone.

But then Cyril stopped and began to tremble all over.

"Someone go now to that other dungeon and tell them to be still! I can't stand it, their howling and crying. Tell them to shut up. Thorne, do it. Do it now while he is on his way away with Marius. Go."

Thorne, who always yielded to Cyril, left on this mission.

Then it seemed everyone in the crypt was busy restoring the place again, except for me as I gave my blood to the wounded Sybelle.

It had been just past midnight when Rhoshamandes took Marius.

Hours later, Sybelle had been dressed again in a new gown of black wool, and lay sleeping, her skin ruddy with blood. Barbara had gone to her apartment for her clothes. She had brought down fresh clothing for everyone. Barbara went on working, doing everything she could.

I decided that I wanted to go upstairs.

A chorus of voices told me no.

"He's not coming back tonight," I said. But they persisted, and so I sat down on the marble bench on which I'd slept, my new home now, and I told them I knew what I had to do.

Once they were gathered around me to listen, I began to speak, and it was in speaking that I thought it out, drew it from the numb wordless shock of knowing and made it into a design.

"I have to talk to the fiend," I said. My voice was a little stronger than it had been before but flat. "I have to reason with him. I have to give myself up to him in exchange for peace. I have to have his word it will be enough, his taking me, and then I'd go with him."

I sensed a silence in the faraway dungeon on the other side of the Château, but how I sensed it, I couldn't have explained.

"I am the one he loathes and despises. I was the one he blamed for everything. I will talk to him, and bargain with him—I will give myself up to him if he will stop his attacks against us and leave the Court forever alone.

"I know him to be a man of his word," I said. "A man still, yes, and a man of his word. Just as I am a man of my word. And I want a quarter of an hour with him, after he takes me, a quarter of an hour in which to explain to him my thoughts on what has happened, and to hear his before I perish at his hands."

At once came the chorus of objections. "Be patient," said Gregory. "The Children of Atlantis are closing in on him. They will have a location for him soon."

"How is that possible?" I said. "He can hear what you're saying."

"You don't know that," said Benji.

"Where is he?" I asked. "On the other side of the world? And how long will it take for them to find his new refuge? No, my mind is made up. All I need is his word. And I will swear to him on my honor, and I do have honor, that none of you will seek to harm him when he comes for me.

"And Amel and Kapetria will restore his property to him, and there will be peace."

Once again came the mingled objections, and from the far dungeon the pleas of Allesandra that Rhosh was indeed a being of his word.

"At any time that he accepts my word," I said, "at any time that he reaches me with his pledge that he will honor this agreement, I shall go up onto the battlements of the northwest tower, and I will wait for him without guards around me, and go with him willingly when he comes."

Again, the voices rose with their objections, but Cyril raised his hand for silence.

"He's speaking," Cyril said. "I hear him."

Gregory obviously could not hear him. But then we'd long known that the first generation of the Queens Blood and the First Brood couldn't hear one another, any more than a maker and his fledglings.

But I could hear him now—faint, calling to me from very far away, a voice as soft as it was distinct.

I am a being of my word.

"Do you accept my terms?" I asked, speaking aloud even as I sent the message to him, picturing him, doing all in my power to reach him.

I accept your bargain. But the Replimoids must restore my property to me, all of it. And your minions must not dare to try to harm me when I come for you or it will be war again. And I will destroy all that I can.

Armand suddenly began to weep.

"Don't do it, don't trust him," he said. "Lestat, he'll just destroy you. And if you are gone—."

Ah, such sweet words from one who only hours ago had been cursing me with his every breath.

"I will see to it that the Replimoids restore your property," I said, speaking to Rhosh. It was as if I could see my voice reaching out over the winds and the clouds. "I am still the Prince here, in these ruins, and I am telling Gregory now that this is my wish. He is the oldest present. And he will get word to Seth of my pledge."

Gregory with the solemn face of the robed Mesopotamian angel nodded and whispered the word, "Yes."

"But I want a quarter of an hour with you, Rhoshamandes," I said, "to talk to you before I meet with your final judgment. I want that before I join my mother and my lover and my mentor at your hands."

I heard a thin hollow laughter.

I give my word. I will give you the quarter of an hour that you want. And then I will do what I want with you. And if your cohorts don't keep your pledge, I will come back for them.

"And if they do keep my pledge in every particular?"

I will leave the Court alone and seek a new existence far from the Court in another part of the world.

"Then we're agreed on everything," I said.

Except for one thing. You do not come up now from your cowardly hiding place. You come in one hour right before the sun rises while you still have the strength to do it. Make your pledge binding upon the Replimoids and then come to the northwest tower right before dawn. If I see any of your cohorts, if I feel their invisible weapons, I will burn you to ashes on the battlements of your father's house and take from your ranks each and every one who ever followed you in your folly. This is our bargain.

Silence.

"Give me the phone," I said to Gregory, "with the connection to the Paris headquarters."

He did as I said. And I did as I had said I would.

Kapetria resisted, but I simply told her over and over that I'd given my word.

"Begin to restore his properties and his resources to him now," I said. And I gave the little slab of a glass phone back to Gregory, who tucked it away in his ancient robes.

I could write another chapter of all the back-and-forth then.

Those gathered in the dungeons left the pathetic Baudwin in his iron wrappings and came quickly to join us in our crypts. Allesandra was convinced that I could prevail upon Rhosh to spare my life, and told me that I must entreat him, that I must persuade him to understand that I had not wanted Benedict to die.

So many arguments. So many hushed and urgent voices mingling in the fractured marble rooms. And the smell of earth coming from the corridors which I'd never lined in granite as I had done the chambers, and Barbara and the new fledgling, Marie, busy with their little chores, and Armand finally sitting beside me, his face crumpled and broken up like that of a little boy as he clung to me, and Cyril against the wall staring off, listening for immortal voices that didn't come.

I was prevailed upon repeatedly not to do what I was planning to do.

Only Allesandra believed I could win the heart of Rhoshamandes, who she swore was infinitely better at loving than hating and had left his beautiful old monastery in the Loire long ago rather than battle the Children of Satan, Rhosh whose heart melted at the strains of beautiful music, Rhosh who used to bring musicians in the ancient times from Paris to play in his cloisters and old book-lined chambers, Rhosh who had wept when the Children of Satan had demolished the old walls and rooms until the forest covered the place where Allesandra and Eleni, and Everard and Benedict and Notker, had been born.

There were moments when Eleni joined in this entreaty. "Say this to him" or "Yes, point out that."

All the while Everard sat sneering at them both. I could see the malice in his eyes. He had never forgiven Rhoshamandes for not rescuing him from the Children of Satan, and he'd escaped their miserable clutches just as soon as he could. He thought them "lovely fools" now and he said so, and the clocks ticked in the empty corridors upstairs, and the pale sky was showing through the shattered walls of the ballroom as Barbara and her fledgling Marie went about with their brooms upstairs, quite convinced of their safety, and the others clung to me as if this were my wake.

And it was my wake.

I sat there knowing, knowing all they told me, knowing who Rhosh was from all of these different angles. And I knew my mother had once run with me through the tall grass on this very mountain, in the spring sunshine, both of us laughing as we climbed higher and higher to look out over the entire valley and the road winding towards the village, I knew because I saw it. And I saw Louis with Claudia in his arms walking through the deep perfumed darkness of the Garden District of New Orleans as the cicadas sang of late twilight, and Claudia with her curls streaming down her back from her bonnet sang a soft song to him that made Louis smile.

And I knew Marius had once drawn me up out of the earth in Cairo and into his arms, because I saw it, and saw him in his great

Mediterranean villa, an eighteenth-century man then after two thousand years, welcoming me, smiling at me, ready to share the secret with me of our great and mysterious parents, those unmovable marblelike beings, Akasha and Enkil in their perfumed shrine.

Incense, flowers. Claudia singing. I listened now for the morning birds of the forest.

I knew Rhoshamandes might well have taken Marius with him across the Atlantic and yet come back in one and the same night because he was that strong. But then again, perhaps he had never gone very far. What did it matter? He was coming now. The birds of the forest knew it was time and had begun to sing.

Time to go.

The shrill ring of a glass phone startled me. Kapetria calling to assure Gregory that Rhosh's fortune had been given back over to him and all the conniving tentacles of her internet reach had been withdrawn.

"For the last time," Armand whispered. "I beg you—."

I kissed Armand and rose to my feet. I embraced Gregory.

"You'll find all my papers in my study upstairs," I said. "You will find directions and codes to make over everything I possess to you. I ask only that should Magnus, my maker, ever succeed in reentering this life, in taking on a body, that you give some portion of my fortune to him, as it was from him that my fortune came into being."

He nodded. "I will take care of everything and everyone," he said—the bearded angel with the long black hair talking and kissing my lips. "Remember you have my blood in you now!" he whispered in my ear.

"Whoever you choose to be your prince," I said, "I wish him well."

I walked towards the stairs.

I turned back and saw them all crowding the passage, with Benji just elbowing through the crush to the very front.

"Goodbye, brave dybbuk," he said.

I smiled.

"Stay below, all of you," I said. For one moment, something immense and very like terror breathed close to me, but I shoved it back. "If you break your word, my friends, remember, he'll destroy me and never let up."

Chapter 17

The snow was falling lightly and soundlessly as I came out of the iron doorway on the northwest tower and walked towards the battlements. I could feel the numbness of morning in me, and wondered if that wasn't some sort of mercy, but he would take me west with the night for certain, and so fast that no one would be able to follow him, and what would follow would happen while all those I loved slept.

I stood still, watching the snow fall on my open palms. And all was stillness and silence all through the Château and throughout the valley, with the smell of burnt timber in the wind.

Suddenly I saw him directly above me, his eyes huge, his dark robes swirling about him—and in that instant, the others betrayed me and sent from all directions their mighty fire.

"No," I roared. "Stop. No." But I couldn't hear my own voice over the swirling force that threw me backwards onto the stone floor.

A great ball of flame rolled Heavenward, and then went out like the flame of a candle crushed between finger and thumb. An arm like iron went around me, and high into the sky I went, so fast the wind felt as if it were scalding my face and my ears.

I saw below me flames in all directions, as if a volley of soundless explosions were sending their dark thick clouds rolling Heavenward,

and then there was nothing but the stars for one instant, the great
far-flung stars too numerous to be broken into patterns, and I realized I was clutching to Rhoshamandes, and he had his left hand on
the back of my neck. By this he held me, this iron hand, and I said
to him:

"I didn't betray you. They broke their word."

Laughter. And his intimate confidential voice saying, "I expected
it, of course."

The pain in my face and in my ears and in my hands was unbearable. I gasped at the wind, trying to breathe it, and then I heard him say the word just as Gregory had said to me: *Sleep.* I couldn't resist it. I felt we were leaving the earth altogether, and it seemed impossible that the drowsiness could feel so warm and so good.

How many hours passed, I didn't know. I knew only that we were someplace over the Pacific, and how I knew that much, I wasn't sure. Maybe it was the strange green tint of the sky, the soft green layers on top of the rosy layers, and the blackness above from which we were descending slowly, until we had dropped down on a white stone terrace just over the glassy and shining sea.

I fell out of his arms and to the ground, dazed. My limbs were numb and useless. But he picked me up and threw me against the stone railing, his hand clamped to the back of my neck.

I looked down at the white-foamed waves crashing on the rocks and saw far away a string of golden lights that meant another shore, or another island, I knew not which.

Beautiful, I thought. The blood rushed through my legs and my feet, and my arms and my hands, again. A wave of sickness came over me. But when I opened my mouth to vomit, nothing came out.

Just a glimmer of a thought sprang to mind and then died into the deliberate silence of my locked mind.

Don't think. Don't imagine. Don't scheme. Don't plan.

"It is so very beautiful," I said.

I felt something brush close to my left side, and then I was thrown a short distance and down again on another stone floor.

He had ripped the ax out from under my coat.

As I got to my knees and turned around, I saw him standing with his back to a row of open arches, beyond which the stars struggled to shine in a rosy mist.

"Yes, it is beautiful," he said. And for the first time I saw him with his golden hair long to his shoulders, and his mustached mouth and bearded chin. He wore a simple robe of brown wool, as monastic as

Benedict's habit had been, which fell to the naked insteps of his bare feet.

"So this is the great Rhoshamandes," I said, "as he looks when he rises, and gives no thought to a razor or a scissors."

He stared at me with an enigmatic expression, certainly not one of scorn or hate.

"You think you know me, but you don't know me," he said. "You, with your arrogance and your vanity, and your shiny little ax." He held it up. It glittered in the low electric light that came from the stone ceiling, a simple fixture of white-painted metal. All the stone chamber was painted white, except for the floor, which was polished to a dazzling luster, and there was the de rigueur fireplace, built of soft sandstone with pilasters supporting its deep mantel and a pile of oak in which the crumpled and broken kindling was just roaring into flame.

I climbed to my feet.

Moving so fast I couldn't see it, he kicked me down on my back and returned to his place, the ax still in his hand.

"Remember when you cut off my hand and my arm with this?" he asked.

"Yes, I do. And if I had it to do over I would not do it," I said. "Think of those who've suffered because I did it. It was rash."

Never mind that his evil plan of that moment had collapsed without my cruel gesture with the ax having anything to do with it. Or that I'd forgiven him all he had done in killing Maharet and imprisoning my son, and told him countless times that I held nothing but goodwill for him and wanted only that we be friends.

I knew this, but I didn't think on it. It just was.

And this time when I climbed to my feet, I did so slowly, dusting off the knees of my jeans and realizing for the first time that my boots were gone.

The wind had ripped them from my feet. And the black velvet

coat I wore was torn at the left shoulder, and my hair was a mass of knots and tangles.

I shook myself all over. It felt good to be standing in my black stocking feet and the stone floor was warm. I sensed a large house around me; I could see electric light streaming in through a doorway to his right as he faced me, and I knew there was a larger archway behind me on my left leading into what was likely the same room.

"Thank you," I said, "for giving me time to talk." I knew suddenly that he was using no telepathic power to hold me where I stood, but I took no conscious note of it. "I want to tell you that Benedict did what he wanted to do, no matter who tried to dissuade him. I hated it. Hated the very sight of it. He wanted to give his blood to the young ones. I loathed all of it, and watched it because he asked me to watch it and he had provided me with a golden throne of sorts. It had been his gift."

He listened to these things without expression, his pale eyes as still as if they were made of glass. They reflected the light like the hourglass eyes of old French dolls.

"He said his time had—."

"I heard what he said," he replied. "Don't speak to me of Benedict, not another word, if you want your full quarter hour. And I know that you pledged your friends to keep faith with you. And I know that your foul little Replimoid friends have restored my fortune as you told them to do. And I know that not one of your friends has been able to come after you, because I lost them before I passed over the great sea."

I hooked my thumb in my jeans and, looking down, I shrugged. I swallowed hard several times, and squinted at the fire until my eyes, sore from the wind, watered at the bright light.

"It would do me no good, would it?" I asked, "to tell you that I never broke faith with you, not ever. That I argued again and again for your life against those who would have destroyed you."

"And how would they ever have done that?" he asked. "You see now my power. You've all seen my power. Which of you can stand against me?"

His eyes narrowed and his face became hard. His lips were as white as his face suddenly until a flash of emotion rendered the whole visage human for a moment with a tapestry of old lines. He appeared now to be in a silent fury. But he wasn't using any of that power to lock a hold on me.

I drew closer to him.

"What can I do to touch your heart?" I asked. "So that you might spare my life?"

Again, he had no telepathic hold on me. He was merely looking at me, his lips working feverishly and his eyes widening as if he couldn't contain the passion, before he narrowed them again.

Closer I moved and then closer and then I fell down on my knees again just a few feet before him.

"Maybe they couldn't have succeeded," I said. "Maybe they had no idea of your power. But it was I who argued for you, Rhoshamandes. It was I who became your advocate time and again."

I bowed my head. I stared at the hem of his brown robe, at the old threadbare cloth, at the naked flesh beneath it, the toenails shining as they always do, the feet as perfect as those of a saint in church. In the high Heavens with their icy winds he had felt nothing in this thin garment as he had carried me here, nothing of the pain that I felt now in every fiber, every limb.

"I admire how you've achieved your purposes," I said. "How can I not admire the choices you made and the way in which you made them? Speed and surprise."

I heard him speak, but I didn't look up at him.

"Are you really trying to persuade me that you have anything but loathing for me?" he asked. "You never knew me. Your cohorts never knew me. You never knew that I did what I did to Maharet only because she contemplated bringing an end to us all."

"But I did know that," I said, my head still bowed. "And I told the others," I said. I inched closer to him, but there was still a good two feet between us. I could smell the wind in the folds of his robes.

"No, you don't know me, you think me a monster even now."

"Yea gods!" I cried looking up at him, and for the first time I did allow myself to invoke the image of my mother, my Gabrielle, on the night I'd come into her death chamber in Paris, on the Île Saint-Louis, and I had shown her what had happened to me, that I was no longer human, and I had seen both the fear and the triumph in her eyes. The tears came exactly as I hoped they would. They came in their usual flood as they always did with me when I gave way to tears, and I trembled violently all over.

Putting my fingers loosely over my eyes I looked up at him as I cried and saw the perplexity in his expression.

"How could I not think you a monster now, Rhoshamandes? What am I to think?" I sobbed. "What am I to pray for as I kneel before you? What do I have to defend me? Oh, if only I had speed. And surprise!"

As fast as I could, I rose up and smashed the crown of my head into his face with all the force I had. His nose was shattered, slammed back into his face, but I held him by the hair on both sides.

He let out a deafening roar of pain, the ax falling to the floor as he stumbled backwards, but I clung to him with all my might, and then I rammed my thumbs right into his eye sockets and, clawing out his eyes, I swallowed them both whole.

"Stop it, stop it!" he bellowed.

I dropped to the floor.

It had all taken place in a second of time.

He spun round, reaching out desperately, and sending the fire all over the whole room. The white paint on the walls blistered and bubbled and turned black. He sent his fire at the plaster ceiling and out the open windows to the sky. Then it was *I* who sent the fire *at him*.

With all my strength and all my will, I sent the fire at him.

"No, you don't understand, stop, listen to me!" he howled.

But the fire had him, the fire caught his long loose sleeves, and burned his face a hideous purplish bloodred. I sent it again and again at him, and I sent my strongest telekinetic power at him, slamming him into the fireplace.

His robes were ablaze and so was his hair. Desperately he tried with both hands to put out the flames, but they were overwhelming him. And I sent the fire over and over, until his head and hands were turning black.

"No, this is all wrong," he roared.

I snatched up the ax where he had let it drop and coming up behind him as he righted himself, as he stumbled in a circle, a great torch burning before me, roaring some mad words I couldn't understand—"*La bait bah so roar, la bait bah so roar*"—I dealt him one fine blow through the flames that struck his head from his neck.

The bait bah so rah!

Quiet. One fragile flickering image of Benedict. *Benedict.* Then nothing.

I flung the head by its long hair at the stone edge of the mantel, hearing the bones crunch, and then again I swung it and again and again, until I held a sack of blood and bones in my hands.

I brought it to my lips, the eyeless face turned away from me, and I sucked the blood from the bleeding neck, sucked it with all my might, and my mind swam with his thick and viscous blood.

It was silent blood. But it was so strong, so sweet and strong, the blood of the brain, so bright and shining. It was electric, igniting every circuit in me, finding my heart and heating it until I thought that I too would catch fire. The power of it was beatific; it was grand beyond imagining, let alone describing. It was the blood of my enemy defeated, the blood of the one who'd slain my mother, and it was all mine.

The only sound as I drank and drank was the sound of the fire and the sea and a horrid thumping and scratching noise that woke me from my swoon. I stood still. I didn't know suddenly where I was.

But Rhoshamandes's blood had become a fine scaffolding of steel supporting me and I was warm, warm as if I'd never ever been cold in all my life.

A listless drowsy breeze filled the room. It was filled with the scent of the ocean, salty and clean, washing me and washing the room, and beyond I saw stars without number, stars of such radiance and such distance that the Heavens were no longer the painted vault of Heaven but a great endless ocean of stars.

I stared down to see the headless body fallen and smoldering and smoking, the robe burnt away to reveal the purplish skin of the back, the headless body moving, crawling, clawing at the polished flags with its great sprawling fingers and pushing through the robe with its knees.

The sight of this was so ghastly that for a moment I couldn't move. A giant headless insect would have been no more horrifying.

Then I was on my knees and, rolling the body over, I drank from the fount of the artery—and the blood flashed through my limbs as if it were molten steel. The hands battered senselessly against my head, against my shoulders. But I could see nothing. I was the blood I was drinking. And I drank as much as I could. I drank when I could drink no more. I gorged on the heat and the power and finally fell back on my hands staring at the broken ceiling. Fine dust fell from a web of cracks in the stucco, and the headless chest rose and fell, rose and fell as the hands rose and fell, imploring with splayed fingers.

The headless body leaked blood, but I could take no more. Its purplish black skin was white already. Even the smashed head lying on the floor, gaping at me with empty eye sockets, was turning from black to white as the last of the blood in it restored the burnt flesh.

I grabbed up the ax again and with both hands chopped open the ribs. The blood splattered from the ugly wound, and the heart beat faster and faster while the hands reached up to me and tried to find me and get ahold of me, until I grabbed the heart out of the body and squeezed the blood out of it into my mouth.

Now the body lay still.

I sat back staring at the distant sky beyond the open arches, my tongue licking the heart, and then I let it drop. I kept trying to find the farthest reaches of the stars, the place where the stars dissolved into a silvery light, but I couldn't find it. With eyes closed finally, I listened to the sea, and it seemed the sea was washing over me; the stars were falling into the sea, and the sky and the sea had become one, and I wanted to sleep forever.

But there was no time for this.

I moved on all fours to the place where the shrunken and battered head had fallen before the fire, picked it up, and lifted the right eye socket to my lips and sucked until the brain itself flowed into my mouth. Ah, such a nasty viscous thing, this brain!

When all the blood had been crushed from it by my tongue against the roof of my mouth, I spat out the nauseating tissues. A convulsion caught me off guard. The eyes came up, mangled and lusterless and sticky with blood, and I spat them out as well. Again, I vomited blood and tissue, tissue my body could not absorb. And the sickness for a few seconds was near unbearable.

Hard to describe such a physical sense of distress. But it passed.

Rhoshamandes was no more.

The surf pounded on the shore beneath the terrace. The fire crackled and ate at the oak logs.

Speed and surprise.

I lay back more exhausted than I had ever been in all my long existence. I could have slept for a year and I imagined, without wanting to, that I was safe at home in my father's house, and the music was playing as always in the ballroom.

But I had to leave here. I didn't even know where I was, let alone that I was safe, or who might come at any moment. Mortals who lived in this place perhaps or fledglings he'd forged to help him in his vengeance.

I sat up. And through a great act of will, managed to climb to my feet and move into the other lighted room.

There, across a great bed, I spied a dark red velvet coverlet and I yanked it free, sending a pyramid of velvet pillows in all directions, and I dragged the coverlet back into the first room.

For a moment, I thought that I might lose consciousness. My head was throbbing with pain, but my vision had never been clearer, and I told myself that I could do what I must. The blood of Rhoshamandes once again flashed in my consciousness as a steel scaffolding actually supporting me, an intricate and endless fabric of steel, and how much of this was Gregory's vintage blood, I wondered.

A sound came from afar, an uneven and unusual sound that denoted something living.

I went still, slowing the beat of my heart to listen. Was there another immortal in this house? But all I heard were the inevitable modern machines, the air conditioner, the water heater, the circulation of water through pipes. The grinding noise of a motor. Possibly a generator. No. Nothing else. I was alone here.

"Start thinking, Lestat," I said.

I threw the headless body onto the coverlet, tossed the smashed and empty head on top of the body, then gathered up even the heart and what I'd vomited of the brain and the eyes, and flung them all together, and then made of the coverlet a sack and threw that sack over my shoulder and staggered out into the cold darkness of the terrace over the sea.

What hour of the clock it was I didn't know, but as I peered up at the stars, as I sought through the shifting mists to see their naked patterns, I realized I was indeed in the islands of the Pacific—and if I had the strength for it, I could rise now and take to the winds and ride them gently west around the globe, hour by hour following the night, over the Orient and over India and over the Middle East until I came upon Europe and France and my father's house in the mountains—without ever stopping for the rising sun. I had to do this.

Once again I thought I caught an unusual noise. Was it the heartbeat of one of the old ones?

A thin telepathic voice spoke.

How on earth did you do it?

Was that really what I'd heard? Was I hearing laughter? It was tantalizingly faint, like someone toying with me, someone watching all this and being mightily entertained by it.

All the more reason to go now. I'd never attempted such a feat before as this great long western journey, but I was bound and determined to do it now. "You slaughtered the great Rhoshamandes, didn't you?" I whispered aloud to myself. "Well, Lestat, you little Devil, rise now, call on all the power in your blood and go home!"

With the ends of the coverlet firmly in my grip, I found myself rising upwards before I had even meant to do it, and I headed west slowly letting the wind carry me higher and higher until I was passing through the cold wet mist of the clouds.

Now the Heavens spread out in all their indescribable beauty before me, the stars like diamonds everywhere that I looked, diamonds of inexpressible brilliance, shining like gifts in the great black vault of Heaven, gifts from whom or what we may never know. "Home," I said. "Guide me home."

Chapter 18

Whenever I did drop off to sleep, I began to fall, and the clouds would catch me unawares and I would rise again and go on. When the mists broke I saw continents that I had known from maps and globes, but they appeared unreal far below, as did the lights of cities whose names I couldn't guess.

At some point over the sands of the Middle East I woke with a start, my body descending fast through hot dry air, and before I could grasp the danger, I felt two hands take hold of me. They gripped me by the waist and propelled me back up towards the blackness of Heaven. I'm imagining this, I thought. And all of a piece I remembered the tale that mortals on desperate expeditions through ice and snow often imagined "another" with them, a helpful figure whose presence they took for granted, a figure of whom they never spoke, but a figure who was known to each of those on the journey. And you're imagining now such a being, I thought, and now he presses you forward and you gain speed and you rise and you travel faster than before, ever more impatient for the finish.

The stars were true. The stars guided me. The night went on and on and there were times when I almost dropped my sack into the dark uncharted lands below. But my hands would tighten on the twisted cloth and I would breathe deep of the wind and see that scaffolding of blood within me.

Somehow I continued. Somehow I moved on.

And gradually thought came back to me. Not just knowing. I had gotten the better of Rhoshamandes. I had done it just as Jesse had said that he and Benedict had gotten the better of the great Maharet, with speed and surprise, and now Benedict was dead and Rhoshamandes had been defeated.

I had slain the greatest enemy that had ever set himself against me, the enemy who had robbed me of all I loved, the enemy who would destroy the Court—and just for a little while, a little while, I felt the kind of happiness I had known very seldom in my life, happiness—as if they were not all dead, not all finished, not all gone.

Keep going. Keep moving. Be a child of the moon and the stars and the wind. Keep going. Think of those times when as a mortal boy you leapt from high cliffs into mountain streams or from the back of your horse, flying out over the fields, as if you were an eagle. Keep going.

Finally I saw the unmistakable lights of Paris shining upwards through the mist and I knew I was almost there.

"My friends," I cried out. "I've come back. Gregory, Armand, David, I've come back." I sent the telepathic message with all my remaining power, and it seemed stronger than me, stronger than the phantom descending slowly from the track of the winds towards the snow-covered mountains.

When the Château appeared before me I felt myself plummeting so fast that I hit the stone floor of the northwest tower with bruising force. A century ago, that would have broken every bone in my body. But not now. Ignoring the shock, I hoisted the filthy sack over my shoulder and pulled open the door to the stairwell.

"Come to the ballroom, all of you!" I started down the stone stairs, aware of feet pounding throughout the house, of voices crying, "He's back. Lestat's alive. He's back." And hearts beating all about me. It was as if the entire Château were alive with movement, the very stones vibrating, a chorus of cries and shouts rising to greet me.

Finally I reached the main floor.

I bowed my head, not looking up at those suddenly crowding about me, staggering on towards the door of the ballroom, and once I'd gained the middle, once I stood firmly on the parquet floor beneath the great embossed coat of arms on the ceiling that marked the very center, I let loose the coverlet and down fell the headless body of my enemy, lifeless white limbs tangled in the burnt brown remnants of the torn robe. Horrors, the remnants of the head and heart, such horrors, and the preternatural flesh as white as it had been before he perished.

"This is Rhoshamandes!" I cried out. Faces surrounded me, Cyril and Thorne, Gregory, Armand, Rose, Viktor, Benji, Sybelle, Pandora, Sevraine, Chrysanthe, Zenobia, Avicus, Flavius, and new faces, eager young faces and aged faces, washed by time of all warmth or expression, the crowd shifting and pulsing about me.

There were cries of "Get back" and "Let him speak" and gasps and the hissing sound of some trying to hush others.

The chandeliers were missing, but countless flickering candles crowded the mantelpieces, and electric sconces burned bright beside the fireplace mirrors, and iron candelabra had been pressed into service all along the walls. The fireplaces perfumed the air with the fragrance of burning oak and powerful sweet Indian incense. And a lovely warmth enveloped me and began slowly to dissolve the painful cold, the merciless cold that encased my whole frame.

I stood rigid as if I were unable to collapse, my body coming alive to its aches and pains.

I saw Seth, Fareed, Barbara, the bald and smiling Notker the Wise with his mossy brows lifted, and the eager round faces of his boy sopranos. Where was Antoine? Ah, there he was with blood-stained face, and Eleni and Allesandra—all of them, all of my precious Court, my kith and kin of the dark country of the night surrounding me, all except for those who most mattered, those who were gone forever, those for whom justice had been done, but no restoration could ever, ever be made.

"Here is the burnt and blackened body of my enemy," I cried. "And here his head, sliced from his shoulders, and there his heart cut from his breast by me." A great new energy was born inside of me, as volcanic as their screams and cries. "Here, all that is left of the one who brought murder and ruin to this Court."

Cries, screams, shouts, and a storm of applause shook the very room.

And how splendid the room appeared, even with its scorched walls and blackened ceiling, with the broken plaster torn from naked stone and charred rafters revealed overhead. The great breaches to the outside had been bricked up, shutting out the falling snow, but the stench of burnt timber and plaster dust lingered beneath the perfume of the fire, and the great crest of de Lioncourt on the shield above me was blackened with soot. But what did it matter? Because the room, quaking now with shouts and stomping feet, held the Court of my fellow blood drinkers, my own, in their macabre finery, each face a lamp illuminating this moment with more light than any other source might give.

"Death to Rhoshamandes" came the shouts, and "Victory to the Prince," and "Lestat, Lestat, Lestat" in a deafening chant.

Something quickened in me, something that demanded understanding, something immense, but I was too weary at that moment to grasp it, too afraid perhaps to grasp something that would prompt retreat into the mind and heart where I was not willing to go. No, I wanted this, this which was happening now, this moment, I wanted it and I heard my own voice soaring above the throng.

"I slaughtered Rhoshamandes," I said. "Fortune was with me and the will to live, and with wit and speed, I brought him down."

The chanting soared in volume, but I went on.

"I claim no great power for this mighty deed. I dealt him one fine blow to the face with the crown of my head and blinded him as he howled like a wounded beast. And then I sent the fire against him again and again. It was a prankster's victory, the victory of your Brat Prince! But we are now saved."

The crowd was delirious, one wave of applause after another rolling towards me, and everywhere I saw fists raised in salute, and the tender young fledglings leaping up and down. Sybelle was embracing Benji, and Antoine had his arms around both of them. And Gregory held Sevraine to his breast, and everywhere I looked I saw these hasty couplings, and those pumping fists, and bloody tears. A memory came back, sharp and clear as a flash of lightning, of the crowd at that long-ago rock music concert when the mighty motor-cycle men with their savage hair and leather armor had pumped their fists in that same manner, and the salutes had come from all around, reverberating off the walls and the high vaulted ceiling, under those merciless solar lights. Ah yes, it was so very like that moment, even to the kettledrums rolling now from the orchestra and from the crash of cymbals—that dizzying moment when, drunk with joy, I had sung from the stage . . . *visible to all the mortal world.*

But this was now, and now was magnificent, and that memory suddenly faded and vanished with amazing speed in the blaze of pre-ternatural eyes and preternatural voices signaling acclamation with blood tears. I raised my voice higher. "And now the great Maharet is avenged," I cried, "and Marius and Louis and my mother, Gabrielle, they are avenged."

One single roar united all their voices, one immense roar that threatened to destroy my equilibrium, but I managed to reach down as I spoke and catch Rhoshamandes's head and lift it high above the crowd.

Ah, what a horror to behold, with hair clotted with blood and eye sockets empty and cheeks withered, and a mouth like the hideous dumb cry of the mask of tragedy.

"He is dead and can harm us no more!"

I could have fallen then. I was losing consciousness. But I forced myself to continue.

"Step aside, open here so I might see the fireplace," I cried. And as they scurried to obey, I pitched the head into the distant flames.

Lost in the deafening ocean of sound, I bent down and picked up the remnant of the heart, ah, the poor shriveled and blackened and empty heart, and squeezing a last bit of blood from it, dark gleaming blood, I pitched it at the bricks behind the fire and saw it drop like nothing but a cinder in the greedy orange flames.

Once more the roar rose and crested and throbbed with rampant cries, and I heard, as it rose and fell, the chorus of voices from other rooms, from rooms filled to capacity as this room was filled, and it seemed all the great Château was filled with triumphant voices, and they were supporting me in my sudden total exhaustion, my help-less loss of balance, my near collapse. Suddenly hands steadied me. Thorne and Cyril had ahold of me, Cyril petting me, petting my head and clutching to my neck like a motherly bear, and Barbara was holding me, sweet Barbara with her lips against my cheek. The crowd pressed in as voices everywhere shouted for others to get back.

"Blood in the remains," I said, crying out above the roar. I waited for silence, my hand raised. "Cold blood, but powerful blood," I cried. "Take it and commit all of him to the fire when you are fin-ished. Ashes to ashes for him who could not forgive himself for what he'd done to Maharet, who could not forgive me that I forgave him and invited him to live with us in peace, who could not love us for what we are, and saw no grand design in our hopes and dreams here. Ashes to ashes when you have taken the last of what he has to give."

Once again, the waves of sound washed over me, like the warmth washing over me, the warm air, the welcoming air stripping away the bruising chill of the winds, melting it as it melted all strength inside of me.

I could say no more, do no more, stand no more.

I saw the vampires closing in to lift the hideous white headless body with its ripped and burnt wrapping of woolen robes. I drew my ax out from under my coat and threw it down. Hands caught it up and I saw the first limb hacked from the body by Benji Mahmoud, that very arm that I had once thoughtlessly hacked away, and then the other arm, and then the crowd came between me and all the rest.

I realized I was being carried by my blessed Barbara and Gregory to the dais and the throne. And for a split second I saw the throne, and realized it had been regilded and was shining as if it were new, the dust cleaned from its red velvet.

How good it felt to rest against the velvet back, to lay my head to the side. Antoine had struck up a wild triumphant dance with the orchestra, and only now, as Barbara brushed my hair free of gouts of blood and Gregory removed my bloodstained coat, did I come to realize what a sight I must have been, barefoot and stained from the battle.

My shirt was stripped away and a fresh shirt put on me. Again and again, the brush sent ripples of delicious sensation through me as Barbara cleaned my hair. New socks and boots were put on my feet. I sat forward to receive a fresh velvet jacket. Ah, crimson velvet, the color so beloved by me and by Marius. Tears for Marius rose in my eyes. "But he's dead, my friend, my beloved Marius," I whispered. "The one who slew you is dead and gone, with all his misbegotten lethal power."

My helpers brought me to my feet, and I heard renewed cries from everywhere.

"Long live the Prince. Long live Lestat."

Lestat, Lestat . . . like the rock concert crowd of long ago, creating one voice: *Lestat, Lestat, Lestat.*

Once again I felt that quickening, that immense thought hovering just beyond my ken, that awesome revelation that eluded me. Grief interrupted it, pushed it away, grief for my Louis, and my Gabrielle, and my Marius. My hand went to conceal my eyes.

"Our Prince . . . our ruler . . . our champion."

Gregory's voice rose above the chorus. "Long live our lord of the Blood Communion." Roars and cheers greeted his words, and then came the chants repeating it: Lord of the Blood Communion.

True lord of the Blood Communion.

Don't see your mother's face. Don't feel her hand reaching for yours. Don't see Louis's sorrowful eyes. Don't hear Marius's voice in your ear, giving you counsel and strength, giving you the fortitude to do what was expected of you.

I collapsed into the chair again. I sat back too tired in mind and body to move. The clocks throughout the Château were heralding the hour of midnight with their singsong melody. Through this din, I picked out their synchronized prelude, and then came the deep heavy chimes that followed. I smiled to think that it was only the very middle of the night since I had left them.

I had circled the globe with the night and come to them at the very midpoint of their first night mourning me, my victory achieved while they'd slept, and I'd caught them before they could do little more than sweep up the broken crystal, rebuild the broken wall, clean away ashes. It seemed terribly amusing to me suddenly, and as I closed my eyes and lay my head against the red velvet padding of the chair, I did what I always do at such times. I laughed. I laughed softly but on and on and I heard someone laughing with me.

Ah, you, you lifted me when I almost hit the desert floor! Yes, well, laugh, because it is too much to do anything else, laugh, let's speak in our laughter, our eloquent laughter.

Where was he, the one who'd lifted me—the one who was laughing with me now? I sat up and looked about the room. The last of

Rhoshamandes's limbs had been thrown into the fire, and the crowd was facing me, facing the orchestra.

"Baudwin!" cried a voice.

"Give us Baudwin!" came another cry, and another, "Yes, Baudwin, give us Baudwin, give us Baudwin now to celebrate the victory of the Prince. We want Baudwin." The whole assembly was alive with calls for Baudwin. "Give us Baudwin who tried to slay the Prince. Give us Baudwin who tried to slay Fontayne and burned his refuge."

The orchestra stopped. Only the drums continued, the kettledrums, beating underneath the chorus of cries that grew louder and louder.

"Do as they ask," said Gregory. "He repents nothing." For the first time I really saw him, beside me in his common modern clothes, with his hair shaved and clipped away, my tall elegant counselor with his quick dark eyes fixed on me, waiting for me to give the word.

"Yes, please do it, sire," came the tender voice beside me of Fontayne. I groped for his hand, found it, and clasped it. "Do it." He was dressed in some of my very own clothes, a narrow-waisted frock coat of green silk, and a shirt of layered lace, and lace fell over his narrow hands with their jeweled rings, his pale eyes entreating me.

And what would Marius say, what would he do, I thought vainly, stupidly. Would Marius give his blessing to all this? And then Marius's voice came back to me confidentially and softly telling me of what I refused to understand, yes, of course—the crowd screaming now for Baudwin, for his blood, for his public execution. *You cannot make angels of us, Lestat. Angels we are not. We are killers.*

"Yes, we are what we are," I whispered, but I don't think anyone heard me.

"Boss, don't hesitate this time," said Cyril. He stood over me with his arm around the back of the chair. "Boss, let them have him."

The drums beat only in a slow insistent rhythm.

"Very well," I said. "Give them Baudwin."

Now you are a true prince.

"Who said that?"

I sat forward oblivious to the restless crowd that was chanting to be given Baudwin, and far off against the patched and restored wall, in a chair by himself, sat a hooded figure, hardly visible in the shadows, but I could make out his green eyes, and a shock of blond hair beneath his dark hood.

"Who are you?"

Chapter 19

No answer came from him.

The drums went into a long roll, the crowd went quiet, as if on a command, and the prisoner, Baudwin, clad in iron was dragged into the center of the ballroom by Cyril and Thorne. The vampire crowd pushed back to make an arena open to the dais. I had to rise to my feet. There was no escaping my duty. I stood uneasily, with my sweet Barbara beside me, and, facing the prisoner, I spoke in a loud clear voice.

"Do you know where you are, Baudwin?"

"Yes, I know where I am" came his muffled but audible reply. "And I curse you and I curse your Court and your house, and I call on my maker Gundesanth to avenge me."

I was about to respond when a voice rang out from the far corner of the room, from the hooded figure.

"No, I shall not avenge you!"

He too had risen, and he pushed his hood back on his shoulders. He was taller than I was tall, with a large handsome face and deep-set vibrant green eyes, and shaggy tangled blond hair to his shoulders. It had the look of straw to it, but it was handsome spilling all over the thin, supple leather of his long cloak. He spoke in perfect English without a trace of an accent.

"Baudwin," he said as he advanced towards the prisoner, "what wisdom did you ever have from me to set you against your fellows?"

The crowd made way for him.

"When did I counsel you to destroy other blood drinkers on a whim, and to use my name as your talisman? I will not avenge you. I will see you executed here, and your blood given to the young as the Court decrees."

He reached the center of the room, the long full leather cloak floating about him, and took his stand beside Baudwin. Now with horrifying ease, he stripped the iron bounds away from Baudwin's head as if they were ribbons, letting the coils fall with a clatter, revealing the mop of unruly hair, and a face red and filled with malice.

There were gasps of amazement from the younger ones.

"I curse you," said Baudwin to him. "I curse you that you let this happen to me, you evil, treacherous maker. Did I ever question you when you burnt the colonies of humans and blood drinkers alike? And now you become a lackey to this Court, another enchanted fool amongst this ludicrous multitude."

The tall blond one, who was most certainly Gundesanth, continued to strip away the iron until the prisoner was now entirely free, a robust figure in leather and dungarees, rubbing his aching arms and hands feverishly.

"What authority have they to do what they do!" Baudwin demanded of his maker. "And how can you, you who broke free of the Queens Blood priesthood, bend the knee to such a Court as this? I curse you! I curse you all"—he looked about himself, at me, at the others—"with your velvet and your satin and your lace and your foolish dances and your poetry and your rules and inane dreams of 'Blood Communion.' I demand you free me, all of you, and you, you cowardly maker."

"Oh, you of such little imagination," said Gundesanth. "Oh, you who have wasted a gift that might have made a hero or a pilgrim of another. Oh, what you have failed to see here."

The word "pilgrim" struck me. But I was eager for him to go on.

He turned and looked at me, his handsome and animated face smiling. His eyes were pale, green in the light and then hazel, but filled with easy goodwill and excitement. It was a face made for conviviality just as much as the face of Baudwin was made for rage.

"Such a place as this has never existed before in all our long bloody history," Gundesanth declared. He looked about him at the others as he went on, his voice ringing clear in the silence. "Never such a place as this—free of all mythologies of dead gods and lexicons of evil and demons invented by aggrieved souls. This is a place existing only for the benefit of all of us gathered here—and all the lost blood drinkers of the world who will come to be one with us. Hail the Prince. Hail the Court. Hail a new revelation—not from the blind stars or the oracles of madness—but a revelation that comes to us out of our minds and our souls, wed as they are to flesh, living flesh, a revelation rising out of our pain and our thirst and our hearts!"

I felt a great shudder pass through me at these words. It was almost, almost, the very concept that hovered so close to me, wanting me to receive it so that for me, and me alone, it would change virtually everything.

Another immense cry came from the crowd and the room shook with the stamping of feet and the sounds of clapping and more random oaths of faith and loyalty.

But the speaker cried out again and at once the room went silent.

"We have found in our souls a better purpose than any ever given us by gods or demons." He struck his breast with his right fist. "We have found inside of ourselves wisdom that surpasses that of ancient kings or queens, and we, we hold the key to our own survival. And those who would reduce us once more to a rabble of monsters inflicting our worst cruelties on one another have no place in this new world that is ours. I say I condemn you, Baudwin. With a maker's authority, I condemn you to death here."

Once again came the praise and acclamation, the clapping, the voices rising in a rumbling roar, but I was deep within myself with the words he'd spoken.

Yes, our own survival. Our very survival, that is what we faced here. I realized I was nodding, and that I'd been nodding with every word he said. I was too exhausted to grasp the full weight of what was happening. I knew only that I was witnessing something wondrous and I had to open myself to this wondrous thing for this moment to be complete.

Still smiling at me, this great blond figure drew a short flat sword from under his long dark cloak of leather, and held it up to me as if it were a gladiatorial salute.

Once more I nodded. Even as I shivered at the horror of it, I nodded. Nodded even though I thought, What must be the agony of Baudwin at this moment, alone, undefended amid a crowd that is screaming for his blood?

Baudwin convulsed as if he were trying with all his power to send the fire against me, but he was held back, held helpless, surely by Sevraine or Gregory or Seth, or all of them who had the power to do it.

Grabbing Baudwin by the hair, Gundesanth lifted the sword and sliced through Baudwin's neck, and then held the head up high for all to see. The crowd was delirious once more, screaming as they had screamed over the remains of Rhoshamandes.

The eyes of Baudwin stared out of the head as if a thinking brain still suffered behind them. The mouth worked with wet trembling lips. How many horrors such as this had I seen in the last many days? And how they sickened me. How alone I felt suddenly, how isolated and cold, and still numbed from the wind, how small in the warmth of this great room with all of its cheering blood drinkers.

As Cyril and Thorne held the body, Gundesanth threw this living head to the ground at his feet, and chopped off the arms and then the legs of Baudwin, and then he put his sword back and walked away from the great frenzy of moving bodies surrounding the feast.

The orchestra began to play another slow and sinister dance like so many that now filled this room night after night, week after week, a dance building and building as the attack continued on Baudwin's head and limbs, the music swallowing the inevitable sounds of the banquet.

Gundesanth made his way along the edges of the throng and came up to the throne, and took my right hand and kissed it, eyes flashing at me as his lips pressed my fingers.

"It was you when I almost fell," I said. "You caught me."

"Yes, it was," he said in a low and casual voice. He stood beside me on the dais looking down at me. He was a big-boned man, with high strong cheekbones and a large agreeable mouth, and a forehead that ran straight up from dark blond eyebrows to the clean hairline of his shaggy manelike hair. "But you would have waked," he said. "You didn't need me. You didn't need me to bring down Rhoshamandes either. And what a good thing that was because I came too late to help you. You're too modest when you describe your defeat of him."

"Once I'd swallowed his eyes, there was no hope for him," I said. "And it all happened so very quickly."

I was vaguely aware that many around me were listening to me. Cyril was surely listening.

"Swallowed his eyes!" Gundesanth said, and his own dark green eyes were wide with amused wonder. How white his skin was, and utterly smooth like that of all the ancient ones, but he was such an animated being that the lines of a human face appeared again and again as he spoke, laugh lines at the corners of his eyes, lines at the edges of his mouth. Third to be made by the Mother. Six thousand years.

"I am so tired my bones have gone to sleep inside me," I said. "That is all there was to it, taking him by surprise and taking his eyes, and . . . his blood. Yes, taking his blood. But my heart and head are falling asleep. I can't say any more and there's no more to say anyway."

He laughed under his breath. If he was as sincere and good-natured as he appeared now, he would be a magnate of the Court.

"Prince, you need a ring for us to kiss," he said without a trace of mockery. He reached into his robes and drew out a gold ring with a face carved on it. He held it up to me. It was the head of Medusa on the ring, with her great mass of writhing snakes for hair, scowling at me.

"Yes, that is a beautiful ring," I said. I watched as he slipped it onto my right ring finger. I felt him forcing it to fit, and slicing away the bit of gold and alloy which was left over. And going down on one knee, he kissed the ring.

"Let me be the first to kiss it," he said. And then he looked up and his eyes fixed on Gregory.

The two embraced. They fell upon each other. And I heard muffled sobs coming from them, and words in a rush, words in that ancient tongue that Rhoshamandes had spoken as he was dying. That was the last thing I saw before I closed my eyes and fell into a deep sleep right where I was on the golden throne given me by Benedict.

Sometime or other—as the orchestra played and the drums beat and the vampires danced—I was carried down to my crypt, waking once as we went down the steps, amused to find myself slung over Cyril's mighty shoulder as if I were a little boy. With great care, as if I'd break, he set me down on the marble shelf. I needed no charm to let me sleep now. And no one need guard the door, I thought. For we are all at peace, and when will we grieve for those we lost? And where is Armand, my poor desperate Armand, who had been beating the walls with his fists, my poor Armand? I had not seen him.

But sleep came and with it dreams, dreams of Rhoshamandes in flames howling and bellowing like a man gone mad. *You don't understand. The bait hah sa rohar.*

And that last plaintive cry for Benedict. Had he seen Benedict as he died? Was there a merciful Heaven that had received them both after their long journey, a journey for which no mortal man is ever equipped, a journey that ends in death no matter how long?

Gundesanth's words came back . . . *Hail a new revelation—not from the blind stars or the oracles of madness—but a revelation that comes to us out of our minds and our souls, wed as they are to flesh, living flesh, a revelation rising out of our pain and our thirst and our hearts!*

Chapter 20

I didn't wake till the following sunset.

Immediately, I had a sense of leaving a great web of inter-related dreams, in which things of the greatest importance had been discussed, and plans laid for mighty achievements. But what truly lay before me was the task of rebuilding the village and restoring those portions of the Château damaged by Rhoshamandes's fatal raids. And I set to work immediately, contacting my architect in Paris, and bringing him and his crew home for the rebuilding.

Funds had to be transferred for the endeavor, and this was a matter of a few crucial phone calls, and then I made an inspection, with Barbara, of what had been done to our lower crypts. The wall of the ballroom had been restored, but there was finishing to be done both inside and out. Plasterers would have to come by day, and the craftsmen who worked with them, to re-create the frames of the silken panels along the walls and the great designs of the ceiling, and the floors had to be refinished, and the two enormous chandeliers had to be repaired and rehung, and on it went, a list that seemed endless.

At every turn I was reminded of Marius, and Louis and Gabrielle, and only by the coldest act of will did I avoid falling into a black pit of grief, so black that it would blind me to anything and everything.

Meanwhile Amel and Kapetria were busy reestablishing their little colony in the English countryside, and I promised to visit them as soon as I was able to do it. Gregory had to assist with this, and he took the legendary "Santh" along with him, who had exacted a promise from everyone to call him Santh rather than Gundesanth, a name he had long associated with infamy. "Gundesanth was a name that struck terror in the runaways of the Queen," he explained. "Santh is a name to inspire trust."

I hated to see him go, as I was eager to talk to him. And desperate to avoid my own pain, I went into Marius's old library and spent the last hours of the night with Pandora and Allesandra and Bianca and Sevraine, who were gathered there. Bianca was obsessed with putting all of Marius's more recent documents in order, and was behaving as if at any minute she might begin screaming uncontrollably, and Pandora frequently drifted into gazing into the fire saying repeatedly under her breath that "both of them" were gone, meaning Arjun and Marius.

But I drew all into some semblance of a conversation in which Sevraine said that we must carry on Marius's work with our constitution and our laws. And Allesandra said the worst pain of the Devil's Road was seeing others drop by the way and not being able to save them.

Other work commanded my attention. Avicus and Cyril wanted to explore the newly discovered dungeons, and set to work with a band of helpful fledglings to clean out the accumulated soil of centuries and bring a merciless illumination to barred cells deep within the earth. Indeed, there seemed no end to the dungeon, as they found one deeper floor after another, and passages that led to other passages, and one to a place of escape beyond the nearest cliffs.

Meanwhile, the house was filling with new visitors—elder blood drinkers of whom we knew nothing, and young ones who'd never dared the journey before—all drawn by the tale of the defeat of Rhoshamandes, all eager to see the Prince who had accomplished it, all fascinated that indeed this new Court with all its promise might actually endure.

But where was Armand?

As another night began, I could think of nothing but Armand. I hadn't seen him since my return. He had not been part of that first greeting; he had not appeared in the Council Chamber; but I knew that he was under the roof. I could feel his presence, and I sought him out.

Gregory had returned with Santh, and the two came with me, Santh having now transformed himself into a spy among mortals, his hair clipped short and groomed to a luster, his jacket and pants of a thick Irish tweed.

Armand was in his own apartment in the Château, a string of rooms he'd designed and furnished on his own—with heavy Renaissance Revival chests and tables, and drapery and carpeting of dark red velvet. The walls held high-gloss paintings from the time in which he'd been born—of haloed saints and veiled Virgins, and magnificent Russian icons that twinkled in the dim light.

Sybelle and Benji were with him when I entered, the two of them sitting on the floor before the fire, Sybelle in a loose dress with her feet bare and Benji in an old worn black Bedouin robe.

But Armand sat apart, on a huge soft modern couch close to the window, looking through the dim glass at the snow. There was a sketch pad on the small table in front of the couch, and I saw a striking face on the page that appeared to be emerging out of a dark charcoal cloud. It was such a vivid fragment that I wanted to say something about it, but I knew it was not the time.

As I introduced Santh, Armand responded with a few polite and colorless words. Then his gaze shifted and he looked up at Santh as if he were seeing him for the first time.

"And out of the deep darkness of Egypt comes yet another great traveler," Armand whispered. "With tales to tell."

"Yes, and very glad to be with you," said Santh with his usual genial smile. He had been receiving the praise and questions of the fledglings since his return. But now he retreated to the shadows, as if to allow us privacy—as if ears throughout the Château were not listening—and finding an armchair in a far corner, he seated himself, hands casually together in his lap.

Gregory sat beside Armand on the couch and took the liberty of clasping his left hand.

Benji drew closer, standing behind Armand, his small brown hands on Armand's shoulders as Armand continued to watch the falling snow.

Armand appeared as exhausted as I felt, his clothes dusty and unkempt, his face wan and hungry, and his brown eyes opaque as he stared through the glass. He heard me out when I told him what he already knew of Rhoshamandes's death, and how Marius's vision of the constitution and laws would be put into practice. I explained that newcomers were arriving even as we spoke. I think what I wanted to say was that no matter what we'd lost we would persevere, and the Court had not only recovered from Rhosh's assault but it had taken on a new strength.

Finally after I had run out of words, Armand spoke, his eyes still on the soundless spectacle of the falling snow.

"You behaved like a fool," he said. His words came low, steady, and heated, with little or no emotion. "You should have destroyed that monster in New York at Trinity Gate when we first had him in our power. The others wanted it. Jesse wanted it. I wanted it. And Gregory and Seth wanted it. Only you didn't want it. Your vanity wouldn't have it."

His voice remained calm, his words coming evenly, as he went on. "No, your vanity would forgive and cajole and seduce and win the monster over. And so you see what has happened—Marius, Louis, and Gabrielle are gone from us forever, and for what? For your vanity." He stopped as though he'd exhausted himself, but he didn't look at me. He continued to look at the snow.

Benji was deeply distressed and pleaded with me with his eyes to be patient. Gregory did more or less the same thing.

"I say nothing in my own defense," I said.

"You have nothing to say in your own defense," Armand replied in the same measured voice, "because there is nothing you could say in your own defense. You've never been able to defend any of your great blunders . . . making a vampire out of a little child, rousing a queen who had closed her heart and soul to nature and history with the fall of Egypt. But you can listen to me now."

He turned and looked up at me, his eyes flashing with malice.

"Listen," he said in the same dull monotone. "Listen, listen when I tell you that you must wipe out to the very last one those Replimoid creatures whom you're nurturing in the very heart of an unsuspecting world."

He paused. I said nothing. He went on.

"Wipe them out now," he said, "off the face of the earth which they could so easily destroy. And wipe out the physical body of that hated spirit Amel that created us and drove us to turn on one another, and nearly took you with him into eternity at Kapetria's hands. Do these things. Don't be a fool again. For reasons I don't understand, the elders of this so-called tribe will not do these things unless you give the order. Well, do it. Issue the order that all of those hideous impostors must die. Do it now for the mortal you once were. Do it now for the mortal world you once loved. Do it now for the mortal destiny you once grieved for. Do it now for the innocent millions out there who have no idea these creatures thrive in their midst, increasing in number with diabolical efficiency. Do it before they have proliferated so that destruction is impossible. Do it for a world that will never know you or thank you, but a world that you can now truly save."

Silence. He turned his eyes away from me and back to the snowfall. "Once you wanted recognition from the humans of this planet; once you were so desperate for their recognition and acclaim that you wrote songs and made films of our very own secret history.

"You flouted your pledge to Marius, all for the love of your mortal brothers and sisters! Desperate for brief moments of mortal fame and recognition, you urged the human race to wipe us out."

Once again he looked at me.

"Where is your love for all those mortals now?" he asked. "Where is your great passion to be a mortal hero?"

I didn't answer.

"You think you've known regret," he said. "You've known nothing like the regret you will feel once those monsters have abandoned you, you and your pitiable blood drinker acolytes, and run rampant underground."

Silence. He sighed as though he had again exhausted himself. He looked at me with eyes full of weariness and disgust and then again through the window. Behind him, Benji was fighting tears.

Gregory appeared to be deep in thought.

"I've heard you out," I said to Armand. "I know where you stand. I've known since the beginning that you wanted them annihilated. I cannot do it. I will not."

"Fool," he said, eyes flashing on me again. The blood rushed to his cheeks. "I pray with all my heart that the human race discovers those beasts before they grow in such numbers as to be unstoppable. I pray that something natural and wholesome in this universe in which we live rises to engulf them—."

"You won't do anything—."

"Oh, no," he said. "I will do nothing. How could I do anything? I won't ever rise against you, and you have the strongest and the most lethal members of your Court at your disposal. Do you think I want to be given to the mob in your ballroom—torn apart for an evening's entertainment before my remains are tossed into the fire?"

"Armand," I said. "Please." I dropped down on my knees in front of him, looking up into his face.

All the emotion he had held back was printed there now. He was in a rage.

"Is your heart totally turned against me?" I asked. "Do you have no faith in what we seek to build here?"

"Fool," he said again. His voice was roughened now by emotion he couldn't suppress. "I have always loved you," he said. "I have loved you more than any being in all the world whom I've ever loved. I have loved you more than Louis. I have loved you more even than Marius. And you have never given me your love. I would be your most faithful counselor, if you allowed it. But you don't. Your eyes pass over me as if I don't exist. And so they always have."

I knelt there defeated. I didn't know where to begin. I didn't know what to say. I felt such a huge exhaustion, I had no way out of it, no way to find eloquence or reason or the vigor to try to reach him, reach beyond his malice to his soul.

He went on again, staring at me as he spoke.

"I hate you as much as I have ever loved you," he said. "Oh, I didn't want for Rhoshamandes to destroy you. Good God, that I never wanted. Never. When I heard them crying out that you'd returned I wept like a child. I never wished for that, for you to vanish into the same darkness that has swallowed Louis and Marius. But how could I not hate you, you who went in search of my maker all those long years ago when I scarce believed in him anymore—and was found by him, saved from the earth by him, welcomed into his lair by him, you whom he loved, you to whom he told the secrets of our beginning, when he had never come to free me from the Children of Satan, you to whom he gave his love, while resigning me to the ruins of all you'd destroyed around me. I hate you! I understand the very definition of 'hate' when I think of you."

He broke off, unable to continue. Benji clung tight to him, resting his head on his shoulder, crying softly. And I heard Sybelle weeping by the distant fire.

I tried in vain to find words, words that would have some meaning, but I couldn't. I had slipped again into knowing, and not thinking. I had slipped again into a purposeless awareness that was a blade turning in my heart.

"You who humiliated me and destroyed my world," he said, his voice now a fragile whisper. "You who later told with such relish how you shattered my coven, my little coven, my little coven of holy purpose. Yet still I didn't want for you to die. And I should have known that you wouldn't. Of course not. How could anyone put an end to you? How clumsy Rhoshamandes must have been in the face of your simple, vulgar cunning." He laughed under his breath. "How astonished he must have been to find himself blinded and burning at your hands. You. The upstart Lestat. The Brat Prince."

I found myself on my feet again. I'd drawn back away from him without realizing it. The air was poison between us. But I couldn't look away or go.

"I love you still," he said. "Yes, even now, I love you, as they all love you, your minions seeking just a smile or a nod or a quick touch of your hand. I love you like all those throughout this palace who are dreaming of drinking just a drop of your blood. Well, you can leave me now. I'm not going anywhere. Where is there to go? I'll be here if you want me. And grant me my wish for the moment, you and your august friends. Go and leave me alone."

He bent forward and put his face in his hands.

Benji came round and moved next to him, forcing Gregory to give way. And Benji held on to him, begging him not to weep, kissing him, and telling him that this would change, this would pass, that he and Sybelle adored him and could not go on without him, that he must live and love for them.

I did not move.

He had looked as ever like an angelic boy as he'd said all these things, and there flashed before my memory the first time I had ever laid eyes on him in the dusty shadows of Notre Dame de Paris, a vagabond angel without wings. I thought of Gabrielle then. I thought of Marius . . . but no, it was not thinking. It was simply knowing. Knowing what was past. Knowing what was present. Knowing who and what were gone.

I couldn't answer him. I couldn't comfort him. I couldn't say anything. There was no point even to try.

It was Gregory who spoke, saying that these were dangerous words from a beloved fellow blood drinker, that it was in dark moments such as this that blood drinkers sought to destroy themselves, and that he, Gregory, did not want to leave Armand alone.

Armand sat up straight. He took a linen handkerchief from his pocket and blotted his eyes. "Have no fear of that," he said, "for my fear of death is greater than my fear of whatever lies ahead here. I fear that death is like a nightmare from which we can't wake. I fear that, once detached from our bodies, we go on in some confused and anguished state in which we are forever lost and unable to escape. You go and do all those many things that the Court demands of you, the busy work of coven building that once so obsessed me and gave me the imitation of a purpose."

"Come with us now," said Gregory. He rose and held Armand's left hand in both of his hands.

"Not now," said Armand.

I wandered away, in the direction of the door, and found Santh there waiting for me.

"Rest and mourn then," Gregory said to Armand. "And promise me that if these thoughts become too great for you, you will come to us; you will not seek to harm yourself."

Armand gave some confidential answer, but I didn't hear it. I didn't separate the syllables from the crackling noise of the fire, or the sounds of Sybelle's sobs. Perhaps I realized that I didn't care what Armand was saying. Perhaps I just knew that I didn't. I couldn't be certain.

Outside the wind gusted, driving the snow against the dark panes.

I was as broken as I'd been by that wind, or the icy winds of the upper air. I was as bruised and exhausted as if I'd just made the long journey back from Rhoshamandes's Pacific lair all over again.

I walked out of the room and on through the rooms of the Château as if I had no feeling in me, no heart to break, greeting the many new lodgers under the roof, listening to this little question or receiving that little compliment as if nothing had happened.

And all the rest of the night I attended to the affairs of the Court, and finally the moment came when I could escape to my bed of marble and so I did, and the last thing I heard before I closed my eyes was Cyril speaking to me in a warm voice, assuring me all was well with the house and that I should sleep well knowing it.

"In all these centuries," said Cyril, "never have we known one whom we could see as our champion. You can't really know, boss, just what you are now to the others. You think you know, but you don't, and that's why I'll be right outside your door again sleeping in the passage, sleeping here so nothing and no one can get at you or hurt you—as long as I live and breathe."

Then I was alone in the chilling darkness—with the villain Armand despised, and the son who had not protected his mother, and the lover who had never protected Louis from himself or others, and the miserable pupil of Marius who had so misjudged Rhoshamandes that now Marius was dead.

The edge of sleep can be such a precious time.

I felt that quickening again, that prodding from the depths of my soul that some great change was taking place in me, a vital change—and another nagging thought, something to do with language. What was it? Something to do with the language Gregory had been speaking with Santh. Dungeons. They were cleaning out all those dungeons. Rhoshamandes had said something . . . and what had I seen? Stairs to a dungeon?

Hours later, when the day had died, and the moon and the stars had risen, I knew what it was that I'd been struggling to remember, those last words coming from Rhoshamandes as he died.

I hurried out of the crypts and went through the house until I came to the Council Chamber—where the lights were warm and the scent of flowers filled the air—and I found Gregory there with Seth and Sevraine, the lovely Sevraine in her gown of white silk, already in discussion about how to carry on Marius's work. Jesse Reeves was there also, a quiet flower in her drab wool clothes, and also Barbara, my dedicated and beloved Barbara, who was scribbling away in a notebook as I came in.

Cyril and Thorne had followed me, as expected, and I asked Cyril to find Allesandra and ask her to join us. "And if Everard de Landen is still here, will you find him?"

"You want the fledglings of Rhoshamandes," he said.

"Yes, that's what I want." And off he went.

I sat down at the table, and realizing they were all looking at me, I began talking. But it was to Gregory that I made my appeal.

"Rhoshamandes said something before he died," I said. "He said something in a foreign tongue, and I don't know what it was."

When Allesandra opened the door, she brought David in with her. They were both in black clothes, simple, the clothes of mourning, and I thought I saw ashes in Allesandra's long smooth hair.

I had not had a private moment with David since the night of my return, because he had been busy in England with Kapetria and Gremt and others settling the Replimoid colony again.

And now we embraced, silently, for the first time since Marius and Louis had been taken. Then he sat down to my left. He looked vaguely clerical in his black suit and simple shirt. And Allesandra might have been a desert wanderer in her black robes.

I knew David was feeling the loss of Louis keenly. No one had to tell me this. But I couldn't entertain the awareness just now that they were gone—all gone. I had to put that completely out of my mind, as I'd been doing over and over again since I pitched the last of Rhoshamandes into the flames.

I had something, something to cling to and investigate, and it supported me rather like Rhosh's blood had supported me with a steel scaffolding when I thought myself too exhausted to go on.

Fact was, I was still exhausted, still bruised all over from the fierce winds, and from all that Armand had said to me, and only a remnant of myself was carrying on. But it was carrying on.

"Go on," said Gregory. "What did Rhoshamandes say?" In his immaculate hands, he played with an old-fashioned fountain pen and finally laid it down.

"Well, I'm going to try to repeat it," I said. "It was a string of syllables. . . . Actually Rhosh said strange things. . . . I remember him blurting out, 'Stop, you don't understand' and I believe he said, 'Wait, this is all wrong,' and then he said these syllables in a foreign tongue, perhaps ancient Egyptian, and it sounded to me like *bait bah so roar* . . . something like that. I caught an image when he said it of stone steps. I didn't even think of it or register it at the time. I was given over completely to one thing, and that was destroying him, and these words went by me. But it was the last thing, well, almost the last thing he ever said."

Gregory was drawing a blank, it seemed. And Santh wasn't in the room. I was about to say something about their ancient tongue when Allesandra spoke up.

"Oh, of course," she said. "The old name he used for his private prison. It's from the Hebrew Bible, the name for Pharaoh's prison, where Joseph is kept in the book of Genesis." She then pronounced it precisely as he'd pronounced it, a cluster of syllables I couldn't reproduce but which I remembered perfectly when I heard her repeat them with such care. She spelled it out for me in our alphabet. *"Bet ha sohar."*

"That's it," I said. "That's what he said."

"Perhaps he was desperately trying to deceive you," said Gregory. "Bargaining that if you'd give up the assault, he'd keep you alive." He was looking at Seth. Then they spoke to each other in a different language for a few moments, and I caught snatches of similar syllables, but it was all too quick for me. And once again, I saw the stone stairs, and this time barred cells, and all the usual things one sees in an ancient prison, and the uncomfortable thought came to me that the old dungeon of this house was being cleaned out for a purpose which no one had dared to confess.

"Well, it was the name of his own secret prison," said Allesandra, "the place where he kept mortals in waiting for when he wanted to feast on their blood."

Yes, and that is very likely what everyone around me is planning for that prison beneath this house. They just don't want to say.

"But, Prince, that old prison is long gone," she said. "The monastery was destroyed centuries ago. All that land is now planted over with vineyards. Machines have plowed those fields. Who knows where those old stones have gone? I saw a garden wall built of old stones in that valley, old stones that might have come from the very rooms in which I'd once lodged. It's gone without a trace."

Sevraine appeared to be pondering.

Allesandra was gazing off as if the past had taken hold of her. "For a while there was a series of archways standing, ah, but that was long ago, when I was with the Children of Satan, and I remember all those white hands pulling at those archways, all those stones falling, and the grass, the grass was like wild wheat."

Her voice trailed off with the last two words.

"What about Saint Rayne?" I asked. "Could there be a hidden prison on Saint Rayne?"

"We went to Saint Rayne," said Seth. "We searched the entire island. There was no dungeon there, only a few easily accessed cells, including the one where he had kept Derek."

David's face was the picture of sadness. "Lestat, why are you putting yourself through this?" he asked. "Kapetria and the others searched the island by day. They went to Budapest and searched the house of his old friend Roland."

"I searched that dwelling as well," said Seth. "There was no real dungeon or prison there either. Only one miserable window-less chamber where Derek had been confined, and a couple of other rooms just like it where, obviously, Roland had kept mortals."

"David, I have to be sure," I said. "Think on it. Why would he cry out like that saying those words? What if there is someplace on Saint Rayne, away from the castle?"

"Prince, that castle is not a real artifact of the Middle Ages," said Sevraine. "Rhoshamandes fashioned it as a blood drinker's refuge and he had no need of deep dungeons by that time and there were none there. I too searched the entire island. I looked, I listened, I roamed every inch of that place. No dungeons."

"Are you absolutely certain?" I said before I could check myself. I immediately apologized. I was talking to immortals so much more powerful than I was. I was crestfallen.

"On the contrary," Seth said, looking directly at me. "We're all in awe of you, Prince. We don't feel superior to you. You brought down Rhoshamandes. We'd thought it impossible. We still don't quite understand how you did it."

I shook my head, and put my hands to the sides of my face. I heard Rhoshamandes's voice, that insistent "You don't understand."

I sat back and found myself staring at the ceiling, at the busy figures so magnificently painted all over it, and then I realized I was looking at the work of Marius, Marius who was gone forever, and suddenly the pain I felt suffocated me, and threatened to become more than I could bear. I almost rose to go, but then where would I go? To Saint Rayne to find nothing? To Budapest to search a house in which Rhosh had likely never lodged?

What was it he had said? *This is all wrong.*

"What could he have meant?" I asked.

"Lestat, it's obvious," said Jesse Reeves. "He was an egotist, a self-indulgent lazy immortal without a particle of depth or true understanding of life. Of course he thought you didn't understand him, because you held him to account for what he'd done to others, and that he couldn't tolerate." She broke off. "Look, must we go over it again? Well, let me say that if you must go over it, I will excuse myself and leave you to it." She rose to her feet and so did I.

"Don't leave without my taking you in my arms," I said. "I never meant to cause you pain, truly I didn't."

"You haven't made me angry," she said.

She softened all over as I held her. I kissed her thick copper hair and her forehead.

"You are my champion," she whispered. "You shed blood for her blood." But she continued towards the door, and Cyril opened it for her, and she was gone. I couldn't blame her.

I settled back into my chair.

"I want to search any place he might have owned or visited," I said. "I feel I must do that. He was trying to tell me something, clearly, about a prison, or a dungeon, or a hiding place, and I must investigate as fully as I can. Doesn't that make sense to anyone else? Why would he mention a prison?"

"Very well. We'll do this with you," said Gregory. "Tonight I'll cross the Atlantic and find those vineyards he owned in the Napa Valley. I'll make sure there is no place there that might serve as a prison."

"Santh knows the house to which he took you, does he not?" asked Seth. "I'll find him and we'll go there and search that house."

"How stupid of me not to have done that," I whispered. And it was stupid. But then I'd been so exhausted, and in such a strange state of disbelief as to what had actually happened.

"What do you want me to do?" asked Sevraine.

I was touched suddenly by their willingness to be pressed into action.

"Ah, yes," I said. "I'd forgotten about those American vineyards. I ought to go with you, but I can't—." I broke off, the mere thought of riding the icy currents above the clouds exhausted me.

Sevraine waited. Gregory waited. David waited.

Allesandra was plainly grieving for Rhosh, and lost in her memories, her eyes down. She was singing something to herself, some hymn, and murmuring under her breath.

"And this place in the Loire Valley," I pressed, though I hated to interrupt her.

"I was so in love with him then," she said in answer. "When he rescued me and brought me there, and he took me down into the prison. He was talking about Joseph in the book of Genesis and Pharaoh keeping him in his special prison all those years. He said he was the Pharaoh of his world. And this was the place where he could leave hapless mortals to languish."

I saw it as she described it, the wide stone steps, the damp glittering on the undressed stone.

"There were monks in his prison, monks whom he'd taken prisoner, pleading for their lives, reaching through the bars to entreat him, begging him if he feared God to let them go."

I sensed that Sevraine and Gregory and the others were seeing it.

"He spoke of the Talmud, I think," Allesandra said, staring off. "Something about God determining the fate of every individual on the holy feast of Rosh Hashanah. And he said that all blood drinkers should keep a prison—he used that very Hebrew word—such as Pharaoh kept for human prisoners, but that he, Rhosh, was merciful and let one prisoner go on the first of every year." She laughed suddenly. "Until Benedict came. Then he fell passionately mad for Benedict, and Benedict begged him to open the prison and let all those monks go.

"'But they're mad now, all of them,' Rhosh protested." She looked at me. Her face was bright and she smiled as she went on. "He told Benedict they would be received as mad creatures when they raved about their captivity and they would be put in chains in some place worse than his prison where he gave them meat and wine every day."

She broke off, drifting back into her memories.

I didn't dare interrupt her. I wanted desperately for her to go on.

"Then Benedict won out," she said. She laughed. "I see it as if it were yesterday, Benedict rushing down and down and down those curving stairs. And monks coming up, a procession of gaunt and ragged monks in rotting robes, singing, all of them actually singing some psalm in Latin and running off into the woods. The woods grew right up to the monastery. The woods concealed it from the world. Benedict was jubilant, and after that Rhoshamandes was a god in his eyes, as he was to the rest of us. Of course Rhoshamandes bolted all the doors, and we kept to the underground rooms ourselves for the next few months as the priests came looking for the fabled place where the raving monks had been kept in the *bet ha sohar* by an Egyptian demon—."

"But what if that prison remains underground, under all the vines," I asked. "Under the forest?"

"It's possible," she said. "But I've searched that land and found nothing. Only several months ago, Sevraine took me there. We found, on a bit of ruin, an old bell tower to an old chapel. The chapel had been a mile from the monastery."

"I have to go there," I said. "I have to go now. Will you come with me? I have to search for anything that remains of that prison."

"I'll go with you," said Sevraine. In her shimmering white gown with her loose hair she seemed scarcely prepared for such a journey, but she asked Thorne if he would get her cloak from the library. The library meant Marius's library and Thorne was off on the errand immediately.

"I will as well," said Allesandra.

"But, Lestat," said David. "What do you hope to discover even if you do find this prison? We've heard not a single solitary word from those he took. They were silenced almost immediately."

"I don't want to think about it," I said. "I want to go, to see, to find out what he meant when he said those words, why he used those particular words. He had to mean his old refuge in the Loire."

"You do realize that Kapetria and Amel visited that land themselves," said David.

"They found some modern buildings," said Seth. "They went there by day and examined every house to which Rhoshamandes held title. They were occupied by families who managed his vineyards."

"Not all of them," said Sevraine. She was on her feet. Thorne came in with her long dark cloak and put it over her white shoulders. "There was an empty building."

"Yes," said Allesandra. "The empty old house with the garden. I remember the garden." When she climbed to her feet, she took on the gesture and demeanor of an old woman again, the old woman she'd been when I'd first encountered her under Les Innocents. David was at her side. He wore modern clothes, a heavy jacket with a sweater underneath that would keep him warm on the journey, but Allesandra wore only a thin robe.

I was about to say something about it when Thorne appeared again with a long black cashmere coat for her, and helped her into it.

"Rhosh was watching us the whole time we were there," said

Sevraine. She turned to me. "And I wanted to take my leave. Finally he came up and asked us what we were doing there on his land. I told him Allesandra wanted to see the place where she'd been Born to Darkness and he said it was all gone. All of it. He asked us to come to Saint Rayne. I didn't want to go with him."

Gregory gestured for all of us to wait. He retired to the corner of the room and was talking in a low voice on his iPhone. I could hear Kapetria on the other end.

He rang off. "We'll go there with you," he said to me. "But Kapetria has already searched this unoccupied house from top to bottom. She swears no one has been there in decades."

"Let us go, Lestat," said Seth. "The prison could still be underground. Very likely it is. We won't come back till we've found it. But you stay here. You need your rest. You need to be here in the ballroom. There's a larger crowd there now than last night. Word of the battle with Rhoshamandes has traveled the world."

"Of course I can't stay behind," I said. "You know I can't."

Chapter 21

It was a house of these times, all right, though not to be called new. I figured it to be at least three hundred years old. It was built of the local stone, and had two stories and a high-pitched roof, with mullioned windows—and it was indeed empty and silent and without any connections for heat or light, and almost no furniture.

There was no one about. Only the bleak winter vines stripped of their grapes, running on for miles, and a distant copse of ancient trees of immense size, and the cold rain, a rain worse to me than snow, falling over all as if it were falling on the entire world, a near-silent rain that felt like needles on the backs of my hands and on my face.

The house was unlocked and had about it the air of a property abandoned, but as soon as we entered the main room, I spied a fireplace with logs in it, and set them alight. There were thick candles on the stone mantel and I lighted these as well. Dust covered the floor, and spiderwebs glittered in the corners. I could smell the dust burning in the fireplace.

Of course we did not need this light; we could see very well in the darkness. But the light did make things easier and I carried a lighted candle with me as I went from room to room. The floor seemed solid everywhere.

Every single flag that I tore up was resting on a layer of concrete. Surely this had been part of a modern restoration, but there was no sign that anyone ever came to this place.

That is, until I reached the last room, a long broad chamber which contained a refectory table with benches on either side. There suddenly I came upon an old upright Victrola phonograph on little curved legs with an old thick black recording disc on the turntable, labeled with the name of a Verdi opera. So perhaps Rhoshamandes had once come here, long decades ago.

Old recordings in brown-paper jackets were heaped in the corner. Verdi, Verdi, more Verdi. And beneath the table I spied what appeared to be a square mosaic with the figures of Bacchus in a chariot surrounded by worshipping nymphs.

"This table's been moved recently," I said. "Look at the marks in the dust." I shoved the table to the side, the legs screeching on the stone, and the bench falling over on its side.

The mosaic was beautiful, and possibly ancient, dating all the way back to the Roman times. I walked back and forth over it, and tapped it several times with the toe of my boot. I could feel nothing and see nothing that indicated it was not deeply embedded in the stone.

"Except that the stone is all new," said Gregory. "This floor is nothing as old as the mosaic."

At once David, Allesandra, and Gregory and I were searching the walls everywhere with our hands for some sort of crank or handle, and finding nothing. I became impatient and wanted to search the rest of the house.

I walked to the double doors that opened into the garden, and there I saw a great pile of what appeared to be sheets of metal glinting in the light of the rainy sky. Sheets of metal!

Now why was that here?

"There could be a thousand reasons," said David. "To patch the roof, to patch walls."

I went out into the rain and examined the heap and saw it was all sheets of steel, each sheet maybe one and one-half inches thick.

"What is steel made of?" I asked.

"Iron, mostly iron," said Gregory.

I was even more excited, and David was even more saddened, wishing for all the world that he could somehow save me from all this.

Now what was this doing here, all this steel, which is mostly made of iron? And it hadn't been here very long at all, because green shrubbery was crushed beneath the loose pile of sheets—and deep rutted tire tracks led to the garden, and they were filled with gleaming puddles of rain.

It was easy to figure that a heavy vehicle had brought these steel sheets here for some purpose.

Gregory stood at my side, oblivious to the cold in his thin worsted-wool business suit and plain shirt and tie. He seemed utterly immune to the rain slowly drenching his short hair and his face. He looked out over the barren fields. And when he realized that I was shivering, foolishly shivering, he removed his long cashmere scarf and wound it around my neck.

I tried to demur, but he wouldn't hear of it.

Another figure appeared in the door. It was Santh.

He was dressed in a tweed jacket and sweater with a rolled neck, and jeans and boots very much like my own. His blond hair was groomed for the first time since I'd met him, hanging like a mantle over his shoulders. He too was looking out at the fields, and I realized that he was listening.

For a long moment, I watched him, watched him intently as if something wondrous was going to happen, and then it did.

"I hear something," he whispered.

Gregory glanced at me and I knew we both were listening. But I heard nothing but the rain on the high roof and on the gables of the roof, and on the leaves in the distance copse. Such immense trees, surely spared from older forest.

"I don't hear anything," Gregory said.

"Neither do I," said Sevraine.

"I do," said Santh. "I hear a heartbeat. I think I hear more than one, but I know I hear one."

"Wait a minute . . . ," Gregory murmured. His hand tightened on my upper right arm. For a moment he hurt me, but I didn't care.

"It's a heartbeat," said Santh. "It's coming from somewhere under this earth and out there."

"I think I do hear it," said Gregory. "It's irregular, tired."

At once, we set to work searching the ground around us, kicking at stones, prying up rocks, digging into the loose earth with the toes of our boots.

Then Allesandra gave a cry. "Ah there, in the trees, yes, the same trees . . . ," she said. She rushed towards the distant copse and disappeared within the dark trunks and wet leaves.

We all came right behind her.

Here were ancient stones turned this way and that by the roots of the trees and relentless vines which sought to bury them. Santh and Gregory pried the stones loose and tossed them out into the open. Then they both began to dig with their hands until they had cleared the remnant of a floor.

"It's just a piece of flooring," Gregory said, dusting off his knees.

Allesandra hung her head and Sevraine put her arm about Allesandra to comfort her. "A foolish journey," Allesandra whispered. "I am to blame for it, and I never wanted to see this place again, never wanted to be under this sky or these stars."

Santh stood transfixed. Then he turned and fixed his gaze on the distant wooded hill beyond the edge of the vineyard and he disappeared.

Of course he hadn't dematerialized. He had simply used his preternatural speed to reach the nearby forest.

Gregory went after him and so did I.

The wet forest was thick and young, and the light of the sky was still plenty for us to see more stones, ancient stones, stones ripped up by more roots, and vines hungry to embrace them. It was a steep ascent, and the mud was wet and slippery, and a cold wind sliced through the forest, clattering in the wet leaves, and cutting into my eyes. But I went on searching, as we all did, pitching the stones right and left.

Suddenly Santh appeared high up the hill. He was beckoning for us to come.

"The old chapel!" Allesandra cried.

We were with him in an instant. "It's close, the heartbeat," Santh said. "And there is definitely more than one heart. But I can hear one heart distinctly. The beat is slow. The being is in deep sleep, but the being is alive."

There was no mistaking the ruins of "the old chapel." We came face-to-face with a long wall of broken-out arches ending perpendicular to the square of a broken bell tower. It rose three stories into the trees, its walls jagged and broken and gaping at the sky.

"I hear it," Gregory cried. "It's under the ground here!"

"I hear it too," said Sevraine. "I hear the heartbeat of two others as well."

I couldn't contain my excitement.

Vines covered the whole ruin, thick winter vines, vines thick as ropes with dark green leaves. And we began to tear at them, stripping them off the stone, and ripping them back from the flooring. Suddenly, underneath the veil of vines, I saw the glint of steel.

It was a door plated in steel, a door into the bell tower. A sheet of steel had been cut to size and bolted on to it.

I smashed it in, and Santh and Gregory followed me inside.

We found ourselves in a rectangular room open to the sky high above, with a broad stone stairway running down to the right. All of this was new construction. I smelled concrete and I smelled new wood.

"Rhoshamandes has repaired all this," said Sevraine. "It's been done since we were here."

But I scarcely heard her words because I had heard something else. "I hear it," I confessed. "I hear the heart—only one heart, but I hear it." It was slow, impossibly slow, just as Santh had said, the heart of an ancient one sleeping. I began to shake all over. David held on to me and led me forward.

We hurried down the stairs, with the others following us, and we found ourselves in a large modern cellar. There lay a stack of sheets of steel, exactly like those beside the house in the old garden. They were new and had their price stickers on them. But all else was thick with dust and the cellar appeared to have no entrance or exit except for the stairs leading down from above.

Frantically we searched everywhere. Then Santh shoved aside the entire pile of steel sheets, sending them clattering at the far wall, and there was the trapdoor, the broad trapdoor with a huge iron ring.

"Wait," said David. He was holding me still, and he stood quiet now until the others were looking at us. "We don't know what we'll find. We don't know what he's done to them."

"Let's go!" I said. "Let me open it."

Santh stepped in front of me to do the honors.

No mortal, indeed no group of mortals, could have pulled open this door. Perhaps I myself could not have pulled it open. But it was nothing to Santh, who opened it and threw it back, revealing its immense thickness.

It was like a rectangular cork in the neck of a bottle, the thing, made of stones bound in iron. The air that rose in our faces was cold and dry, and I smelled blood, not human blood but our blood. And something else, a strong smell that was familiar and unfamiliar.

Santh disappeared into the square of darkness, landing on a floor far below with a loud thud. "Come on down," he called out, his voice echoing off the walls. "It's a short drop."

He was right. The jump was not hard for any of us, but Allesandra was afraid of it, and I took her in my arms and carried her down with me.

"This is part of the old house," she cried as she was placed on her feet. "*Mon Dieu*, look at the torches in the corners." There were four of them, and they had been dipped in fresh pitch. It was the pitch that I was smelling. It had been a very long time since I'd held a torch like those in my hand. Santh lighted all of them with the power of his mind, and then took one in hand to illuminate the high-arched entrance to a catacomb.

"This runs all the way to the old monastery cellars," said Allesandra. "This was a way we could escape if ever the Children of Darkness surrounded the monastery; we'd come here by this catacomb, and go out through the tower."

The catacomb was broad and had been swept clean. There were more torches on the walls, and I lighted them as we went along, just wanting the comfort of the illumination, though we could see perfectly by the torch Santh carried in his right hand.

For five full minutes we walked briskly through this passage, following several sharp turns which appeared to send us back in the direction from which we had come. I couldn't tell. But finally we came to a vast room, a room with its own torches to be lighted, and a table against a far wall, and other random items here and there, and sheets of steel glittering in the flickering torchlight.

And there on the barren floor lay a long row of iron coffins, of the old-time elongated-heptagonal shape, the great part of them empty with their lids open, and only three of them closed, and those three being the coffins nearest us.

Now David and Allesandra could hear the heartbeat. And I could hear three heartbeats in all.

The others looked at me, waiting for me to move first, but I found to my shock that I couldn't do it. I stared at the coffins, prepared for a horror that I could not yet imagine.

But Santh stepped up and immediately ripped open the lid from the first one. And we found ourselves staring at what appeared to be

an adult body wrapped entirely in a steel shroud. For a moment, I didn't know what to make of it.

"He's taken the steel and molded it to the form," said Santh. "He's wrapped it tight, tight as you wrapped Baudwin."

"Clever miscreant," said Cyril. "He knew what I'd done to Baudwin. He knew steel is mostly made of iron."

Santh peeled back the steel sheathing as though it was nothing, and slowly revealed the body of a woman in a torn white shirt and jeans and boots, her arms and her feet flopping as he lifted her, her head entirely covered by her hair. He set the body down on the stones.

I knew it was Gabrielle. I knelt beside her.

"Mother," I whispered. I could hear the rhythm of her heart, agonizingly slow.

I reached out to part her hair, to uncover her eyes, and then I realized what he'd done to her.

It was the back of her head facing me. He had turned her head completely around on her neck. He had broken her neck. I let out a gasp.

"Be careful," said Gregory. "No, don't touch her. This is a matter for our vampire doctor. He's broken her spinal cord, and only Fareed will know precisely how to repair it."

"If it can be repaired," whispered Sevraine.

Of course it can be repaired, I thought. Why is she expressing such a doubt, she, one of the eldest? But what if she knows something that I don't know? Finally fear took the place of words inside me.

"Fareed will know," Gregory said impatiently. And he called to Fareed, begging him to come immediately, describing the strange route and the forest above the vineyards and bell tower.

I remained beside Gabrielle and I kissed the hair on the back of her head and told her in a soft voice that I was here. I took her limp hand in mine, and I kissed it, and I laid my hand gently on her heart and I told her that I could hear her heart beating. "Let my words find your mind, Mother," I said. "I'm here. I've come. And I'm taking you home. I'm taking all of you home."

No sound issued from the body, not even a telepathic sound. But I knew Fareed was on his way, and these next few minutes would be the longest I'd endured in all my life.

In a daze I sat watching as the others removed the remaining two bodies. With immense care Gregory and Santh folded back the steel wrappings.

I recognized Louis's simple dark wool suit and lace-up shoes, and Marius's loose red velvet robe. And they too had suffered the same fate.

No sound came from any of them but the beating of their hearts, and that had to mean that they were alive and could be restored. It had to mean that. But who knew? What book contained pictures of such disasters and the directions in bold scientific terms as to what one was supposed to do with the blood drinker subjected to such indecencies? Would Fareed someday add these horrors to the books he was writing, and spell out how such bodies could be reanimated?

"I've never seen such a thing done," said Gregory. "But I understand now how he silenced them so quickly. He broke their necks. And how he managed to bring them here without their being able to utter the smallest cry for us. They are in a deathlike sleep."

I couldn't bear the sight of them lying in a row like that, the three of them, their faces turned to the floor. I fell back against the wall. It was as if I'd traveled miles on the wind again, I was so tired, and I began to laugh almost hysterically as I gazed at the three of them with their white hands and their clothes just the same as they'd been the night they'd been taken away.

I had seen so many horrific things in these last few nights I knew that my existence now was completely altered, but we had found them, they were here, they were safe, and I was certain, certain, based on all I knew, that the three of them would be fully restored.

Rhoshamandes's words came back to me, his claiming that I didn't understand him at all, his claiming that he was not a monster, but what cruel game had he meant to play?

Suddenly the body of Marius began to move.

We were all astonished.

One knee rose under the dark red velvet robe, and the heel of his boot scraped the stone floor. Then the body slowly sat upright, and the hands moved sluggishly up to the head. None of us dared to move or to say a word.

The hands took their time, feeling the skull through the hair, and then the hands began to turn the head slowly. We heard snapping noises, popping sounds, and even a low grinding, but the face of Marius was now directed towards us, and the eyes quite suddenly snapped open and were fired with life.

Marius stared at me, and then at the others, and then at me again, and a slow smile appeared on his lips.

"I knew you'd come," he said. I rushed forward and helped him to his knees, though of course he did not need it. And as he rose to his feet, I wept in his arms. The only thought in my mind, the only image, the only idea, was of Armand, and how Armand would feel when he too could hold Marius like this and know that Marius lived, that Marius had been restored, that all of them were safe and secure, and using my strongest power I sent the word to him. I sent the news. And I sent my love to Armand with it.

"And the monster?" Marius asked. His voice was hoarse, and not quite his own. "What's happened to him?"

"Dead, destroyed, gone from the earth," I said.

"You're certain of it."

"Oh, yes," I said. I laughed. "I am quite certain of it." I couldn't stop laughing. "I destroyed him with my own hands. I saw his remains burned with my own eyes. He's gone, vanquished. You can place your trust in me."

I gave him to know how it had come about. I lavished upon him the bits and pieces of my memory in a little torrent, and I saw the relief course through him. He closed his eyes. "Lestat," he said, "you are the damnedest creature! May the gods protect you always. You are indeed the damnedest creature."

Fareed had just arrived. He broke in on our laughing and I had to get control of myself, or I would pass into crying like a boy.

But I was so convinced now that all would be well, I couldn't hold the tears much longer.

Fareed studied the two bodies, and then asked if Rhoshamandes was right-handed. "Yes," I said. "He held my ax in his right hand."

"Exactly as I thought," said Fareed.

Then he knelt beside my mother, and taking her head in his hands, he carefully turned it, listening to every tiny snapping or popping noise as if they were confiding some secret to him. At last she lay as if in a deep sleep, no breath issuing from her lips, and only her heart beating.

"Mother!" I called out. "Mother, wake up. It's Lestat. It's me."

For a few long torturous seconds she lay there inert with her eyes half-mast, but then the eyelids fluttered and she looked up at the ceiling. She took a long shuddering breath. And her full expression came back to her as she appeared absorbed in what she saw, her breath rising and falling with one deep breath after another.

"Can you see me?" asked Fareed. At once, she looked at him, as if seeing him for the first time.

"Yes, I see you," she responded in a sleepy roughened voice. Her eyes moved from right to left. When she saw me she said my name.

"I'm here, Mother," I said to her.

Fareed drew back, studying her intently. I picked her up as a man picks up a bride, and kissed her on the lips. I could hear the blood rushing in her veins. I could feel its heat in her face. I set her down on her feet gingerly and held her as tight to myself as I could, my senses flooded with the scent of her hair and her skin. I was trembling. I raked at her hair with my fingers. It was smooth new hair, grown back after he had cut her hair from her. I swallowed, refusing to show her tears. I said "Mother" because I couldn't help it, "Mother," as if it were the only word I knew. "Mother."

"My champion," she said, in the same hoarse voice. "And where the Hell is the villain?"

"Gone from the earth," I said. I tried to get her hair away from her face.

"Lestat, stop fussing with me," she said. She was obviously eager to stand on her own two feet, but at once she began to fall, and I caught her and held her once more in my arms. When she spoke again, her words were slurred. "Where are we? What is this place?"

"An old cellar belonging to Rhoshamandes," I explained to her. "He brought you here. We all thought he'd destroyed you. He wanted us to believe that he had. He wrapped you in steel, the way Cyril had wrapped Baudwin in iron. But you are safe, completely safe now."

She lay against me for a long moment but then stood on her own and told me that I had helped her quite enough.

I didn't argue with her. The time for tears had passed, thankfully, and I turned to watch Fareed with Louis.

For Louis, I was most afraid.

I could see that Fareed was taking extreme care. He turned Louis's head very slowly, listening to the inevitable sounds again as if they were confiding something vital to him, and finally Louis's face was as it should be, but Fareed still held it waiting for the eyelids to show the first signs of life.

It seemed an eternity before those dazzlingly beautiful green eyes opened, but finally they did, and Louis looked about himself drowsily, and whispered something incoherent which I couldn't catch. But I knew it was French.

"Talk to me," said Fareed. "Louis, look at me. Talk to me."

"What is it you want me to say?" Louis asked. His voice was as hoarse as Gabrielle's voice had been, and I saw him wince as if from a sharp pain. "My head aches," he said. "My throat is on fire."

"But you see us clearly," said Fareed.

"Yes, I see you," said Louis, "but I don't know where we are. What's become of him? Is he dead?"

When I told him, yes, that Rhoshamandes was dead, he shut his eyes as if he meant to fall asleep, and that was what he did. Gregory picked him up for the journey home, assuring him that we were all safe now.

Chapter 22

It was just past midnight when we returned to the Château. We could hear the shouts and the clapping and the cheering before we ever reached the ballroom, and there we discovered the largest crowd that had ever filled the room. Blood drinkers crowded the terrace and the nearby salons. It seemed the full Blood Communion had come to share the joy and join in the thanksgiving.

Rose and Viktor, with Sybelle and Benji, begged for the three victims to explain everything.

It was Marius who took command, and related the story; but without disclosing the salient details of how the three of them had been rendered powerless. The enclosing of their bodies in steel, that much he did explain, but not how a snapping of the neck had put them into a silent dreamless state in which they could communicate nothing. I saw the wisdom of his not disclosing this and marveled at how he described the rescue as the heroic work of "the Brat Prince" who had held out hope that those whom Rhoshamandes had abducted might still be in existence.

There came cries of my name, cheers, a chorus chanting "the Brat Prince," and then Marius raised his stentorian voice to remind them all that the Brat Prince was also the Prince, and he turned and took my hand and kissed the golden ring of Medusa's head and gestured for me to be seated on the throne.

My Prime Minister.

As he looked about the ballroom, at the evidence of Rhoshamandes's fury on the walls and ceiling, and at the bright and eager faces of the fledglings surrounding him, he declared there would be a grand ball in ten nights' time—when the ballroom was fully restored—and until then the young ones must go back to their hunting grounds, and the elders who had no need to hunt were welcome to remain quietly under the roof, while he, Marius, meant to give the ceilings of the room the fresh murals they deserved before the ballroom would be reopened.

"The worst foe this Court has ever faced is now vanquished," he said. "And the word goes forth from this palace that on the tenth night after this, all should come together to celebrate the Court and its purpose. As for now, I bid you all go your separate ways, as I must seek a quiet time with those who are closest to me."

Armand was not in this gathering. And Marius had taken note of this, and he had exchanged looks with me as he pondered this.

"He needs you," I whispered to him.

"Ah, I have been waiting for that for a very long time," he confided. "His heart is finally no longer shut against me."

I was quietly stunned by those words. Did Armand not fear that Marius had renounced him? Had they been at cross-purposes with one another? Perhaps not. Perhaps it was the truth that Armand had only now come to the point when he could open his heart to Marius as he had opened it centuries ago in Venice. I couldn't know what these two immortals had to say to each other.

I couldn't know the stories of immortals all through the Château, immortals in couples, or groups, or loose gatherings, or wandering solitary and unmolested through the different libraries and studies and salons, immortals with so many tales to tell that they would fill volume after volume on endless shelves yet, tales that other immortals might inherit and read as part of the promise of this strange place which was defining itself before my eyes.

The assembly was over. Gregory came forward to ask me to authorize more funds for the rapid restoration of the village, and Barbara was at my elbow asking for more equipment in the old kitchens I'd installed when first I renovated the building. Somehow I found myself at my desk signing one document after another, scarcely noticing that I'd agreed to the installation of bathrooms throughout the dungeon "complex" and to the purchase of giant refrigerators. I glimpsed a map of the underground prison floors for less than a second, and then came more papers to sign for the restoration of the stables, the repair of the roads, and an extension of the hothouses in which our flowers were grown so they might provide fresh fruit and vegetables for the mortal carpenters. The walls needed plastering on the outsides where Rhoshamandes had broken them out, and there had to be scaffolding for Marius to do the painting he wished, and Alain Abelard, my humble architect, was asking for another team of roofers. On and on it went.

Meanwhile Marius had gone off to find Armand, and Pandora and Bianca had gone with him. And I heard voices coming from countless rooms, and the sound of a film playing in one of the libraries.

I experienced a great sigh of relief when I thought of Marius and Armand, but I found myself staring numbly at an order for the installation of a great furnace adjacent to the dungeons. Why in the world did we need a furnace of that size, I wondered, but I didn't care really, and so I signed where I was told to sign, and I was glad when I could escape to go down into the village street and see how the rebuilding had been progressing. It was deliciously cold, and the night was clear and crisp and filled with a bounty of stars and the scent of oak fires, and fresh wood, and paint, and the soft murmur of a few mortal voices behind closed curtains in the townhouses.

It was just before dawn when Gregory and Seth found me and put the question to me that I should have foreseen. Gregory foreswore the seductive power of his lordly robes and Babylonian hair for the encounter. He was businesslike and honest. If we did not keep mortal prisoners in the dungeons, the young vampires might sooner or later do mischief in the cities close to us, which was strictly forbidden. Or they would give up on the Court altogether. They could not endure the thirst of being away from their hunting grounds.

"It's too easy for us to forget that thirst," he said. "And true, they could endure for far longer than they do, but it's painful to them, and that is not how we wish it to be for them, not at all, when they come to us."

We were standing on the paved road leading up to the drawbridge, and I found myself looking up at the great castle with its scattered lighted windows and the paling sky beyond with its remnants of starlight.

The morning birds sang in the forest. And a last automobile left the grounds, speeding over the drawbridge and past us bound at great speed for the highway.

"So this is what I must do?" I asked. "Preside over a dungeon of condemned men beneath my father's house?"

"It was always just a matter of time," said Gregory. "The young ones have to feed. And more than ever they want to be here. They want to see you, talk to you, dance at the balls. Stories of your victory over Rhoshamandes are being written by them in poetry and song." He smiled as if he couldn't repress it. "And some of the ballads are rather good, and they want to perform them for you."

Shock of memory. Shock of knowing—how once I'd stood on the stage in a jam-packed auditorium outside of San Francisco singing my own ballads to the raucous and deafening accompaniment of guitar and drums, the Vampire Lestat, the rock singer, the creator of a string of luminous little "rock videos" that had told the world about our tribe, that had baited the world to believe in us, to come find us, to wipe us out. I was back in the moment, on that stage again under the burning solar lights—so proud, so arrogant, so visible.

You know what I am.

And the agony of irrelevance had been banished, the dull despairing awareness of utter insignificance in the mortal scheme of things. I could hear those roaring voices, those pounding feet, those delirious shrieks and howls. *Visible.*

How quickly the mortal world had closed over that night, and all its reckless abandon—over slick black remains on the asphalt of vampires burned in a flash by the will of the great Mother of us all; over witnesses claiming they had seen my preternatural skin, they had touched it! Time had rolled over the entire experience, flattening it to the pages of a book. Where were those little films I'd made? What the world remembered was just another rock singer with long hair and a French name. The few true believers who would not deny the evidence of their own eyes had ended up on the margins of life, ridiculed, ruined, and slightly mad, and eventually questioning themselves and why they had risked so much to insist upon the truth of something so obviously fictive and predictable. Rock singers, vampires, Goths, romantics.

"Lestat," Gregory called me back to myself. "Let us keep mortal victims for them. They are desperate to stay with us, and think what we can teach these young ones."

"No one has ever given a damn for the young," said Seth, though he was marveling at it.

And Benji's radio voice came back to me. "We are a parentless tribe. Where are you, old ones? Why don't you spread your wings to shelter us?"

"Yes, mortal victims, very well," I said.

The following night, as I sat in my comfortable apartment in the Château with Louis and Gabrielle, we pondered the vitality of the

Court that was increasing in size around us. We talked of Rhosh and why he'd kept his prisoners alive, rather than destroying them.

"He wanted you to suffer what he had suffered," said my mother. "That much he told me. It's the last thing I remember before I found myself unable to move or breathe and falling into a kind of emptiness." I couldn't bear to picture it, my mother in the arms of that demon. But why had he not crushed her head, which he might have done with one hand as he spirited her away from us?

I saw Louis shuddering, hugging the backs of his arms. He was still battered by the abduction, and gave no hint of how he had experienced it.

"I think he meant to use us after you were dead," my mother said. "I think he meant to destroy you and then sue for peace, offering to return us to the tribe."

"Yes, I think that is a very good guess," I said.

But we all agreed we'd never really know. As for the words he'd spoken in his last moments, Rhosh was bargaining for his own life with me.

"I will never be able to convey," I said, "how quickly it all happened. One moment he had me at his mercy; the next he was blind, and essentially helpless. And no matter how great is the power of one to burn or to destroy, no blood drinker possesses a gift for putting an end to the flames once he's engulfed by them. Only water will do that. If he'd fled the room and plunged into the sea, he might have saved himself. And it was an easy thing to do. But I gave him no time to realize it."

I saw him again, stumbling, pressed back against the fireplace by all the force I could muster against him. Surely he had known which way to flee. But then I'd pounded him against the stones, and sent the fire in one swift blast after another.

I felt no pity for him in those moments, no pity for him anymore at all. That was plain enough. It seemed impossible that I had ever felt pity for him. But I was keenly aware that something else had prevented me from condemning him to death, and that was simply my respect for him as a living being.

I didn't like having the power of life or death over others in a formal way. God knows, and God alone, how many lives I've extinguished. But to formally condemn a creature of my own ilk to death, that is not something I would ever be able to do with ease, no matter how the council might press me on it. I saw in my mind's eye the death of Baudwin, and my heart went cold remembering those calls for it. There is killing and there is killing. There is murder; there is massacre; there is slaughter. And what I willed for this Court was something that was now in great peril.

But how could I explain this to Gabrielle and Louis, Louis who had confessed long years ago that the taking of a human life was his unequivocal definition of evil? Louis who was hungry now and pale, and had asked me more than once if I'd come with him to Paris, Paris where he might hunt in the early hours, alone with only me at his side, hunt for something neither of us ever really found.

For the first time, I told them both the story of my return with Rhoshamandes's remains, even though I knew they'd heard it from others. I told them of how Baudwin had been brought up, and how Santh had beheaded him. I told them of how the ballroom reverberated with merciless cries as an immortal being, a being immune to sickness and natural death, had perished along with all he'd ever seen, and all he knew, as Antoine waited to strike up the dance that would celebrate the being's passing.

"And this little ritual you despise, is that it?" It was my mother who asked this question, sitting back on the antique velvet couch in her jungle khaki and boots, her hair once more braided behind her back. "Is that what you're telling us?"

"Yes," I said. "I despised it." I looked away. Her eyes were no harder now than they usually were, and her tone no less cynical and remote.

"But they loved it," said Louis. He had not spoken all this while. "Of course they did."

"As we speak, the old dungeons under this house are being repaired," I said. "An even lower level of cells has been discovered. The filth of centuries is being removed."

"Lestat, the fledglings long to be here with you," said Louis, "and you know their need for blood."

"Ah, so you too are for it," I said.

"And you are not?" he asked. He was genuinely puzzled.

I didn't answer.

"It is the young ones who need you," Louis said, "far more than the elders. It is the young ones whom you must prepare for the Devil's Road. And the young ones must drink or suffer agony."

"I know," I said dejectedly.

I realized suddenly and silently that Louis was regarding me the way the others did, that he was actually looking at me with a mixture of awe and wonder.

"Good Lord, don't tell me you are starting to believe all this!" I said.

A shadow of disappointment fell over his face. He implored me as he spoke:

"You mean to tell me that you *don't* believe it?"

My mother laughed softly under her breath. "He believes it, Louis," she said. Her voice had a cheerful ring to it. "He believes in it and he believes it, that the Court has changed our world forever. And it's what he wants, and what he's always wanted."

I had always wanted *this*? How could she believe such a thing, but I knew she was speaking the truth, and I had the deep disconcerting suspicion that she knew more about the truth of the matter than I did.

"The mortal prisoners," she said, "this was inevitable. Had you not found those old dungeons under the southwest tower, you would have had to create them. You have the council behind your decision. You should have—." She broke off with a short apologetic gesture.

"I know, Mother," I said. "I know. I should have listened to them about Rhoshamandes a long time before. I do know that now."

I couldn't read the expression on her face. I couldn't read the expression on Louis's face either, but they were both looking at me, and then my mother came close to me, and though she did not touch me, she sat beside me on the floor in front of the fireplace.

"You're not alone," she said. "No matter how strong you are, my son," she said. "You are not alone anymore."

Louis gazed at me with a faint smile on his lips, and I felt a tenderness for both of them suddenly that I couldn't express. Louis's words came gently and slowly from his lips.

"You have all of us."

Chapter 23

Three nights later our dungeon cells were filled with wretched mortal reprobates, drug dealers, slave traders, mercenaries, terrorists, pimps, gunrunners, and assassins. The old kitchens I'd installed when I renovated the Château were now pressed into service in feeding them. And the furnace stood ready with its belly of fire for whatever refuse would be fed to it. And when I closed my eyes, I could hear the babble of voices down there in the darkness, where the wine and the food never ran out, speculating on which tyrannical government had dared to put them in this unspeakable place and how they might buy their way out of it. The dregs of Mumbai, Hong Kong, San Salvador, Caracas, Natal, Detroit, and Baltimore were soon thrown into the mix, along with fabled gangsters, and arms traffickers from Moscow, Afghanistan, Pakistan, and Spain.

I insisted against all objections that there would be no public ritual of feeding these hapless thugs to a crowd, but that the hungry could go down the winding stone stairs to pick their victims silently by torchlight and have them brought to a large richly furnished chamber; and there the feeding would take place, as it had so often in the past, against the backdrop of plastered walls, darkly varnished paintings in ornate frames, damask chairs, and a great canopy bed hung with silk and golden embroidery. Amongst pillows or on the thick wool carpet, the condemned would succumb to the fatal embrace, with only the silence to witness it.

"That is how it must be," I said. "We are not barbarians."

Chapter 24

The rebuilding of the village was happening very fast, in spite of the cruel winter, and as more mortal carpenters and craftsmen poured into the valley, I made the decision to offer the Dark Gift to my head architect, Alain Abelard, when all the rebuilding was done. Of course I didn't confide my decision to him. I wanted to discuss it with the council before I did that.

Marius was hard at work once again on the documents that would embody our basic laws. He had much to say on the making of blood drinkers, and was struggling to get his best ideas into a manageable form.

Amel, Kapetria, and the colony of Replimoids were completely resettled in England within a week. I visited often, sometimes without seeing anyone in particular, and just walking about their little British village and the restored church and the spacious grounds that surrounded their manor house and the restored asylum building in which their laboratories were hard at work with research so technical and baffling to me that I resolved never to underestimate it or fear it, trusting Amel's love to keep us all safe.

It was clear to me that Gremt, the spectral founder of the Talamasca, was now part of Kapetria's community along with Hesketh and Teskhamen, though Teskhamen often came to Court.

I knew that at least one of Kapetria's projects was making a study of the flesh-and-blood body that Gremt had formed for himself, and I did find myself curious about that. Magnus also was in residence with Kapetria in England, and that made me curious as well. Could Kapetria make a flesh-and-blood body for Magnus? For Hesketh? For any of those Earthbound human souls that clung to the atmosphere around us, listening to us, watching us, wanting to reenter the life they were slowly forgetting as the years passed?

Armand's warnings were ever on my mind.

More than once I sat with Kapetria in her office discussing her long-ago commitment to do nothing that would ever harm humanity, and I was convinced that she believed in this old vow.

"We will always be the People of the Purpose," Kapetria assured me. "Let me tell you about one small bit of evidence we've collected about ourselves so far. Every clone child born of my parts has this full commitment, and almost all of my knowledge, at least all of that knowledge with which I was initially endowed—and it's that way with the direct clone children of any of us who make up the original team.

"Allow me to point out that there is no end to the number of such clone children we can generate. Severing the very same limb each time I want to give birth to another works as effectively as choosing another limb. But . . ." She paused, her finger raised to insist on my close attention.

"But," she continued. "If I should make a clone child from a clone child, the purpose and the knowledge are not as firmly imprinted as with the direct clone. And then if a clone child is made from that third-generation clone child, there is even less knowledge and less emotional conviction to the purpose, and so on it goes so that by the time we reach the fifth-generation child made from the fourth generation, there is almost no innate knowledge, no innate grasp of science or history or logic, and there is no knowledge of the purpose at all."

I was slightly horrified.

"This fifth-generation clone child is not dim-witted so much as passive, with a malleable and agreeable personality which seems to be the pale shadow of my own. Now, to know, as I had to know, I have gone on to produce a sixth generation and a seventh. But the seventh is so obedient and compliant, so easily led and manipulated, that I hesitated to go further. But then again, I felt that I had to go on, and with the tenth generation I produced a perfect slave."

"I see," I said.

"Now the slave, even with her diminished intelligence and total lack of ambition or curiosity, nevertheless knows pain and seeks to avoid it, and appears to want only the simplest comforts and peace. The slave likes nothing better than to sit outside in my garden and watch the movement of the trees in the breeze."

"Is the slave capable of anger, or malice, or the will to do harm?"

"Apparently not," she responded. "But how can we know? I can tell you think that if I were to present you with a present of such a tenth-generation Replimoid she would be content as your guest for-ever supplying you with blood whenever you desired it. Teskhamen has put that to the test. There is a slight response in the slave to being praised for obedience, a certain happiness in knowing that her blood has nourished another, but almost no real sense of the differ-ence between herself and other clone children or blood drinkers or incarnate spirits such as Gremt. To the tenth-generation slave, all beings register socially in terms of what they say and how they smile or frown."

"This is a power that could be misused in hideous ways," I said.

"Absolutely. So right now, it is forbidden amongst us for any clone child to propagate. We alone propagate—Derek, Garekyn, Welf, and I."

"What became of the line of generations?" I asked.

"Well, there are two—one line from me and one from Derek,

and the results were about the same. They are all valued members of the community here, but the tenth generation has to be watched. Should I ask Karbella, the tenth-generation clone of me, to sweep the paths of the garden outside, she will sweep them hour by hour, day and night, week after week, month after month, until told to stop."

"I see."

"The generation right before Karbella is far more useful in terms of service, in that it possesses what we call common sense and a broad simplified awareness of our overall objectives here. What comes after Karbella, I do not know." She gave a sigh at that point, but then continued. "But sooner or later, I will want to know," she said, "because I must know everything about us, and I must discover why it is that our clones inherit 'the Purpose' as we redefined it for ourselves before the city of Atalantaya fell, and not the original purpose given us when we were sent here—to destroy the city of Atalantaya and the whole human race."

"Which of your fields of study excites you the most?" I asked.

"Figuring out why the body I grew for Amel has so many faults."

"But what are the faults?" I asked. Amel appeared not only to be a beautiful healthy male, but to have an immense passion for life.

"He cannot procreate at all," said Kapetria. "And he does not experience the pleasure of attempted procreation."

"Oh, of course," I said. "And he's aware of this deficiency, he has to be."

"Oh, he is aware of it, but he suffers no desire, so doesn't feel the lack of anything, and indeed loves everything equally whether it is embracing me or drinking a glass of fine wine, or listening to a symphony. In fact, he's convinced that his erotic passions pervade his entire body and mind, and that he approaches all of life with an orgiastic fervor that he's not eager to lose."

I thought of him, of the joy he found in listening to music, of the way that he loved to dance, of the manner in which he could be distracted and obsessed with the spectacle of the rain falling on the pavements in the lamplight or the moon slipping behind layers of cloud.

"That's how it is with us," I said, "except that when we drink blood, when we take the victim to the brink, there's a . . . a satisfaction we don't know in any other way."

"I know," she said. "He's explained all this to me. His mind is running over with observations and discoveries to the point where he can't organize what he knows, or focus on any one topic, and is forever asking me for some sort of medication to slow down the process, if for no other reason, so that he can sleep."

"I can understand."

"He says that when the vampires lie dormant in the hours of the day, their minds and bodies experience all manner of essential processes, that it is not merely paralysis because the sun has risen, that it is part of a cycle triggered by changes in the atmosphere prompted by the sun's rays."

"He must have a great deal to teach us as well as you," I said. I reflected on my battle with Rhoshamandes, and the long journey westward to return to France. My exhaustion had become excruciating, as it can be with human beings. We blood drinkers could be tortured by eternal wakefulness just as humans can.

"Yes," Kapetria said, addressing my comment, "but until Amel can get some control over his impulses, he won't be teaching people anything. The reason he likes to be with you, and not with us, is that you can think as fast as he thinks, and you keep bringing him back to the subject, and also, well, he loves you in a special way. Each of us loves you in a special way. All the Court, all of them love you in unique and special ways."

"Isn't that true of everyone?" I said.

"I was driving at something particular to you, your seeming gift for making each person you encounter feel connected to you. I suspect others have the gift, but in you the gift is strong."

I felt uneasy with this topic. I didn't really want to talk about myself. I changed the subject, asking if she and the others would all come to the up and coming ball.

"Our invitation has gone out to the whole world," I said, "and we're finding that blood drinkers who ignored us in the past are coming to us. Gregory and Seth are receiving letters. Fareed has the idea that there might be two thousand of us when the ballroom opens. I suppose there will be dancing on the terrace and dancing in the corridors and in the adjacent rooms."

"I believe it is best if we do not come," she said. "I don't think you need include us in your special entertainments. I think it is better for you and for your fellow blood drinkers that we not be there—that it be a night for only you and them."

I was about to protest when something prevented me from doing it. "All know that you're under our protection," I said. "And that you come and go when you please."

"Yes, Lestat, and we love you for it. But the balls are becoming a different matter, and this one in particular is really for all of you."

"Perhaps you're right. There will be so many newcomers, more than ever at any one time in the past."

"Yes," she said. "We know we can visit you whenever we like, just as you're welcome always here."

"Something *has* changed," I said. "But it has nothing to do with your safety, nothing at all like that."

"How would you describe the change?"

"That's just it," I said. "I don't know. But there's something in the air now in the palace. There's something different about it all."

"Is this a bad thing or a good thing?" she asked.

"I think it's good, but I don't know."

"You do realize you astonished everyone, don't you?"

"Well, if I did, luck had a lot to do with it, luck and impetuosity, and my usual devil-may-care attitude. I mean it was the simplest thing, all of it."

"That's what you keep telling others, isn't it?" she said. "It's as if you are ashamed of all the adulation."

"I'm not ashamed of it," I said, "but I think anybody could have taken Rhoshamandes down with the same collection of movements. We never stop being human beings no matter how old we are. I didn't bewitch Rhoshamandes. I just . . ." I didn't say any more. I rose to go, and I took Kapetria's right hand and kissed it, and then I kissed her upturned mouth.

"I'll always protect you," I said. "I'll never be so stupid again as I was about Rhoshamandes. I'll never let anyone harm you."

She smiled at me before slowly rising to take me in her arms.

"I don't know why you're so uneasy," she said. "It's all coming together the way you always wanted it."

"I? The way I always wanted it?" I asked. We walked out of her office and through the garden and towards the gates of the manor-house grounds. It was a lovely evening, and surprisingly mild for December, and the enormous spreading oak trees gave me a deep feeling of peace. Perhaps they made me think of the great oaks of Louisiana, and the long avenues of oaks that often lead to houses such as the house of Fontayne.

"Yes, it's all exactly what you wanted," she said when we had reached the gates.

"Kapetria, I never dreamed of a Court for us. Never dreamed that my father's house would become that Court or that I'd be called upon to be the Prince. Believe me, this is not what I always wanted because I could never have imagined it."

She was smiling at me, but she said nothing.

"What on earth do you mean?" I asked.

"Ah," she said. "Amel is right. You don't know yet. But let's stop with all this. The times are happy times. You go back and I will see you very soon. I'll be with Fareed in Paris for the next few nights. Perhaps I'll see you there."

And that was the end of our conversation, and it was back to the Château and to the report from Barbara that the work on the crypts had been completed, ceilings replastered, marble tiles replaced over the granite walls. New crypts were being dug in the slopes behind the castle, and soon another building would go up there, an annex of comfortable apartments to supplement the rooms in the Château.

Barbara walked beside me through the salons leading to my apartment, allowing the newcomers to greet me, and be greeted by me, then politely ushering us steadily along to the safety of my rooms.

"The chandeliers have been fully repaired and rehung this afternoon," she reported. "And the parquet floor is entirely refinished. You'd never know that it had been burned." She wore an artist's long smock over her usual dress, and her raven hair was loose down her back.

I marveled at how all of this busy work enlivened her, and how all that I had to give in return was my appreciation of the results. I made a mental note to buy something precious and lovely for Barbara, a string of natural pearls, perhaps, or even a necklace of diamonds to show my gratitude. It saddened me suddenly that I knew so little of her that I couldn't think of anything more significant than that.

Before I let her go back to her endless chores, I said again that we must keep sending out the invitation to all the world of the Undead to come to the ball.

"Do you realize how many are already here?" she responded. "Lestat, if there is a blood drinker anywhere on this Earth who doesn't know about what is happening, then that one has shut himself off of his own will."

She was right.

The word had gone forth night after night from the Château that all immortals should attend the coming Ball of the Winter Solstice, that no one should stay away out of timidity or fear, that the Court was a place to which all blood drinkers had a right to be received, and that all of the elders of whom we knew would be in attendance when the ballroom again opened its doors.

It was a feudal pact that we were offering: Come to the Court, acknowledge it and its rules, and you will forever after have its protection, no matter where you go.

All the rooms of the Château, other than the ballroom, had been open since the night that Marius, Louis, and Gabrielle had returned.

And Fareed had been busy questioning every newcomer, and recording as much of his or her story as he could. He had a staff of helpers in this endeavor, ranging from those who typed what they heard directly into their laptop computers to those who wrote the stories down in large leather-bound diaries, and still others who recorded the accounts to be transcribed later on.

Many discoveries were being made.

It turned out that Baudwin, who had tried to destroy me and destroyed Fontayne's house in the process, had been the maker of Roland, the unfortunate blood drinker who had imprisoned the Replimoid Derek for ten years. And learning of Roland's destruction at the hands of the elders of our Court, Baudwin had vowed to destroy me for it, though he knew full well I hadn't been present when the elders destroyed Roland. Why he had not struck at the Replimoids, I didn't know. A long story lay behind the making of Roland, and Baudwin's making by Santh, and all this and more went into Fareed's history, along with the tales Santh told Fareed of his wanderings in the time before the Christ.

Santh was secretive as to where he had been during the centuries of the Common Era, but of those long-ago nights, he had plenty to say. It was during that time that his fast friendship with Gregory had been forged, and now, when Santh was not talking to Fareed, he was usually at Gregory's side.

Meanwhile Louis and Fontayne had become fast friends. Fontayne had been given a spacious apartment in the new southeast tower, and there they read *War and Peace* together in English, with Fontayne sometimes reading the novel in Russian to Louis, who was picking up the language very fast.

Gregory had sent funds to America for the rebuilding of Fontayne's house, for which the nearby towns were extremely grateful, but Fontayne wanted to remain with us and was eager to sell the place as soon as it was restored to the locals, who wanted it as a famous lodging to draw people to their district. Fontayne's expansive personality invited everyone to like him and accept him. He spent time with Pandora and Bianca, and with Benji and Sybelle.

Meeting Benji had been a precious moment for him, as he had heard Benji's radio broadcast for over two years, and was well aware of the role that Benji played in bringing us all together, and establishing the Court.

As the date of the ball drew near, I had evergreen branches brought in to decorate every mantelpiece and every hearth. Barbara ordered truckloads of holly for more decorations, and evergreen garland which was hung in great festoons from sconce to sconce throughout the hallways and the salons.

Soon the entire palace, as the newcomers were calling it, smelled of the green forest, and I had a Christmas buffet set out in the high street one evening for all the mortals working on the village and went down to serve the wassail myself. Notker supplied a small string quartet of blood drinkers to play for this event, quiet uncomplaining creatures who easily passed for human as they played the familiar French carols in a way most appealing to human ears.

Of course, I wore a hooded wool garment for the cold—black velvet lined in white fur, and leather gloves, and pale violet-tinged glasses to shield my "sensitive" eyes from all the flickering torches lining the streets. But it was exquisitely pleasant to be standing amid my mortal workers, passing for human, and talking with them as if nothing divided me from them as we celebrated this special time of year. I had a comfortable sense of how very important it was for these innocent mortals never to guess for a moment the true nature of those who inhabited the Château, and I felt confident that I could preserve their innocence indefinitely. But I kept my eye on Alain, my architect, who had been in residence longer than anyone else now, and I could see what I often saw in him, an awareness that something very mysterious was happening around him, something beyond restoration and reclamation, something that just might be revealed to him eventually and perhaps very soon. (I had hinted to him that I had secrets to share, and would do so when "the time was right.") He was somewhat isolated and alone at the Christmas gala, and though he chatted with others when they approached him, he spent his time under the sign of the inn, resting against the wall, staring at me, his wool collar pulled up around his ears.

A bonfire had been built round which the mortals gathered until they were drunk enough not to care about the cold. And a small choir of Notker's boys sang to the beat of a tambourine the medieval "Gaudete Christus Est Natus," and the mortals began to clap in time and sing.

I found myself reflecting on my happiness, my strange sense of satisfaction, so very unusual to me, so very unlike me, and my mind wandered back to Kapetria telling me that I had what I always wanted. I fancied she'd completely misunderstood.

When had I ever not hated my invisibility as a vampire? When had I ever not cursed my separation from the great stream of human history in which I now accepted that I would never play a part?

No one knew better than I that secrecy was imperative to the world we had constructed here in these remote mountains, and even

Benji had come to accept that the radio broadcasts had to be for the cognoscenti and could no longer go out to all the mortal world.

I was on the verge of realizing something, something of immense importance—that feeling again, that feeling—and just for a moment, I began to see how a great many things all came together to produce something I hadn't allowed myself to acknowledge let alone accept . . . when Alain came up to me and slipped his arm around me and said,

"Monsieur, may I steal you away?"

"Of course," I said. And we walked together out of the warm light of the fire and the torches until we had come to the darkened alcove of the church.

"Monsieur," he said again, glancing from left to right to make certain we were in private. "I've come to a conclusion. I don't want to leave here when all the work is finished. I think somehow I've been ruined for the normal world."

"And whoever said that you would ever have to leave here?" I asked.

"It's taken for granted, isn't it?" he replied. "That someday all the restoration will be complete, and you won't need us anymore. The speed with which all this has come back after the fire, I can see that if anything the time is closer than ever. But I want to stay. I want you to find room for me somewhere, where I can still be useful to you, where I can still do things here and live here and . . ."

"You're worrying about nothing," I said. I put my hands gently to his face and turned his head so that he was looking at me, and I saw deep into his hazel eyes. How very young he was still at forty, with so few lines at the corners of his eyes, and skin so healthy and beautiful here in the shadows. So very perfect.

"Alain," I said. "I want you to stay here forever. I promise you. I will never ask you to leave my service."

I had taken his breath away.

"Monsieur, I am honored. Why, I am so honored, yes, yes, I will work for you always. I will find things to do, I will . . ."

"Doesn't matter, young one," I said.

Tears sprang to his eyes. He looked like a boy to me, rather than a man in his prime. I took the liberty of running my gloved fingers through his thick ashen hair, as if I were an old man, and of course I must have been an old man to him, an old man who had known him as a little boy when his father had brought him to the Château to begin the restoration, though how he accounted for my unchanging appearance I did not know.

He was aware of this; this I did know.

I had seen him grow up, go away to university, come home. I had seen him become the man he was now, a widower with a broken heart and one son who lived on the other side of the globe. Such a fine and strong man. Perfectly groomed. *Ready.* I felt through the thin leather of the glove the smoothness of his square jaw. Perfect. I took his bare hands in mine, his cold hands, red from the cold, and looked at his perfectly groomed nails. What about himself would he change if he could? Nothing, it seemed to me.

I turned and opened the doors of the church with the Mind Gift. There came the click of the lock and the doors opening, and I heard him gasp in surprise. I took his hand and led him into the darkened church and closed the doors behind us without looking back.

We stood in the nave under the high Gothic arches. Ahead lay the old altar covered in lace-trimmed white linen with its golden candlesticks and beeswax candles, and banks of flowers fresh for morning Mass.

I turned to him and took him by the shoulders. "You know what I am, don't you?" I asked.

He couldn't answer. He was staring at me, struggling to see me in the darkness through which I could so easily see him.

"I believe you are the very being you wrote about, monsieur, in your books. I have always known it. I have seen things, things I never confessed to you. . . ."

"I know," I said. "The night that Rose and Viktor were married in this church, you were watching. You broke the curfew and you were watching from the window in the inn. I could have sent you home, but I didn't. I let you watch."

"It's all true then," he said. His eyes were gleaming.

I closed my eyes and listened to the rhythm of his heart. I stripped off my gloves and took his hands again and felt the beat of his heart in his hands, and then I kissed the palm of his right hand.

"There's no going back," I said.

"I want it!" he cried. "Give it to me."

"Some night a very long time from now you'll come to see that what I am doing is very selfish, but when you do remember this, remember please that I held off for many years. I've done many an impulsive and foolish thing in my life, but what I do now, I do with great care."

Two hours later, I brought him down from the mountain stream in which he'd cleansed away all the fluids of his physical death and I took him across the drawbridge and through the gates into the lower court of the house. I'd wrapped him in my hooded fur-lined cloak and he wore only this garment as I took him into my apartments, and carefully dressed him from the wealth of shirts and jackets that crowded my closets, and then I led him down into the crypt.

I saw him shiver as he stared at the coffin, the old-fashioned lacquered coffin in which he would now sleep. I saw him settled in it, and I knelt beside him and kissed his lips. His eyes were already closing.

"I'll be here when you wake," I said.

Chapter 25

Two nights before the ball, the Great Sevraine sent trunks of gorgeous glittering feminine garments to be freely given to all who might make use of them; and Barbara and I saw to it that there were rooms filled with jackets, frock coats, tunics and robes, cassocks or soutanes—almost all of which were made from velvet—for the males.

Velvet had become the cloth of the Court. I wore only velvet, and always white lace. Marius too wore velvet, and always red in color; and it was the fabric of countless gowns.

But there were many garments popular among us—of satin damask, and silk, including sherwanis trimmed in jewels. Opera capes, capes lined in fur, boots, and fine shoes, shirts, leather jackets of all styles, dungarees—these were all there to be enjoyed by the vagabond blood drinkers who came to our doors. But one might wear rags to the Winter Solstice Ball if one wished.

Fareed meantime had revised his estimate of our population to three thousand worldwide, but only about two thousand blood drinkers were known to him in person. And we heard tell of blood drinkers in the Far East who had had no contact with the blood drinkers of the West for thousands of years. Nevertheless we used our telepathic powers to keep sending the invitation.

As the ball drew near, I found myself dreading it, and I didn't know why. The house had been filled for nights with blood drinkers eager to make my acquaintance, and I was mightily intrigued by the older blood drinkers who, after the death of Rhoshamandes, had overcome an earlier reticence to see the Court for themselves. So it wasn't a need to be alone that fueled this dread I was feeling. It was something else, something to do with that quickening in me I'd felt the night I brought the remains of Rhoshamandes back to the Château and the roars of the throng had put me in mind of my long-ago rock concert.

In fact, I was enjoying life in the Château as never before—really enjoying it. Yet there was this dread, this dread perhaps of something inside of me that was changing, something I couldn't anatomize yet, something that might not be bad at all, but be splendid.

The night before the ball, Marius invited the council into the ballroom to see his completed work on the ceiling.

We were astonished. We'd expected the usual pantheon of Roman gods, and instead we found a great dancing procession overhead of the blood drinkers who made or make up our history, hands clasped here and there to suggest an immense circular chain. All were done in the full robust and colorful style of the baroque—the regal figures of Akasha and Enkil with their golden crowns and long braided Egyptian locks, faces dark, remote, seemingly mindless; and following them the figure of Khayman, poor Khayman, in Egyptian robes as he might have looked when he had been the steward of the royal household, and the red-haired twins with their fierce deep-set green eyes, their slender bodies garbed in soft billowing gowns, and Santh, the mighty figure of Santh, with his huge blond mane covering his shoulders, clad in bronze-studded leather armor with his hand on the hilt of his sword, and Nebamun (our Gregory), resplendent as the Babylonian angel who had given me his blood, and Seth, the son of the Queen, in full Egyptian linen, and Cyril, my Cyril, enshrined right there with the ancients, with his dark smiling face and mop of unruly brown hair. His worn leather coat and boots had been painted as carefully as if they were royal raiment. But nothing outshone his expressive face. Beside Cyril stood Teskhamen, spare of build, in long Egyptian robes. Next came the strangely lifeless figure of Rhoshamandes, with a face that signified nothing, in the austere brown robes he'd worn when I somehow managed to destroy him, and his tender Benedict in a monk's robe of white, cleaving to his master with a beguiling and boyish smile. Clasping Benedict's hand was the queenly Allesandra in the ornate and bejeweled garb she might have worn in the days of her father's reign. Beside her, but apart from her, and alone, stood my maker, the hunchbacked Magnus, in his dark hood and cloak, his gaunt white face and hooked nose infused with an undeniable beauty yet paling in the radiance of his enormous dark eyes. After Magnus came Notker in his usual monastic attire, surrounded by a cluster of his singers holding lyres like angels in a painted celestial choir.

Then the Great Sevraine appeared in her Greek-goddess gown of white, glittering with precious stones, and the delicate and imperious Eudoxia, the long-lost fledgling of Cyril, of whom Marius had told us and whom he pointed out now, followed by the tall muscular figure of Avicus and his blood bride, the ever-beautiful Zenobia, and Marius himself, Marius in his familiar red velvet robe, his long hair completely white, with Pandora, the elusive Pandora, all in shades of brown in her simple gown and sandaled feet, and then Flavius in his old Roman tunic with the ivory leg that had once been his crutch.

After these came the blond Eric who had perished long ago, and cold-eyed Mael who'd disappeared as well and now the vibrant and dazzling Chrysanthe known to all of us, and Arion with his beautiful black skin and pale eyes, clad in an ancient Greek chiton clasped at the shoulders and bound about the waist by a leather belt. And there appeared other Children of the Millennia—some new to Court and some known only in legend, impressive figures all, figures to ponder in time, figures to talk about—until the great procession moved on to the magnates of the present age.

Armand had been rendered with undisguised devotion in velvet the color of blood, his youthful face angelic, his soft brown eyes infinitely sad, and beside him stood the lithe and beguiling Bianca in her stately purple Renaissance gown. Beside her stood my mother, Gabrielle, her hair long behind her back, her tall slender form quite dignified in her khaki jacket and boots, her face serene with only the smallest smile. Next appeared Eleni in swirling skirts of embroidered blue, and Eugenie and Laurent in striking eighteenth-century garb, these being the faithful servants of the Théâtre des Vampires in its early years. There followed Fontayne in his old-fashioned frock coat, lace studded with pearls, his lean face bright as if illuminated from within, and Louis, my handsome Louis, in dark wool and old-fashioned high-collared linen, gazing down on us with a look of thinly veiled amusement, but with a secret in his hypnotic green eyes. At his side was Claudia, my tragic little Claudia, in her puff sleeves and blue sash and golden ringlets—the only real child vampire in the procession, reaching out with one small dimpled hand to David Talbot in his trim Anglo-Indian body who, in turn, reached out to Benji Mahmoud, Benji who had been exquisitely outfitted in his black three-piece suit with his round cheerful face, black eyes laughing beneath the brim of his black fedora, and the sweet Sybelle, our gifted pianist, Benji's ever-faithful companion, the wan and mysterious Sybelle in her simple modern gown of black chiffon.

Jesse Reeves followed, so slender and fragile with her long rippling coppery hair identical to that of the twins who'd been her ancestors, and black-haired Rose, the fragile girl I'd sought to protect from every bad thing when she was living, who was now one of us, and her spouse in the Blood, Viktor, my beloved son, Viktor, taller than his father, just as blond, and perhaps a bit menacing with eyes that were cold and more reminiscent of my mother's than mine. Next came his mother, Flannery, in the simplest modern garments, wrapped in silence and mystery, who had become one of us many years after Viktor's birth. Fareed was beside Flannery, handsome as always, his golden skin irresistible, his eyes fierce and almost mocking, dressed in his simple white doctor's coat and pants. There followed other blood drinker physicians and scientists, secretive, reluctant, as if quietly suffering as Flannery was under the painterly hand that rendered them with the same care lavished on all the others; and then, Barbara, my lovely self-effacing assistant in her handsome dress of magenta wool, and finally Alain, the very last to complete the great circle, hand raised to point to the figure of King Enkil. Alain was in the fancy duds I'd forced on him, supple suede tailored as if it were velvet, and antique lace, his face ruddy and his hazel eyes filled with optimism.

This was the great circle of dancing figures who encompassed all of the ballroom ceiling.

In the very center, on a great shield that was equidistant from the chandeliers, was a figure of the Prince in his red velvet, fur-lined cloak, wearing an actual crown of gold and holding in his hand a scepter.

I blushed when I saw it. I felt Marius patting me on the shoulder and I heard him laughing that I'd blushed. I shook my head and looked at the floor. Then up again. It was a perfect likeness, as were all Marius's likenesses, and surrounding the Prince was what appeared to me to be the wilderness of the Savage Garden.

Behind these large blazing figures, the figures of the procession, and the shield that framed the Prince, the night sky covered the ceiling in a pale luminescent blue sprinkled with the smallest stars forming their inevitable patterns and constellations.

If only words could capture the art of Marius's work, and the remarkable flow of colors through the great procession, and the subtle touches of gold and silver, and his preternatural skill at capturing the glitter of jewels and the vitality of eyes—if only, but words cannot.

It was a gorgeous achievement. Marius noted that there was room on the ceiling to make another circle within the grand circle, and room enough to add figures behind the existing figures. And we left the ballroom convinced that all would love this new work.

Why was I apprehensive? Did I not want the Court to succeed? Of course I did. Was I not glad that I'd destroyed Rhoshamandes? I was more than glad. So what was changing in me that so confused me? Whatever it was, it had to do with me. It was private and vital to my well-being.

Chapter 26

The night of the ball came. While the gates were still locked, and the ballroom still closed off, the orchestra was arranged to the far-left side of the room and the back, which still provided it with ample space for some one hundred musicians, and a chorus behind it of one hundred singers.

And a new large dais now stood at the very center of the back wall, with the throne given me by Benedict in the middle of it and towards the front. A row of gilded French chairs had been placed behind the throne in an arc, and I was told by Gregory that these were for the council.

This all seemed very fine to me, but the position of prominence given to the throne—that it now faced the distant double doors to the room—made me very uneasy. Seeing myself rendered in brilliant color on the shield in the center of the plaster ceiling also made me uneasy.

The dungeons were packed with murderers, assassins, and cut-throats of every kind, so as to provide for the fledglings. And on the lower floor of the Château just inside the inner court were the rooms filled with garments to be freely offered to all comers. But I made a point to Barbara and Alain and others who were managing these rooms that no one must be pressured to take finery against his or her will. All were welcome.

Just before the ball was officially to commence, the members of the council placed a lectern near the entrance to the passageway, at the head of the grand stairway, with a great black leather reception book laid open on it, and an artfully made modern pen ornamented with a quill for the guests to sign their names. I had to confess I was curious as to which vampires would take the time to sign this registry.

Meanwhile the council was poised to split up and line the walls of the passage on either side from the entrance to the ballroom doors to greet the newcomers. All the family of the house was dressed in spectacular clothes, and the ancients had chosen to let their facial hair and the hair of their heads be long and natural. Gregory, Seth, and Santh were the oldest vampires in the house, and they all wore embroidered satin robes and gilded slippers. Marius, Notker, Flavius, Avicus, and other male Children of the Millennia wore long gold-etched tunics for the most part, with only Thorne and Cyril dressed in handsome sleek leather coats and boots, each with an ornate lace shirt with lace at the cuffs as well as at the collar. I had never seen them like this and I was delighted.

Of the female vampires, Sevraine was the most remarkable in her slender Grecian gown of gold cloth, her satin hair like a veil, and her shapely naked arms like marble. But Bianca, Pandora, Chrysanthe, and Zenobia wore ball gowns of sumptuous velvet in a spectrum of muted and dazzling colors. And the young members of the household wore the finery one might expect at a formal ball of these times, with Viktor, Benji, Louis, Fontayne, and Alain in white tie and black tailcoats, and the younger women, including Sybelle and Rose, in the streamlined gowns currently in fashion. The display of jewels was breathtaking, with rubies, emeralds, diamonds, sapphires everywhere that one looked, or ropes of pearls and barrettes and pins of gold and silver.

As for me, I was dressed as I usually am, in a frock coat of red velvet with cameo buttons, and layers of embroidered lace at the neck and the same snow white lace dripping over my hands—with the invariable pressed dungarees and high shiny black boots, and the gold Medusa ring on my finger. My hair was groomed as it always is. And I wondered if I might not be a disappointment on the throne in the very middle of the ballroom facing the open doors and the long passage to the grand stairs, but I wasn't all that concerned about it. If I disappointed, it would be for obvious reasons—that the newcomers drawn by word of the ball, and our recent story, would find me ordinary, young, and uninteresting. As I said, I fill the bill of a matinee idol in looks and always have. And until I decide to really hurt someone, I look harmless too, which doesn't help. Enough on that subject.

Now let me explain about the newcomers.

Ever since we had opened the Château, newcomers had been arriving. But for the most part they were young vampires—vampires Born to Darkness in the twentieth century. There were even some who had become blood drinkers after the year 2000. But the elders who came, the older powerful blood drinkers, were largely connected with someone already at the Court or known to someone. Notker, for example, brought a pair of blood drinker intimates from his alpine refuge to see the Court, and of his boy sopranos many were ancient. And Arion had become part of the Court, a beautiful dark-skinned vampire with yellow eyes who boasted at least two thousand years in the Blood, introduced to us through his connection to the convicted enemy of the Replimoids, Roland. Another Child of the Millennia, a hermit by nature, and a friend to Sevraine, had also come to see the Court and stayed with us for months before taking his leave with thanks and blessings.

But by and large, the newcomers were young, very young, and they were the ones most desperate to be part of the Court and to be protected by it, and now to be allowed to feed upon the miserable prisoners in the dungeon.

It had become clear as Fareed made his lists and tried to gauge the size of our population that most of the blood drinkers of the world perished in the first three hundred years of their existence. And that is why Armand, encountering Louis in the nineteenth century, had presumed himself to be the oldest vampire in the world, having been kidnapped by the Children of Satan in the 1500s.

Now, after the death of Rhoshamandes, more and more young vampires came to us, and some of these recent visitors were four hundred or even five hundred years old, but without the powers or sophistication of Armand, and eager to learn whatever the elders of the house would teach them.

But on this night unusual things happened.

First and foremost, just about every blood drinker who had ever visited us had returned, and every single one welcomed the invitation to the wardrobe rooms and appeared on the grand stairway in glittering garments that increased the air of merriment and excitement.

And as I took my place on the throne, as the doors opened, as all the young residents of the house filled the ballroom on the right and on the left, as the orchestra under Antoine's direction began to play a magnificent canon composed by Antoine—born of Pachelbel and Albinoni—I began to realize, in spite of my anxiety and uneasiness, that something of historic magnitude was happening. I could hear the soft unmistakable heartbeats of vampires in such numbers that I knew this crowd would exceed any other we'd ever hosted.

I heard heartbeats, I heard greetings on the floor below. I heard cars moving down our deserted and out-of-the-way roads towards us. And I was aware of others appearing out of nowhere in the snow-covered fields around us.

My nervousness increased. A great pathway through the crowd gave me a view of those strangers just coming to the top of the faraway stairs, and I felt myself struggling desperately to conceal my confusion.

But then a ravishing woman appeared, seemingly out of nowhere, smiling at me as she approached, her hand out to greet me.

Her hair was gloriously done up in the old French style of which Marie Antoinette would have been proud, and her bodice of gold damask revealed a slender waist descending to great skirts of dark purple silk, flanking an underskirt open in front of layer upon layer of embroidered lace that covered her feet to the tips of her slippers. The shape of her arms in the close-fitting upper sleeves, the sight of her bare arms emerging from the lower open sleeves of dripping lace, and her graceful hands, all of this was tantalizing and lovely and drew from me an immediate smile—until I realized this was my mother.

Gabrielle! These brilliant blue eyes, these rose-tinged lips, this soft confidential laughter—belonged to my mother.

As she mounted the podium and took her place at my side, I started to rise to embrace her, but she told me gently to remain as I was.

"*Mon Dieu, Maman,*" I said. "I've never seen you more beautiful." There were tears of gratitude gathering in my eyes. The room swam with color as I struggled to regain my composure, and the music and the color melded in some great pervasive intoxicating brew that made me faintly dizzy.

"You didn't think I'd be the Queen Mother for you tonight?" she asked. She looked down at me, lovingly. "You think I don't know what is going on in your mind and has been for nights now? I can't read your thoughts, but I can read your face."

Her hands, warm from the kill, clasped my right hand, and she lifted my hand and kissed the golden Medusa ring that very soon others would also be kissing.

"I'll be at your side," she said. "Until you tell me that you don't want me."

I breathed a deep sigh of relief that I didn't attempt to conceal from her.

And now the first of the newcomers were streaming into the room and coming right towards me. Younglings as expected and proud and merry in their fine clothes, some rushing up to confess how much they adored me for vanquishing Rhoshamandes, and others shrinking back until my mother motioned for them to approach.

"Come meet the Prince," she said in a cheerful voice I don't think I had ever heard before from her lips. "Don't be afraid. Come!"

And then came ancients, ancients such as had never visited us before, moving slowly towards the throne, blood drinkers as stately and pale and powerful as Marius or even perhaps Sevraine, with eyes like gems. I extended my hand, and over and over they kissed the ring rather than simply clasp my hand in greeting.

Their voices came low and intimate, offering names with little preamble: Mariana of Sicily; Jason of Athens; Davoud of Iran; Kadir of Istanbul.

I heard Cyril's voice beside me on the right, just behind my mother, also offering his greeting. And then he whispered in my ear, "Don't worry, boss, got it covered."

And I gave him a quick grateful smile, though to be afraid, genuinely afraid, had not even occurred to me.

As these impressive figures moved into the swelling crowd, I saw Seth approaching them and offering them a cordial face and hand. Meanwhile others came, young, bright, still ruddy with human flesh, sometimes babbling in their enthusiasm that they were grateful, so grateful, to be welcomed here.

"All blood drinkers are welcome to the Court," I said, over and over again. "Keep the rules, keep the peace, and this is your Court. It belongs to you as much as to us."

And now another ancient one approached, lean and with the same severe features of Seth and the same solid-black hair and a beard as lustrous as that of Gregory.

Old, so old. So filled with power. So filled with power as Rhosha-mandes had been filled with power, able to destroy the village in one wanton quarter of an hour, and able to destroy all that had been achieved here.

But there was no hint of malice, no taint of hostility, no breath of resentment.

The music had increased in volume.

"They're waiting for you to dance," said my mother. "Come, lead me in the waltz so they can dance also."

I was speechless. Had we ever observed such a formality before? I found myself taking her hand and leading her out into the middle of the floor, with one quick glance up at that blinding image of myself on the shield. Then I pressed my hand against her small waist, and we were moving fast in circles as the orchestra filled the room with the spirited strains of a dark and original waltz threaded through and through with mystery, with enchantment.

How perfectly lovely she was, her delicate feet moving effort-lessly with the steps, and her hair such a radiant halo for her face, for her exquisite eyes. Well, if they are disappointed in me, I thought, they will look at her and they cannot find her anything but gorgeous.

Then it came to me. I had seen her like this, yes, very like this so many long years ago in this very house: I had seen her in this very gown in a small lacquered portrait of her with my father, a painting that hung on her bedroom wall and was surely gone now forever.

She was laughing as I turned her round and round, going faster and faster. The music goaded us to fantastical speed and I had the distinct feeling we were rising into the Heavens in the dance, just the two of us, turning in circles, and all the sparkling light surround-ing us was starlight. But I could feel the floor beneath my feet, I could hear the click of her heels, such an erotic sound, the click of a woman's heels, and then I saw Gregory, Gregory in his splendid robe taking her hand from me, and offering the hand of his magnificent Chrysanthe.

"Yes, my dear," I said to Chrysanthe, "and what a pleasure." All around us others were dancing, many partnered as we were, and the younger blood drinkers alone, swaying with their hands raised and their eyes closed, and some of the males dancing as Greek men dance in tavernas, that wonderful dance in which side by side they move one way and then the other, their hands on one another's shoulders. The waltz had broken into a form entirely new with the deep beat of drums and the clash of cymbals and the chant of the boy sopranos, and preternatural dancers everywhere made their own patterns, their own little circles or larger groupings, describing arabesques on the dance floor.

I danced with Zenobia, and with Pandora and with Rose, my precious little Rose, and with the regal Mariana of Sicily.

"Prince, you do realize, don't you, that there has never been such a Court as this," she said, her face white and cold as that of Marius.

"I had that distinct feeling, madam," I said. "But I wasn't sure of it. Now I am, if you say so."

Suddenly she smiled and the mask dissolved into a warm, ingratiating vital expression. "Never have such things been done before, Prince, as you and your friends have done," she said. "And you are simple and straightforward and your smile is quick and open."

I couldn't think of what to say, and I think she knew it, but it didn't concern her, and in a moment I was given over to the Great Sevraine as she, Mariana of Sicily, moved on to Teskhamen in a soutane of silver and gold.

The dancing swept me up again, wordless and wonderful, and I pondered what this great spectacle might look like to mortal eyes, or even to the eyes of my young Alain, so mortal still, but I couldn't imagine it, and quite suddenly the strangest thought came to me, that I didn't care what it looked like to mortal eyes. I couldn't imagine any speculation to be more irrelevant. I almost laughed aloud. Sevraine assured me in a hushed voice that she and Gregory and the others had things "under watch" but that all was as it looked, gay and friendly.

"Yes, it is that way, isn't it?" I said.

Sevraine fell into the arms of Marius, and I retreated to the throne, and sat back to watch the dance, to study each and every individual I could pick from the crowd, and I saw, saw perfectly, how distinctive each being was, and also I saw something else—something I'd never noticed before in the ballroom. I saw how completely at ease they were. Slowly, as my eyes moved from figure to figure, I saw how dress and dance were the full expression of the wishes of each individual; I saw how completely at peace these dancers were, talking animatedly to one another or lost in the rhythm, or just rocking on the balls of their feet, gazing about themselves as if in a swoon. I saw what I'd never seen before, that for all of them, even those who'd been at Court for the last year or more, that this was a wholly new experience. Nothing like this had ever been attempted, not in size or scope or generosity.

And there was an extraordinary atmosphere uniting us, of comfort in being amongst our own with no thought given to the mortal world whatsoever.

It was not the imitation of mortal life I'd once achieved with Louis and Claudia in our little bourgeois townhouse in the French Quarter of New Orleans. It was a different kind of life, *our life*, defined by how we wanted to dress, to dance, to speak, to be together. And mortal life had nothing to do with it.

A thought occurred to me. I stood and moved out among the dancers. I looked for Louis, and I found him almost at once. He was dancing with Rose. They were dancing in the conventional way that men and women dance, and then breaking into other simple variations, turns, new embraces, making it up as were so many others. The music was beautiful now, or so it seemed to me, liking melodic music as I do, not taxing one to become ecstatic or crazed. I watched patiently as they danced until Viktor appeared and reached for Rose's hand. Of course Louis released Rose and then he bowed just as if he were at a ball in old New Orleans after the opera. I came up beside him and took his hand.

"What are you doing?" he asked.

"Dancing with you," I said. I turned him easily this way and that to the music. I could see he found this immediately awkward, to be dancing with me as a woman might dance with a man, and then something playful and vibrant came into his eyes. He gave himself up to it. I turned us around fast twice and then three times, and we broke the pattern and then my arm slipped around his waist and I danced beside him, in step with him, like the Greek men do it. "Do you like this better?" I asked.

"I don't know," he said. He appeared brimming with happiness. But I was the one truly brimming with happiness. The music seemed to move us as if we were powerless, borne along exquisitely, and then we faced each other again and we were simply dancing in a loose, comfortable embrace, intimate, making one body and then two bodies, and one body again. All around us were dancers, dancers pressing in so that at last we were dancing without really moving our feet. But what did it matter? One can dance that way. One can dance a thousand ways. Ah, if only I could reach back over the centuries and bring the light of this ballroom into the world I had once shared with someone else. . . .

"What's the matter?" he said to me suddenly.

"What?"

"I saw something, something in your eyes."

"Just thought of a boy I once loved a long time ago."

"Nicolas," he said.

"Yes, Nicolas," I answered. "Seemed all the little victories of life and life after death were so hard for him, happiness was so hard for him . . . joy was an agony I think, but I don't want to think of it now."

"Some of us are infinitely better at being miserable than happy," he said gently. "We're good at it, and proud of it, and we get better and better at it, and we simply don't know what it means to be happy."

I nodded. My thoughts were as thick and confused as the dancers, the music. But the dancers and the music were beautiful. My thoughts were not.

I could not recall ever having spoken of Nicolas to Louis, never ever even mentioning Nicolas's name. But then I do not remember everything, as I once thought I did. There is something in us, even us, that will not allow for that, something that pushes the memory of suffering that is unbearable slowly away.

"I have no gift for being miserable," I said.

"I know," he said. He laughed. Such a human face. Such a lovely face.

There must surely have been twice as many blood drinkers now in this ballroom as there had ever been, and I sensed that I had ought to stop having such a marvelous time and return to greeting newcomers as the Prince should. But not before holding Louis for a moment, and then kissing him and telling him low in French that I loved him and always had.

It was a struggle just to make our way back to my golden throne.

I took my seat, and Louis moved off to my left in the shadows, and I watched the spectacle of the dancers, as I might the beauty of a storm.

An ancient one entered the ballroom.

I heard the heartbeat. Then I sensed the effect of the heartbeat on the crowd, the subtle awareness taking hold of the others—the awareness registering with our ancient ones. This was a creature as old as Gregory or Santh. The dancers were making way for him, stepping aside to make a path for him as he came towards me.

Slowly he approached—this tall white creature, a male with

deep-set black eyes and flowing black hair, who offered me a subtle smile long before he reached me. He was a gaunt figure, taller than me, with broad shoulders and enormous bony hands, his body clothed in a simple cassock of black velvet.

I saw Gregory following him and then Seth. I felt Cyril press in close. Thorne was beside me as well.

The newcomer bowed before me.

"Prince," said the newcomer. "Centuries ago I knew members of your Court in Egypt. But they might not remember now; I was a servant to the Queens Blood but not a soldier."

Gregory stepped up to take the figure in his arms.

"Jabare," he whispered. "Of course I remember you. There are no servants or soldiers here. Welcome."

"Old friend," said the newcomer. "Let me kiss the Prince's ring." I felt myself blush as he did so. I was glad suddenly that I hadn't fed in many nights, that I was starved actually, as there wouldn't be so much blood to flood my cheeks when someone of this venerable age paid homage to me.

"Why so shy?" Jabare asked, and there was that miracle again when the masklike face, washed clean of all expression, suddenly reflected the feelings of the heart with unmistakable warmth and sincerity.

"He doesn't know what he has done, Jabare," said Gregory. "That is one of Lestat's many charms, that for all his mischief and ready wit, he is self-effacing. He doesn't quite understand what is happening around him."

But I do understand, I wanted to say, and suddenly there came that quickening, that deep threat of an insight so powerful it would carry me to recesses of my heart I'd never explored before, and would most certainly take me out of this moment.

And I didn't want to be taken out of it. But then I realized something. As I watched Jabare talking to Gregory, as I saw them clasp hands, as I saw them kiss, as everywhere I looked I saw contented and trusting faces, as everywhere I saw animation and discovery and heard all about me the ring of friendly voices and the ring of sweet laughter, I realized that what I feared in that quickening was embodied by this moment, this radiant and immense moment.

I almost caught it, the full thought that had been stalking me night after night since the moment when, having brought Rhoshamandes's headless body to this very ballroom, I'd heard those raucous cheers rising, seen those pumping fists, and thought of the rock concert stage, the old rock singer moment when mortals had been screaming my name, and raising their fists in that same manner and I'd felt so visible, so wholly known, so recognized.

Mon Dieu! It was almost there, that moment of inward turning which would redirect everything inside me.

Suddenly the music stopped. My mother came off the dance floor and stood behind me on my left, and Marius took his place on my right gesturing for all to be silent.

He introduced himself simply as Marius, known to some as Marius de Romanus, Born to Darkness in a Druid shrine some two thousand years ago.

"I promised my young friend here," he continued, "that he wouldn't have to speak to this assembly. I told him that I would speak and it's my pleasure to do so. After weeks of ridiculous work, I've reduced our voluminous constitution to a few simple rules which I want to share with you. But I think you all know what they are, and how vital they are to all of us."

Suddenly Benji cried out, pushing his way to the very front of the throng, "Slay the evildoer for one's own peace of mind. And keep the secret always of our presence, our nature, and our powers!"

As Marius nodded smiling, fledglings on all sides were sharing in the approbation and laughter.

"Yes, yes, yes, forgive me, all of you young ones who have listened too long to me hold forth," said Marius. "But truly, my brothers and sisters, those are the commandments on which our survival is built. And we welcome all of you, all of you blood drinkers of this world, to the Court, to believe in it, to honor it, and to be forever protected by it!"

Clapter, soft roars of agreement, and before me strung all through this glittering assembly I saw the pale forbidding faces of the ancients rapt and approving. I saw their nods, saw them looking to one another, saw even this one, this ancient Jabare, nodding.

"Hunters we are," said Marius, "and from the human race we take what we must have to live and we do it without regret. But we are gathered here tonight to declare our loyalty to one another, and our embrace of what we are, not just in ourselves but in all who share the Dark Blood with us, regardless of age or history."

He paused, letting the applause come. Everywhere I looked I saw eyes fixed on him, faces waiting. And he went on now, raising his voice effortlessly without the slightest distortion.

"You know how we came together," he said. "You've heard how, from the simple desire to help one another against a common enemy, we came out of the darkness which concealed us from our fellows. You know the story of how the common enemy proved to be Amel, that spirit who gave birth to us. You all know how that one was freed from his innumerable invisible chains without bringing harm to a single one of us.

"But what has brought us here tonight is the overwhelming need to celebrate events which have now changed our history forever.

"I don't speak of the stories and films made by Lestat de Lioncourt that gave to each and every one of you the history you might never have learned in any other way; and I don't speak of this young one's great generosity in creating this great edifice that can contain every single blood drinker of our tribe. Those are good things and things that benefit all of us.

"But I speak now of Lestat's battle with Rhoshamandes."

I felt my face grow warm. I lowered my eyes. In a flash I saw it all, and didn't care who read it from my mind, for it was truly next to nothing. And slowly I realized that Marius had paused and was looking at me.

"I speak," Marius said, "of the simple fact that when it seemed a certainty that Rhoshamandes would destroy everything that had been constructed here—and the cynical ones among us were saying it was bound to happen, and if it were not Rhoshamandes, it would have been another—the Prince did something no blood drinker in the history of our tribe has ever done, and strangely enough he did not himself even take note of it."

Silence. The room was so silent it was as if nothing living were in it. All faces were turned to Marius. I too was looking at him.

"The Prince, without a second thought," said Marius, "offered his life for the Court. He offered to die so that the Court might continue."

I was shocked by these words. I looked at him and I couldn't conceal my perplexity.

"Oh, I know," he said to me in a soft immediate voice that all could nevertheless hear. "I know that you meant full well to bring Rhoshamandes down, of course you did. But you had no way of knowing that you could. And no one would have predicted that you could. And with the willingness to die, you gave yourself over into his hands . . . and you disarmed him and destroyed him."

Again, the silence. And I myself was speechless.

"No blood drinker in our dark history of six thousand years has ever done such a thing," he said, his eyes on me. "And with that gesture—and the destruction of a deadly enemy—the word went out around the world that all the lofty notions of this Court were rooted not in fancy and idle dreams but in our very blood, and of our blood, and that if you, Lestat, could do this for us, then we can come together to make this Court endure forever for one another."

The silence broke.

It broke in murmurs and whispers, and a soft mingling of voices giving their assent and then other voices, and more voices cried out to declare it was true, and then came the applause and the applause grew stronger and stronger, and then came the stomping of feet, and the roar filled the room, and Marius stood still gazing at me.

"Stand up!" my mother whispered.

I climbed to my feet, and now as Marius stood back, I realized I had to say something, but what in the name of Heaven could I possibly say, because it had been so quick, so natural, so simple. But then the word, the word I'd just used in my deepest thoughts, the word "natural" came to me, and I knew I could never put into words what I was feeling, what I was coming to understand, that deep secret that I couldn't share with others, though it was all about others, all about us as we were gathered here.

I raised my hand and then my voice.

"This is what I dream for us," I cried. "That this Court live forever!" Cries came from all over the room once more. "May we never again be reduced to lone wanderers as suspicious of one another as we are of the mortals who despise us. May we never again drink the poison of self-loathing!" Louder and louder came the cries. "We must love one another if we are to stay together," I said. "And it is loving one another, and nothing else, that will give us the strength to write our own history."

The cries and applause overtook me. I had some more pathetic words inside me still, or so it seemed, but they were lost in the burst of shouting and cheers and applause. And I knew it didn't matter now to say more. It was clear what was happening.

I saw Armand gazing at me, I saw a faint smile on his lips, and I saw Louis standing beside him, and I saw my beloved Alain with them, gazing at me in wonder, and at his side Fontayne and Barbara.

I looked at Armand. He was splendidly attired in burgundy velvet, himself once more, his fingers covered with jeweled rings as he clapped along with the others. I could not quite believe the calm, accepting expression on his face, but then he nodded. It was just a small nod, a nod no one else would have noticed, but I saw it and I saw him smile again.

Marius embraced me and quickly stepped down and away, and I found myself seated once more, settled back on the red velvet throne, face flushed again—and the orchestra gave its loud voice to the applause and once again the entire throng was moving to the ecstatic music.

I sat back and closed my eyes, and the realization I'd been avoiding since that night, that night that I'd brought Rhoshamandes's remains back, the realization that I'd avoided as impossible, that realization fully took hold of me.

Visibility, significance, recognition! All that I'd ever wanted when I took to the rock music stage, all that I'd ever wanted as a boy heading to Paris with a head full of dreams, all I'd ever wanted I now had right here with my brothers and sisters! I had all that I had ever hoped for, and I had it here and now in this place and amongst my own people.

The old human story simply did not matter. I had this, I had this moment, I had this recognition, and this visibility and this significance. And how could I ask for anything more? How could I look from right to left, at immortals who had witnessed all the epochs of recorded history, and want more than this? How could I gaze at immortals who'd been drawn to this very spot by something more immense than they'd ever witnessed, and long for more than the recognition they were now giving me?

The victory of our own tribe to embrace one another, and let go of the hatred that had divided us for centuries, was my victory.

"To the Blood Communion," I said in my heart. And I felt the cold numbing shell of alienation and despair which had imprisoned me all of my life among the Undead—I felt that shell cracked, broken, and dissolved utterly into infinitesimal fragments.

What had been taken from me by Magnus had been repaid a

thousandfold. And what had been snatched away that night in San Francisco when Akasha visited death and horror on our rock music spectacle had been given back a thousandfold. And I knew now that I could be the monarch that my people wanted.

Because they were indeed my people, my tribe, my family. And whatever happened hereafter wouldn't be just my story. No, it would be the story of us all.

The End.

September 26, 2017

A NOTE ON THE TYPE

This book was set in Janson, a typeface long thought to have been made by the Dutchman Anton Janson, who was a practicing typefounder in Leipzig during the years 1668 to 1687. However, it has been conclusively demonstrated that these types are actually the work of Nicholas Kis (1650–1702), a Hungarian, who most probably learned his trade from the master Dutch typefounder Dirk Voskens. The type is an excellent example of the influential and sturdy Dutch types that prevailed in England up to the time William Caslon (1692–1766) developed his own incomparable designs from them.

Composed by North Market Street Graphics,
Lancaster, Pennsylvania

Printed and bound by Berryville Graphics,
Berryville, Virginia